BURIED
IN A BOOK

Lucy Arlington

BERKLEY PRIME CRIME, NEW YORK

THE BERKLEY PUBLISHING GROUP
Published by the Penguin Group
Penguin Group (USA) Inc.
375 Hudson Street, New York, New York 10014, USA
Penguin Group (Canada), 90 Eglinton Avenue East, Suite 700, Toronto, Ontario M4P 2Y3, Canada
(a division of Pearson Penguin Canada Inc.)
Penguin Books Ltd., 80 Strand, London WC2R 0RL, England
Penguin Group Ireland, 25 St. Stephen's Green, Dublin 2, Ireland (a division of Penguin Books Ltd.)
Penguin Group (Australia), 250 Camberwell Road, Camberwell, Victoria 3124, Australia
(a division of Pearson Australia Group Pty. Ltd.)
Penguin Books India Pvt. Ltd., 11 Community Centre, Panchsheel Park, New Delhi—110 017, India
Penguin Group (NZ), 67 Apollo Drive, Rosedale, Auckland 0632, New Zealand
(a division of Pearson New Zealand Ltd.)
Penguin Books (South Africa) (Pty.) Ltd., 24 Sturdee Avenue, Rosebank, Johannesburg 2196,
South Africa

Penguin Books Ltd., Registered Offices: 80 Strand, London WC2R 0RL, England

This is a work of fiction. Names, characters, places, and incidents either are the product of the author's imagination or are used fictitiously, and any resemblance to actual persons, living or dead, business establishments, events, or locales is entirely coincidental. The publisher does not have any control over and does not assume any responsibility for author or third-party websites or their content.

BURIED IN A BOOK

A Berkley Prime Crime Book / published by arrangement with the author

PRINTING HISTORY
Berkley Prime Crime mass-market edition / February 2012

Copyright © 2012 by Penguin Group (USA) Inc.
Excerpt from *Every Trick in the Book* by Lucy Arlington copyright © 2012 by Penguin Group (USA) Inc.
Cover illustration by Julia Green.
Cover design by Lesley Worrell.
Interior text design by Tiffany Estreicher.

ISBN: 978-0-425-24619-1

BERKLEY® PRIME CRIME
Berkley Prime Crime Books are published by The Berkley Publishing Group,
a division of Penguin Group (USA) Inc.,
375 Hudson Street, New York, New York 10014.
BERKLEY® PRIME CRIME and the PRIME CRIME logo are trademarks of Penguin Group (USA) Inc.

PRINTED IN THE UNITED STATES OF AMERICA

10   9   8   7   6   5   4   3

Writer's Block

Back in Novel Idea's reception area, I smelled Marlette before I saw him. Once again, that stale scent of unwashed flesh and clothing permeated the space, despite the aromas created by my tray of hot drinks. The espresso and steamed milk failed to mask the distasteful odor.

"Mr. Marlette." I put the beverages down on the coffee table and cast a quick glance at him out of the corner of my eye. I was surprised to see that he was leaning against the sofa with his face resting against one of the back pillows. He had clearly fallen asleep. "Sir. You can't rest here."

When he didn't respond, I sighed in exasperation and decided to deliver Zach's beverage before it grew tepid. I couldn't just shoo Marlette away. Bentley had stated that he often came to the office twice a day. If he was going to be a regular fixture in my life, I wanted to lay down some ground rules with him. And truth be told, I was dying to read his query letter.

I gave Zach his double espresso and then quickly returned to the front, hoping Marlette had awakened, but he hadn't moved an inch since I'd left the room. His head was still resting against the cushion, and his shoulders were slumped forward as though he were in a deep slumber. Yet something was wrong about his posture. Then I realized exactly what was amiss.

Marlette's shoulders were not gently rising and falling with each breath. They weren't moving at all.

To aspiring writers of all ages.
The world needs more stories.
Don't give up on yours.

Chapter 1

I THOUGHT I'D BE WRITING ARTICLES ABOUT CHURCH bazaars and Girl Scout cookie sales until I retired, so you can imagine my surprise when, at forty-five years of age, I was handed my very first pink slip.

Okay, I'm exaggerating. I tend to embellish otherwise uninteresting stories. There was no pink slip. In fact, no one gave me anything until I started to cry, and then my editor, who'd been cantankerous and impossible to please since the day I submitted my first article for the Features section, unceremoniously tossed a box of tissues on my lap.

"It's nothing personal, Wilkins," he said, squirming uncomfortably in the face of my tears. "Budget cuts across the board. I've gotta let a dozen people go today."

"But what will I do?" I asked. "I've given this newspaper twenty years of my life! The *Dunston Herald* owes me *something*!"

My editor shrugged. "How about a glowing reference?

But only if you leave without pilfering office supplies or lighting a fire in your trash can."

I rose from my seat. "I'm not that desperate for a box of paper clips, thank you."

I walked back to my cubicle with as much dignity as I could muster and began to take down the yellowed clippings of my best articles. When I pulled the thumbtacks from the corners of my son's graduation photo, I was nearly paralyzed by fear. Trey would be a freshman at UNC Wilmington in the fall, and I'd only paid for his first semester. Without my job, how would I cover the cost of another three and a half years of college? And knowing Trey's subpar work ethic, I'd need funds for five or six years of higher education.

This was not the time to panic. I needed work, and I needed it right away. Surely there was a job out there for an experienced writer. I reached for today's paper and rapidly flipped to the Classifieds section. It only took a few minutes to realize that unless I was a registered nurse or could drive an eighteen-wheeler, I was out of luck.

Then, an ad I remembered seeing before caught my eye.

Help Wanted: *Intern for the Novel Idea Literary Agency. Help us sign the next bestselling author. Read and answer queries, attend conferences, edit manuscripts. Excellent communication skills required. Competitive salary. Suitable candidate must be available to travel. After a successful three-month internship, candidate will be promoted to junior agent.*

It sounded perfect. I called, and after a five-minute phone interview with the agency's terse and commanding president, a Ms. Bentley Burlington-Duke, I was told to report to her office tomorrow, nine o'clock sharp, prepared to put in a full day's work.

So I walked out of the squat concrete building that housed the *Dunston Herald* that Thursday afternoon for the last time, not in tears, but smiling like an inmate released from prison. Instead of indulging in a midlife crisis, I was embarking on a new adventure. Who knew what this change of direction could mean? My head was filled with glorious possibilities. Fame, fortune, and romance featured prominently.

If I became a full-fledged literary agent, I would get paid to read! Every day, I'd be the first to sample the work of scores of author hopefuls. I envisioned my name in the acknowledgments section of dozens of fabulous books. This image was quickly replaced by the dedication page in an international bestseller.

To Lila Wilkins. I couldn't have come this far without you!

Delving deeper into fantasy, I created more interesting dedications, penned by the next John Grisham or Jodi Picoult. *To Lila Wilkins, agent and friend. For Lila, with gratitude.* Or this one by J. K. Rowling, whom I convinced to write a standalone about Harry Potter's children: *Lovely Lila, you are a treasure!*

I should have known that something was amiss. The Novel Idea Literary Agency ran an ad for an intern position every few months, but I was foolish enough to believe the job kept coming open because it had yet to be filled by the right person. I was also foolish enough to believe that person was me.

I was so giddy by the time I got home to the little house I shared with Trey that I wasn't even annoyed to find the kitchen sink full of dirty dishes, potato chip crumbs scattered across the rug and sofa in the living room, and a pair of mud-encrusted socks at the top of the stairs. Trey had left a note saying he'd be out late. He was going to the movies and then to a party at his best friend's house. He suggested I not wait up for him.

I didn't. I was starting a new life tomorrow, and I needed my beauty sleep.

THE NEXT MORNING, I decided to take the train into Inspiration Valley. The Inspiration Express was more expensive than driving my car from Dunston, but it was faster, and I wanted to read through the information I had Googled about the Novel Idea Literary Agency during the commute. Not only that, but riding the railroad is far more poetic than fighting traffic, especially since the gleaming silver train was transporting me to my new life.

The last time I rode the Express was with ten-year-old Trey on a special birthday trip to visit my mother. The interior was the same as I remembered, with red plush seats, carved wooden armrests, and small crystal chandeliers hanging from the ceilings. I was delighted to see that the train still maintained a white-gloved porter who pushed a pastry cart through the aisles, distributing chocolate croissants on china plates and pouring coffee from a silver carafe. It brought to mind the Orient Express, and for a moment, I imagined I was steaming toward Zurich or Istanbul as Hercule Poirot interviewed murder suspects over a cup of tea.

Smiling, I stared out the window and tried to absorb the fact that I would soon be a literary agent. Trees whipped past in blurs of green interspersed with splotches of bright blooms, and I soaked in the kaleidoscope of colors. Hazy mountains ascended in the distance, and the gentle rocking of the train allowed my mind to wander. Finally, I pulled my attention away from the scenery, opened my folder containing information on Novel Idea, and began reading.

I discovered that my new boss, Bentley Burlington-Duke, was instrumental in revitalizing Inspiration Valley. Years ago, when my mother moved to the tiny hamlet, it was called Illumination Valley and was a tourist trap for New Agers. Althea, my mother, found it was the perfect place for a psychic to set up shop. But when both the Yoga and Meditation Center and the House of Holistic Healing went bankrupt during one of the country's worst recessions, the rest of the town began to die.

Therefore, it was no surprise that when Bentley bought up a prime piece of property in the middle of town to establish her agency, the locals welcomed her with open arms. She motivated other business owners and friends to relocate, and soon the town was reenergized and renamed. Despite her success as a Manhattan-based agent, Bentley was determined to return to her country roots and establish the finest literary agency south of the Mason-Dixon Line. According to my online research, Novel Idea had quickly become one of the nation's top agencies and Bentley had lured away several top-notch New York agents who now proudly called North Carolina home.

Before I had finished reading the agency's dossier, the whistle blew and we pulled into Inspiration Valley Station. Stepping off the train, I inhaled deeply and looked around. I knew exactly where to go, having read that the Novel Idea Literary Agency took up the second floor of a prestigious office building on High Street.

I loved High Street. It was a narrow cobblestone road that only allowed pedestrian traffic. Lined by cherry trees and ceramic urns overflowing with vibrant annuals, it called to mind a picturesque village in the English countryside. I knew Inspiration Valley well, as my mother lived on the outskirts of the isolated hamlet, but I'd never imagined I might be one of its inhabitants. It seemed like an enchanted place, set aside for those blessed with high levels of creativity. Having written nonfiction my entire life, I felt a bit like an imposter in a town filled with artists, writers, bakers, gardeners, and the merchants who catered to them.

I deliberately headed for the middle of High Street where it intersected with Dogwood Lane, because I wanted to cut through the charming little park that stood in the heart of town. Well-tended garden beds surrounded a gurgling fountain rimmed with cobalt tiles. Sculptures of nine beautiful women in classical Greek dress stood inside the fountain, their lithe bodies frozen in graceful poses. Some of Inspiration Valley's residents perched on the fountain's edge with their coffees and newspapers, relishing the company of the famous muses who permanently bathed beneath arcs of soft rainbows and the water's gentle spray.

I didn't have time to toss a lucky penny in the fountain today. Hustling into the spacious lobby of the building where the Novel Idea Literary Agency was housed, I was greeted by the delightful smell of brewing coffee and chocolate chip cookies fresh from the oven. I realized that I'd discovered a side entrance to Espresso Yourself, Inspiration Valley's sole coffee shop. Sunlight streamed through the massive windows in the lobby and I couldn't help but smile.

Talk about a job perk. I pictured myself beginning each morning with a caramel latte and a croissant.

"Let's actually make it through a day of work first," I chided myself. Taking a deep breath, I smoothed my skirt and hurried up a set of wide, sweeping stairs that led to a well-lit reception area. A leather sofa, two plump club chairs, and a polished mahogany coffee table dominated the empty room.

On its slick surface, books had been arranged in a perfect circle around a slim vase of calla lilies. I took a moment to examine the titles. If the Novel Idea Literary Agency represented all the authors on that table, then I had stepped into a workplace representing a remarkably diverse group of writers. From Idiot's Guides to erotic romance to graphic horror novels, no genre seemed to be off-limits. Excitement surged within me. I felt as though I already belonged.

There was no receptionist's desk, only a small table stacked with manila folders, unsorted mail, and a telephone. A sign said, "Dial 1 to announce your presence." Ignoring the instruction, because Ms. Burlington-Duke had told me to come straight to her office, I hesitantly made my way down the main corridor, noting the agent names on brass placards on every closed door. Suddenly, a door to my right opened and a very short, very round woman in a floral dress ran right into me. She bounced backward with a high giggle.

"Oops! Silly me!" Her round cheeks flushed pink. "Can I help you, dear?"

The woman reminded me of the librarian at Trey's elementary school. With a big, soft body and a generous heart, she, too, had favored flowered dresses and orthopedic footwear. The entire student body adored her.

"I'm the new intern," I answered and then added, doubtfully, "Are you Ms. Burlington-Duke?"

The woman guffawed, her bosom jiggling in mirth. "No,

dear. I'm Flora Meriweather. I handle the children's and young adult acquisitions. See?" She gestured inside her office.

Leaning over the threshold, I took in a whitewashed wooden desk covered by disheveled stacks of paper, a Tiffany-style lamp, and a computer. There was a butter yellow file cabinet in the corner and a set of forest green bookshelves lining the longest wall. As for the walls themselves, they had been hand painted to resemble the art of a famous children's book illustrator. I waited for the name to surface in my brain. "Tasha Tudor?"

Flora was delighted. "You're the first intern to recognize her work!" She clapped her pudgy hands. "Oh, I think this means you're meant to be here."

I could have hugged her, but I restrained myself and settled for a grateful smile. "I hope so. My name's Lila."

"Oh, that sounds just like a storybook character! Maybe a fairy or a flower princess." Her merry face dimpled with pleasure. "Do you read children's books?"

I thought back to the days when I used to read aloud to Trey. "When my son was little, he was crazy about the Hardy Boys and anything by Roald Dahl, but the books we read over and over were Judy Blume's *Superfudge* and Beverly Cleary's *Ramona the Brave*." I traveled down memory lane even further. "Personally, I loved the *Little House on the Prairie* books."

Flora clapped her hands with glee. "I recently sold a series of chapter books called Laura Ingalls, Prairie Detective. Anyone who ever liked Laura Ingalls or Nancy Drew will just yum these books up!"

"They do sound wonderful," I agreed.

"Come this way, my dear. Bentley's in her office, neck-deep in contract negotiations." She lowered her voice. "She's working on a major deal for a thriller writer. The man's desperately been trying to get published for years, and it seems he's finally penned a winner! Bentley says he'll be even bigger than Patterson. His name is Carson Knight. Wait until you meet him. He's so charming he'd cause a catfight among the Disney Princesses."

We stopped at the end of the hallway. Flora wished me luck and hastily retreated. With her last words hanging in the air, I couldn't shake the image of Snow White pulling Sleeping Beauty's hair or Belle biting Cinderella on the hand. Once composed, I knocked on the door.

"Enter!" an authoritative voice ordered.

I stepped into the president's office.

It was all glass, chrome, and black. A large, black-framed, arched window covered most of the wall facing the door. In one corner, three black leather chairs surrounded a round glass table with chrome legs, upon which sat three tidy and very tall stacks of paper. The austere white wall was broken up with a series of black-and-white abstracts framed in chrome. Black bookshelves with glass doors lined the opposite wall.

This was definitely not meant to resemble the work of Tasha Tudor. More like Ansel Adams.

Dominating the room was a sleek glass desk with a chrome lamp in one corner, a black phone in the other, and a laptop computer in the center. Behind it sat a tall, thin woman wearing a tailored peach-colored suit—the only color in the room. Her dark hair, cut short with a line of razor-straight bangs, accentuated well-defined cheekbones.

Perched on the end of her nose was a pair of diamond-studded half-moon glasses connected to a gold jeweled chain.

Ms. Bentley Burlington-Duke.

She had a decade on me and sat in her chair with the regality of a queen. Attired in a suit that likely cost as much as one of my mortgage payments, she radiated refinement and wealth. I reminded myself that I was a seasoned reporter and this agency was lucky to have me.

"Hello, I'm Lila Wilkins." To my relief, I sounded cool and collected. "We spoke on the phone. I'm the new intern."

"Sit." She waved her hand at the chrome and leather chair opposite the desk.

Perching myself on the edge of the seat, I smoothed my skirt over my knees and wondered what task I'd be given for my first assignment.

Bentley typed a few more words, then closed the laptop and took off her glasses. They hung around her neck like an art deco necklace. She folded her arms and studied me. "In order to become a literary agent, you need to be able to read a query letter and instantly determine three things. One, can the author actually write? Consider voice, diction, pacing, and the use of correct grammar. Two, is there a market for the author's idea? Three, is the author sensible and professional or a narcissistic, daydreaming drip? Here." She slid a piece of paper across the desk. "One of these paragraphs was written by a current client. The other is by an unpublished writer who, if I had my druthers, would remain unpublished until the end of time. You tell me which is which."

I reached over and picked up the paper. Slightly perplexed to be given an examination within minutes of my arrival, I started reading.

Query A: *Annabelle is a nurse. She lives with her cat, Furball, who Annabelle believes is the reincarnation of her best friend, Shirley, who was also a nurse at the same hospital when she was alive. When a patient named Ray comes to the ER with mysterious wounds, Annabelle tries to figure out the truth behind his injuries. Annabelle eventually solves the mystery by talking about it to Furball, who shows her who the real culprit is. Annabelle and Ray also fall in love, but they have trouble staying together because Furball gets jealous.*

Query B: *A killer walks among the small population of Solitary, an isolated farming community in Wisconsin. On Halloween, a Methodist preacher is found dead in an abandoned barn, and suspicion is thrown first on Will Bradley, the local tavern owner. When Bradley is absolved and a herd of valuable livestock succumbs to an unidentified virus, the townsfolk point their fingers at Fred Hammer, the large animal veterinarian. Yet even after his incarceration, the loss of life continues. The idyllic community begins to crumble. Neighbors turn against neighbors. Secrets come to light that threaten to tear apart families and friends. When state police investigator Sara Carter is called to Solitary to track down a murderer hiding in plain sight, she must negotiate her way through a web of lies and deception to discover the truth hidden deep in the town's dark and troubled history.*

Was my new boss joking? The difference between the two paragraphs was so obvious I almost grinned. Looking up at her I said, "Query B was written by your client."

"Well done," Bentley said, though the agency head didn't seem too dazzled by my powers of deduction. She pushed three fat tomes across the desk and stood. "These reference books will provide guidelines as to what makes a good query. Read them on your own time. Starting now, you will fulfill a quota of one hundred queries per day along with doing a critical read-through of two or three proposals as well as an assortment of other tasks. Because our last intern was rather inefficient, we have a shocking backlog of queries in our email inbox as well as in hardcopy form."

She paused, using her slim hands to mime a mountainous stack of papers. "I am only interested in stellar queries," she continued. "Once your laptop arrives, you can email those to me. As far as the rejections, you're responsible for emailing out a form letter to each author. Be sure to keep electronic files for the rejects and the possibilities. For now, you'll have to organize hard copies in folders and deliver the possibilities directly to the appropriate agent." She walked around her desk and shook my hand. "Welcome to the Novel Idea Literary Agency, Lily."

"It's Lila," I corrected, but my new boss appeared not to have heard. She breezed out of the office, shutting the door firmly behind her.

Befuddled, I retraced my steps to Flora's office. "I'd like to ask you something. Do you happen to know the location of my desk?"

Flora giggled, her multiple chins wobbling in mirth. "The first one you lay eyes on when you come up the stairs to our reception area, sweetie. Bentley will give you a real desk and a laptop on Monday. She wants to make sure you're really coming back before she sets you up at your own station. For now, I'm afraid you only get a cup holder filled with pens and a few file folders."

"Thank you," I told her and headed back down the hall.

When I located my desk, I laughed, thinking I was the butt of a hoax traditionally played on the newest intern, but no one popped out from behind the sofa or potted palm to witness my reaction. In the quiet space, I was forced to admit that no one had noticed my arrival at all.

However, I was expected. I hadn't seen it earlier when I first arrived, but there, in a corner between the sofa and the wall, to the right of the table with the telephone, sat a student desk with a paper-stuffed file folder resting on its surface. As Flora had warned, there was also a cup holder filled with ballpoint pens resting on top of the folder.

Serf! Indentured servant! Peon! my reporter self silently screamed in indignation.

"It's only for a day," I spoke loudly into the empty space, hoping someone would hear the determination in my voice. "If they think I'm going to complain because I've been assigned this Little Rascals office furniture, they're wrong. I'm more the Steel Magnolias type!"

Still, it only took thirty seconds of sitting at the student desk—it was the one-piece kind with the tiny L-shaped writing area and the seat back that not only provided zero support, but also mercilessly poked into the dead center of one's spine—for my bravado to lose its force. I couldn't possibly work hunched over like some nearsighted scientist while my rear end ached and my lower back grew more and more fatigued.

Determined to mark myself as an independent thinker,

I stacked the client books from the coffee table and placed them on the student desk. Next, I neatly laid out my materials on the coffee table, kicked off my shoes, and sat down on the carpet. With my back and neck supported by the sofa, I felt right at home.

Before delving into the query file, I decided to call my mother and surprise her with the news of my change in employment. I should have known better, since she makes her living telling fortunes using a combination of palm and tarot card readings and therefore claimed to have been fully aware of my new job.

"I had a *feelin'* I should lay out the cards for you last night!" My mother stated theatrically. She never missed an opportunity to be dramatic. "I saw a *major* change. You got the Wheel of Fortune card in the Present position, after all. Even a monkey could've seen this comin'."

As always, I allowed her to believe she had an accurate foreknowledge of everything that was going to happen in my life. "Well, you're not called Amazing Althea for nothing."

My mother sniffed, as though I'd caught her crying. "Oh, sug! I can't hide the truth from you. Your readin' was the *scariest* thing I ever did see. You got the Tower card in the Reason position and the Devil in the Potential spot. You gotta get outta there, honey! For *once* in your life, listen to your mama!"

I rolled my eyes and tried to control my feelings of annoyance. "Stop it. I know you're punishing me for not calling you yesterday. I'm forty-five years old, Mama. I do not need to call you each and every day, and right now, I have to get to work." My parting line was meant to make her feel guilty. "I wish you could have just been happy for me."

"*Happy? HAPPY!*" my mother shrieked. "I dealt the Death card in your Future position, Lila! How can I be happy?"

Now she was stooping really low. "I don't know much about those cards of yours, but you've told me time and time again that the Death card is not to be taken literally."

My mother sniffed again, and when she spoke next, I felt a tiny spark of trepidation, because her voice had gotten quiet and small, and she never spoke like that unless she was extremely distressed. "*This* time it's the real deal. Death is comin' to the place where you work and he's comin' *soon*. I'm not sayin' he's lookin' for you, but he is gonna take somebody with him when he leaves that office. Baby, *please*. Just walk on outta there."

I stared at the query file and then at the books on the desktop, proudly showcasing the names of all the prestigious authors the Novel Idea Literary Agency represented. I thought of my mortgage and Trey's college tuition payments. I thought of how much I wanted to become an agent with this firm.

"Sorry, Mama. If Death shows up, he's going to have get by me first." I picked up a pen and gripped it in my hand. "Because I'm not going anywhere."

Chapter 2

AFTER MY MOTHER'S DISTURBING PHONE CALL, I WAS
more determined than ever to shine as the Novel Idea Literary Agency's newest intern. It was time to begin my quota
of reading one hundred query letters, but I paused to savor
the moment, touching the stuffed file on the coffee table and
wondering whether the next Booker Prize winner might be
waiting within. With a rush of anticipation, I grabbed the
first letter and read:

Dear Sir:

I wanted to give you the privledge of hearing about my
amazing book, Pitch Black. *My book is a 55,000-word*
thriller that is a quick read and is written in the break-
neck speed style of bestselling author Don Brawn. In
Pitch Black, *a coal miner goes crazy after a number of*

years worked in the dark and decides to murder first his
family then anyone foolish enough to cross his path.

Whoa. I didn't need to consult the reference books Bentley had given me to know that this query contained several
major errors. In my opinion, his title was cliché, his opening line rather pompous, and he'd called his work a thriller
when it sounded like a horror novel. Definitely more Stephen
King than Dan Brown. It also contained spelling and gram-
matical errors. I read through the rest of the letter, but nothing about his query hooked me as a reader.

After digging out a pair of blank folders that I found
beneath the query letter file, I labeled one tab with the word
"possibilities" and the second with the word "rejections." I
hesitated for a moment before placing *Pitch Black* in the
rejection folder.

This query was to be my very first rejection. Within the
space of two minutes, I would forever crush the writer's
dreams of getting a step closer to one of the agents working
down the hall. It was momentarily paralyzing. What if the
author was depending on this query letter to change his life?
What if he slaved at some manual labor job during the day
and then burned the midnight oil composing his novel all
night? What if he had five children to feed or, heaven help
him, to put through college?

"I can't think about those things," I informed the letter
resolutely, but with compassion. "My job is to look for an
idea that readers would find compelling, something they'd
rush out to the bookstore to buy, and that's not what you've
got. Sorry." Into the rejection folder it went.

The next query was utterly baffling. The name and

address of the Novel Idea Literary Agency and a date from last week had been written at the top of the document in an angular scrawl. Beneath that, there were only four lines of text reading, "Return my story. I gave it life. It belongs to me. You will regret your actions."

Now here was a quandary. Did I put this in the rejection folder or create a new one termed "Nutcases," "Crackpots," or "Agents Beware"? I rubbed the sheet of paper between my fingers. It was not ordinary printer paper, but quality stationery, watermark and all. It also smelled faintly of the outdoors, but I couldn't pinpoint the scent.

As I raised the sheaf to my nose for a second whiff, a man in his midthirties with tight black curls and formfitting designer jeans jogged over to the table. He slapped a ten-dollar bill on the coffee table and shouted, "Zach Attack!"

"Excuse me?"

He thrust his hand right under my chin, and I instinctively jerked away, trying to protect my personal space. "Zach Cohen, aka Mr. Hollywood—the man who gets the screenplays onto the big screen." He pumped my hand up and down and then let go. "I also represent sports writers. *All* the elite athletes who are able to string a sentence together come to me. Especially the B-ball guys. I just sent out a proposal for a tell-all by one our most famous Dunston players. Can't name names, but I'm *sure* you know who I mean." He stood back so that he could take note of how impressed I was by this declaration.

I was not impressed, because I didn't know a thing about basketball. This is a grave sin considering I live in central North Carolina, home to several elite basketball programs, but I didn't care. "I'm Lila Wilkins," I replied flatly, and then my Southern upbringing kicked in. "It's very nice to meet you. Do you mind telling me why you're offering me money?"

"Caffeine run, baby. The Zach Attack has to have his double espresso every morning to work his magic." He cracked his knuckles repeatedly as though already experiencing caffeine withdrawal. "I wanted to treat you to one, too, seeing as it's your first day on the job. I was hoping *you'd* run downstairs and get them for us. I'm waiting on a call from New York, and your queries aren't exactly going anywhere, so what do you say?"

I swallowed a mouthful of irc and tried to address Zach as pleasantly as possible. "I'd be glad to go this *one* time, but I did not accept this position in order to fetch your espresso."

Zach smiled and dusted a fleck of lint from his formfitting black crewneck. "You're a sassy one. That's good! You actually stand a chance of surviving the summer. The last girl spent half her morning doing coffee runs and spilled at least one latte a day. I kept telling her she couldn't handle the stairs *and* a tray of coffees wearing those wedge-heeled sandals she liked." His mouth stretched into what I'm sure he thought was a charming smile.

"I doubt 'the last girl' enjoyed playing waitress, and I'm a *woman* with twenty years of journalism under my belt. I'm here to become an agent, and that's all." I gave Zach a hostile glare and then realized I'd better start off on the right foot with the young man. After all, I wanted to be one of his equals in three months. "But it is very kind of you to buy me a coffee. I never say no to a free latte, but I'm not ready to take a break just yet."

He looked at me with new respect. "Twenty years, huh?

I heard you worked for the *Herald*. You know, you're *totally* overqualified to be an intern at this place, but the Zach Attack is glad we've got someone with an experienced eye to sift through our queries."

Mr. Hollywood wasn't so bad after all, though I prayed he wouldn't continue to refer to himself in third person. I asked him if the other agents would come around to introduce themselves.

"I'd just knock on their doors if I were you," Zach suggested. "But don't bother looking for Luella Ardor. She never gets in before ten. I think she stays up late reading those erotic romances she represents."

Slightly put off by the manner in which Zach licked his lips, I excused myself and marched back down the hall. I stopped at the first door on the right, which was marked as belonging to Franklin Stafford.

A low and soothing voice responded to my knock. "Come in."

"Hello. I'm Lila Wilkins, the new intern."

Stafford was the image of a Norman Rockwell grandfather. A ring of fluffy gray hair surrounded the shiny dome of his head, and a mustache the same color hovered on his top lip. Twinkling blue eyes appraised me through silver-rimmed glasses. He wore a crisp white button-down shirt and brown slacks held up by a pair of striped suspenders. Behind his chair, a plaid suit jacket and an umbrella hung from a coat tree with shiny brass hooks. Franklin's office was as subdued as Flora's was colorful, and I began to picture the agency's offices as little shops in a small town. Each one had a markedly different flavor based on the wares it sold. Flora's room reflected her love of fantasy and adventure, while Franklin's space spoke of refinement, tradition, and order.

"Welcome to the Novel Idea Literary Agency. Pleased to meet you." The older man stood up from behind his desk and approached me, offering his hand. "Franklin Stafford, the agent for most of the nonfiction work we represent." He gestured to a wall covered with framed book covers. "It seems we have that in common. I understand you've worked for the *Dunston Herald*."

"That's right." I walked over to the frames and looked at the covers. An Idiot's Guide to writing poetry. A how-to on feng shui. A book on fishing in the South. Another on planning for retirement. A golfer's advice book. "Quite an eclectic selection," I said, looking around the rest of the room. In addition to a pair of wing chairs upholstered in soft tweed, polished cherry bookcases and a large wooden file cabinet occupied the rest of the space. On the floor beside Franklin's dark mahogany desk was a long green runner with a little metal putting hole at the end. A putter and yellow golf ball rested beside it.

"Heh, heh. That's my stress reliever," he said, picking up the putter. "Do you golf?"

"I'm afraid I was never athletic and don't follow a particular sport," I admitted. "But my son has tried them all. Surfing is his latest love."

"I have a splendid reference book on surfing." He removed a hardcover from the nearest bookshelf. "It's signed by my client, and I have several copies, so please give this to your son. Consider it a welcome gift."

I was touched by his generosity. "Thank you. Trey will love this." That was partially true. Trey would love looking at the beautiful photographs at least.

Grinning, Franklin tucked his thumbs under his suspender straps. "Are you a nonfiction reader?"

"Not really. As a reporter, my whole life has revolved around facts, so when I want to relax I turn to fiction," I answered. "However, I do buy biographies and memoirs on occasion. I read a wonderful biography last month. Mitch Albom's *Have a Little Faith*."

"An excellent book." He tapped his large ears. "I listened to an audio recording of that work while driving to the Masters this spring. I found it quite moving."

Just then, a breeze blew in from the open window behind his desk, fluttering some pages. Franklin put his hand down to stop them from flying onto the floor. "I need to get a paperweight. I love to breathe the fresh air, despite the humidity."

I smiled at him. I preferred to inhale Freon-free air as well. "I'd better finish my rounds. See you soon, Franklin."

"I have a feeling we're going to be great friends," he said, returning my smile.

I rapped on the next door but received no response. I checked the name. Jude Hudson. He must not be in yet, either. Bypassing Bentley's door, I returned to the lobby.

I was just about to leave for Espresso Yourself when a man emerged at the top of the stairs. His appearance was so startling that I froze on the spot, Zach's ten-dollar bill hanging limply in my hand. It took me several seconds to react, because the man seemed so incongruous with the surroundings that I believed he might be an apparition. He had the appearance of someone I'd expect to see on the street corner with a shopping cart filled with possessions, but not here, in the pristine offices of the Novel Idea Literary Agency. What had brought him upstairs? Was he lost? Confused? Off his meds?

"May I help you, sir?" I spoke gently, as if I were addressing a frightened child or injured animal.

The man scratched his long, knotty beard and stared at me with a pair of dark, deep-set eyes. Though partially obscured by wild, bushy brows, those eyes seemed haunted. The man's dirt-encrusted fingers abandoned his beard and traveled to a spot on his scalp, which he clawed roughly. The action seemed to further entangle the mat of unkempt hair, which was the color of steel wool. I couldn't see the other hand, as it was hidden behind his back.

My eyes traveled from the man's weathered face to his dingy clothes. Despite the warm temperature outside, he wore long pants and a long-sleeved denim jacket over a striped T-shirt. None of his apparel looked as though it had been washed recently, and judging from the shade of the feet protruding from a pair of tattered leather sandals, he hadn't seen the inside of a shower stall for quite some time, either. My heart went out to him. How had he become this decrepit and troubled creature?

"You're new," he croaked as though his throat were parched and raw.

"I am," I agreed with a warm smile. "Would you like some water? It's so humid out already."

He nodded humbly and withdrew a handful of wildflowers from behind his back. I had never seen flowers like the ones he held forth. They were shaped like snowballs, made of dozens and dozens of tiny white blossoms, and at the base of each individual blossom was a reddish purple ring. The leaves were large and waxy, and the stem was brown and wiry, as though the stalks had been clipped from a bush.

23

"These are for you," the man said in his gravelly voice and gently laid the flowers on the coffee table.

I stared at the blooms for a moment, totally taken aback by the bizarre scene in which I was somehow a player. And I had thought a quota of query letters would consume my entire day.

Shrugging myself into action, I removed the bottled water from my purse and handed it to the man. "I'll accept your gift if you'll accept mine."

"Thank you." He smiled, displaying a set of surprisingly white and perfectly aligned teeth. The frightened look in his eyes abated. He took a deep, grateful drink of water, and I wondered if it had been a long time since someone had shown this man any kindness.

"My name's Marlette." He spoke softly as though wary of attracting attention. "Have you read my letter yet?"

A homeless man had submitted a query letter? "I don't think so. This is my first day, and at this point, I've only had the chance to read two."

He cast a glance at the folders on the coffee table. A look of pleading crossed his face. "There's one in with the flowers. I always put one in with the flowers."

Suddenly, the sound of voices tripped down the hall. Eyes widening in alarm, Marlette turned and fled down the stairs, leaving a waft of foul-smelling air behind him.

"There goes our resident lunatic," Bentley Burlington-Duke said to me. "He'll be back. He always comes in twice. Just give him an hour or two in the sun to get a little riper. That man has absolutely no sense of personal hygiene." Without warning, she grabbed the flowers from the coffee table, gave them a disgusted shake, and dropped them onto the floor. Turning to the incredibly attractive man who'd accompanied her down the hall, she said, "Dispose of these in the Dumpster, would you, Jude?"

This must be Jude Hudson. My, my. He was so handsome that I couldn't take my eyes off him. Focusing on his chiseled features, I briefly forgot about Marlette's query letter.

Jude must have felt my gaze, because he turned to me and held out his hand. "Jude Hudson. I represent thrillers and suspense novels. You must be the new intern."

"I . . . am," I breathed. Shaking his hand, I swear I felt a spark. It wasn't carpet static, because we were standing on a hardwood floor. He had dark wavy hair, chocolate brown eyes framed with long lashes, and a rugged chin with a hint of a beard that I found very sexy. I bet he spent time in the gym, judging by the way his snug dress shirt revealed the outline of well-defined muscles. For a middle-aged man, he was a fine specimen.

"Lily!" Ms. Burlington-Duke spoke my name too loudly. I jumped. "It's Lila."

"See that no more vagabonds enter our office." She waved toward the staircase. "I don't want anything to disturb my meeting with our client Carson Knight, who is due to arrive any minute. Here. I printed out the week's query letters mistakenly sent to my personal email account. You can add these to your current file." She handed me a wad of papers, turned, and disappeared down the hall.

"Zach said you were heading to Espresso Yourself. I'd accompany you, but I have more contract details to review with Carson." Jude's velvety voice felt like a caress. He bent down to pick up the flowers while I enjoyed the view.

"Don't worry. I'll take a rain check." I couldn't believe I'd said that. I wasn't normally so forward. Grabbing my purse, I made my exit before Jude could realize that I'd been staring at every inch of him.

There was no line in the cramped café downstairs. Coeds with laptops occupied most of the tables, and two patrons waited for their drinks at the pick-up station next to the barista.

I made my way slowly to the counter as I took in the art on the wall, an array of wonderful watercolors and oils. One of them, a lively rendition of the town, was marked by a sign declaring: *All paintings by local artists. Support your community by buying an original.*

Acoustic guitar music played over speakers. Beside the counter stood a carved wooden shelf holding uniquely shaped and colored mugs. *Mugs by Christa*, a notice posted on the shelf proclaimed.

I was greeted by an African American clerk in her mid-twenties. Her head was shaved, accentuating her fern green eyes. Her skin looked like chocolate silk and was infused with a radiance that made her appear ageless.

"You are gorgeous!" I couldn't help exclaim. "Your eyes are dazzling, and you have the most beautiful skin I've ever seen."

"Woman, you have made my day!" she beamed. When I recited Zach's order, her fingers paused over the register keys. "Are you the new intern?"

"I am. Though it seems like no one is able to last long in the intern position. Any insights?"

The woman laughed, a sound that reminded me of wind chimes. "Not a clue. All I can say is don't take anything too seriously. Life's about small pleasures, right? A cup of coffee, a great song, someone telling you you've got nice skin. You see what I'm saying?"

I nodded. "How did you get so wise at such a tender age?"

She grinned. "You learn stuff when your job is to give folks the boost they need to make it through another workday. And I read a *ton* of books. We have sort of a lending library in the corner there." She gestured to a niche filled with three stuffed bookshelves. "I also keep one behind the counter for when things get slow. A girl can only wipe a counter so many times, you know what I'm saying?"

I laughed. "So what are you hiding back there now?"

She held out the cover of a tattered paperback with a flourish and then put it down the counter again. It was the latest novel by Nicholas Sparks. "That man's words melt in the mouth like sugar! And a girl needs a good dose of romance every now and again." She uncapped a pen and drew a heart on a paper napkin. "Still, next time you get in line I could just as well have J. D. Robb or Malcolm Gladwell under the counter. Even *I* don't know what I'm going to read next. I walk over to those shelves in the corner, close my eyes, and pick a book. I'm Makayla, by the way. I run this little corner of heaven." She favored me with another stunning smile.

"I plan to start all of my days off here, Makayla," I said after introducing myself. "Coffee *and* books? This place is paradise."

"Stop by tomorrow and your next latte is on me. It's my way of welcoming you as a new regular customer. And feel free to sit and talk to me about books anytime. I'd love it!"

Glad to have made a new friend, I carefully carried the coffees upstairs to the office. To my credit, I didn't spill a single drop of Zach's espresso.

Even so, things were about to get *very* messy.

Chapter 3

BACK IN A NOVEL IDEA'S RECEPTION AREA, I SMELLED Marlette before I saw him. Once again, that stale scent of unwashed flesh and clothing permeated the space. Despite the aromas created by my tray of hot drinks, the espresso and steamed milk failed to mask the distasteful odor.

"Mr. Marlette." I put the beverages down on the coffee table and cast a quick glance at him out of the corner of my eye. I was surprised to see that he was reclining on the sofa with his face resting against one of the back pillows. He had clearly fallen asleep. "Sir. You can't rest here."

When he didn't respond, I sighed in exasperation and decided to deliver Zach's beverage before it grew tepid. I couldn't just shoo Marlette away. Bentley had stated that he often came to the office twice a day. If he was going to be a regular fixture in my life, I wanted to lay down some ground rules with him. And truth be told, I was dying to read his query letter.

I gave Zach his double espresso and then quickly returned to the front, hoping Marlette had awakened, but he hadn't moved an inch since I'd left the room. His head was still resting against the cushion, and his shoulders were slumped forward as though he were in a deep slumber. Yet something was wrong about his posture. Then I realized exactly what was amiss.

Marlette's shoulders were not gently rising and falling with each breath. They weren't moving at all.

I quietly approached the sofa and placed my hand lightly on the man's ratty shirt. I patted him on the upper arm, and when he didn't respond, I gave the arm a mild shake.

Finally, I was forced to push a mat of hair from the man's face in order to put my fingertips under his nose in hopes of feeling an exhalation, but my hand stopped midair the moment I saw that Marlette's eyes were open. Open and unblinking with a trail of dried tears leading down each cheek.

Having long been a fan of television medical dramas, I knew to check for a carotid pulse by locating Marlette's Adam's apple and then moving my fingers outward until they encountered a ropy muscle. The flesh on Marlette's neck felt doughy, and as I searched, I noticed his lips were abnormally large and the flesh on his face was swollen.

"Nothing," I whispered, feeling the panic rise in my chest. Next, I grabbed Marlette's bloated hand, and turning the dirty palm over, I pressed firmly on the wrist. "Come on," I entreated. "Come on."

But the limpness of his wrist and the slack weight of his arm made it perfectly clear that the life had gone out of Marlette. There was already a hollowness to him, as though he had run away from his body and would never return. I backed away from the flaccid cheeks, the inert chest, and the repellent smell of a man who had walked in with an offering of flowers earlier that hour. Yet his skin was warm to the touch. Maybe there was still life left in his body.

Wracking my brain, I tried to recall everything I once knew about performing CPR, but my mind drew a blank. All I could remember was that if I did it wrong, the lifesaving procedure could do more harm than good.

I rushed down the hall and banged on Bentley's door.

"This had better be good!" Bentley sounded most displeased. "Lila? Is that you?"

I went in, too upset to acknowledge that she'd finally said my name correctly.

"I need help! Does anyone here know CPR? Mr. Marlette . . ." I swallowed hard and then forced myself to calm down. "I think he's dead." I gestured behind me. "He's out there on the sofa. I couldn't find a pulse."

Bentley scowled. "That man is infuriating. Is there anything he won't do for attention?"

Jude, who had leapt to his feet during my startling announcement, shouted, "Call 911!" and then ran off toward the reception area.

"How awful," said the man seated in a leather chair across from Bentley's desk. I nodded gratefully at the voice of compassion, locking eyes with Carson Knight, the thriller writer who was in the office to review the lucrative deal from Doubleday. He must have arrived while I was downstairs getting acquainted with Makayla. A good-looking man in his late forties, Carson had a lean body, sand brown hair, and intelligent gray eyes that were gazing at me with concern from behind a pair of silver-framed glasses.

Bentley waved me away. "Go on. Phone the authorities."

I pulled out my cell phone and hurried toward the foyer. As I passed Flora's office, her door opened and she peered out.

"What's all the commotion?"

I pointed down the hall. "Marlette. I think he's dead, but someone has to try to revive him." Rushing off, I almost knocked over Franklin, who had just stepped out of his office.

"I know CPR. One of my clients wrote a book on reacting to emergency situations," he said. "Where is he?"

"Follow me!" I said and ran to the lobby with Franklin right on my heels.

Jude was at the couch, leaning toward Marlette, who was no longer hunched over but lying flat on his back. "We've got to get him breathing," Jude said, spinning around to face us.

Franklin dashed over and began to rhythmically press down on Marlette's chest. "One and two and three and," he huffed.

Suddenly realizing I hadn't yet called 911, I punched in the number on my cell phone. Making the report to the emergency operator, I watched Franklin give mouth-to-mouth to Marlette, ashamed at the relief I felt that Franklin was touching those chapped lips while I spoke to a calm woman who promised to dispatch a team of paramedics immediately. "There's an emergency crew en route," I announced as I hung up. "They should be here soon."

Jude leaned over and whispered in my ear, "Are the police coming, too?"

"Probably." I edged away from him after noticing that Flora was positioned behind us anxiously wringing her hands. "Why?"

Jude glanced at Marlette, then back at me. "I think this may be a homicide."

"You mean . . ." Flora dropped her hands and looked aghast. *"Murder?"*

"That's ridiculous," declared Zach, who had materialized in the lobby. "Why would anyone kill a homeless guy?"

I was wondering the same thing when Bentley came out of her office with Carson. The attractive forty-something author had donned his suit jacket while Bentley was wearing enormous Chanel sunglasses and carried a Louis Vuitton duffel in her hand. Striding down the hall they looked as though they were embarking on a trip.

Bentley halted at our little group. "Jude, let's go."

"You're kidding, right?" Jude looked stunned. "You need to deal with this situation. I think Marlette's been murdered."

"Murdered?" Carson's surprised gaze moved from Jude to Marlette. "Looks more like an allergic reaction. His face is terribly swollen."

We all turned toward the couch. I thought about Marlette's puffy fingers and how doughy his neck had felt. "But from what?" I wondered aloud. Certainly not the water I'd given him.

Carson shook his head in dismay. "I don't know. Maybe there was a bee in those flowers he was carrying."

Jude shook his head. "No way. I noticed—"

"We're wasting time," Bentley interrupted impatiently. "My plane is already sitting on the runway. Lila can handle this."

"M-me?" I stammered, flabbergasted that she would even consider jetting off to New York with a dead man in her agency. "Don't you need to be here when the police arrive?"

Apparently, she found nothing amiss in her behavior. "My dear, Mr. Knight, Jude, and I have a late lunch meeting with a senior editor in New York. We have a few minor details to work out, and after that, Mr. Knight will officially become the highest-paid author of the Novel Idea Literary Agency." Her eyes glimmered with dollar signs. "As for this unfortunate incident"—she gestured at Marlette without looking at him—"I'm confident that I can entrust you to manage the police as well as your daily allotment of queries. A woman with your experience and maturity can certainly give a succinct account to the authorities. Come, Jude."

Jude shook his head. "I'm staying, Bentley. This needs to be taken care of. You can handle the details in New York."

"Suit yourself. See you Monday." And with that, she was gone. Carson gave me an apologetic bow, shook Jude's hand, and followed the clip-clop of Bentley's heels down the stairs.

"Oh dear." Flora began wringing her hands again. "Oh dear, oh dear."

I looked over at Franklin, who continued, without any sign of success, administering CPR. I marveled that he refused to give up despite his obvious weariness. "Has anyone ever read Marlette's query letters?"

Flora shrugged. "My goodness, I have no idea! The interns were all warned about his regular visits and his . . . quirks. To tell the truth, they were a bit scared of him. He's been coming here for almost a year now, and he brings flowers every day. Such a nuisance."

"And his letters were always attached to the flowers?" I asked, wanting to confirm what Marlette had told me earlier.

"Yes." Flora sank into one of the club chairs and began

to dab at her flushed face with a tissue. She then continued the motion across her neck and down the deep V of her cleavage. "But I have no idea what they said."

I felt anger on Marlette's behalf. No one had bothered to spend five lousy minutes reading his letter? And yet, he had remained undeterred. Day after day, he reappeared at the agency, clutching his bouquet and his query, only to have his hopes dashed afresh each morning. "Everyone just assumed he was crazy," I murmured sadly.

Flora stood. "Yes, dear, that's about it." She patted my arm. "Don't judge those young interns too harshly. That awful man didn't always make sense. He often babbled or talked to himself and could be a tad frightening. I can't begin to imagine the germs he carried into the office. I encouraged Bentley to get a restraining order against him, but the rest of the agency thought he was harmless, so we never bothered. I guess . . . we all got used to him. He was a fixture, if a rather odoriferous and unsavory one at that."

"But no one saw him as a person, just a nuisance. A brief blight on one's day," I grumbled. "When in truth, he was more of an odd, flower-bearing writer wannabe."

Flora's eyes darkened. "It is terrible that we can become *so* immersed in our regular tasks that we ignore a person right under our noses." She blinked, and the hostility in her eyes evaporated. "Perhaps I've been unfair to him. I don't even know his last name. Or if he had a home or a family. I feel terrible." She hurried back to her office.

Franklin straightened up. "It's not working. He's definitely dead." He brushed his hand over his brow and shrugged. "I did what I could."

"You were amazing," I told him. "Don't blame yourself. I think it was hopeless from the start."

As Franklin shook his head and disappeared down the hall, Jude touched my arm. "I'll be in my office if you need anything. Let me know when the police arrive. I want to talk to them. I'm sure Marlette's death is a result of foul play."

"Why do you believe that?" I asked.

"Okay." He looked from left to right, then directly at me. "When I was straightening him on the couch, I noticed a puncture mark on his neck."

"Like a bee sting?"

Jude shook his head. "Maybe that's what we were intended to think, but I know what a needle puncture looks like, and that's definitely what it was."

I couldn't keep the shock off my face. Not just at Jude's insistence that Marlette was murdered, but over his statement about needle marks. "But why . . . and who?"

"I don't know, but I have to tell the cops."

Watching him walk away, I picked up my latte from the coffee table. Just as I took a sip of the unappealingly cooled brew, I heard the heavy tread of several men on the stairs.

A pair of officers from the Dunston Police Department met me at the top. The one in the lead, a stocky, thick-necked man in his late twenties, walked directly over to Marlette. A couple of paramedics carrying a stretcher pushed past me and followed him. The second policeman, an all-American-looking blond with blue eyes in his early fifties, held out his hand. "Officer Griffiths. Are you all right, ma'am?"

I was charmed by the fact that he asked how I was faring before peppering me with questions. I told him I'd had a heck of a first day on the job and explained how I'd found Marlette dead on the sofa.

Officer Griffiths wrote down every word I said, and his bright blue eyes and professional, courteous manner were a balm.

"That's *some* first day," he commented when I was finished. "Would you like to sit down?"

I shook my head, feeling more unnerved than I let on. My mother's gloomy premonition kept repeating in my mind. Every now and then, her foresight was accurate, but the circumstances were usually positive. She'd stop a young couple in the grocery store and predict that they would soon be married or tell an expectant mother the gender of her baby. Sometimes, she knew the location of a lost pet or a missing object, but she'd never known about a death before it happened. I rubbed my arms, feeling chilled as I recalled her certainty that someone would die in this office.

The medical examiner arrived and quickly moved toward his patient. After inspecting Marlette's lifeless body, he conferred with the paramedics and the stocky police officer. I tried to listen in on their conversation but only caught snippets, words and phrases that put my senses on high alert and caused my brain to start whirring. "Fresh needle puncture," I heard the ME say. "Doubt it was self-administered because there was no . . ."

I wished I could have heard the whole conversation, but I did catch part of the cop's response: "Possible homicide."

Jude's suspicions were right! Someone had murdered Marlette. Even the police thought so. At that moment, I decided I would do everything I could to discover who had harmed a man who just wanted to have his query letter read.

"Do they know what happened to him?" I asked Griffiths as the two paramedics began to unfold the legs of the gurney.

Griffiths made a noncommittal shrug. "Nothing defini-

tive until an autopsy is done. Results could take anywhere
from six to twelve weeks."

"And that's it? He just goes . . . in some refrigerated
drawer until the autopsy?" I felt as though someone should
be concerned on Marlette's behalf.

"We'll search for next of kin." Griffiths looked over his
notes. "So he came here every day carrying flowers? I should
probably talk to someone who's been here a bit longer than
you about his past behavior." He said this with a smile.
"Would you take me to your boss?"

I shifted on my feet. "She left to catch a flight to New
York."

Griffiths raised his brows. "Before or after this man died
in her office?"

I glanced around the officer's shoulder in order to watch
the men strap Marlette into the gurney. One of them grimaced, no doubt over the pungent smell emanating from the
corpse. The second paramedic was all business and quietly
directed his partner to prepare to hoist the gurney. I felt
sorry for the two men. It couldn't be easy to bear Marlette's
weight down a flight of stairs. Suddenly, I wondered how a
person with a physical disability would make it up to our
office and whether the Novel Idea Literary Agency represented any handicapped clients.

"Ms. Wilkins?"

Returning my attention to the policeman's patient face,
I answered, "Ms. Burlington-Duke left afterward, and I'm
sorry to say that I doubt she, or anyone else in the back
offices, could tell you much more about Marlette. I believe
he was assigned to the interns. No one else interacted
with him."

"Do you think you could get me contact information for

the most recent intern?" he inquired, his grin transforming from friendliness into something intangibly flirtatious as he handed me a business card.

I told Griffiths I'd be glad to help. Why not? He seemed like a sweet guy, and I wanted to talk to that intern myself. Not only would I like to find out more about Marlette, but I'd also love to know why my predecessor hadn't been able to hack it at the agency for more than a mere three months.

I took the card and returned the lawman's inviting smile. "I'll get back to you soon."

As the professionals concentrated on their tasks, the literary agents drifted out of their offices. Jude pulled the stocky policeman aside and talked to him. I wanted to listen in on the other cop's reaction to Jude's murder theory, but Officer Griffiths kept demanding my attention.

"Ms. Wilkins, we need to conduct a search of the premises. If you and your coworkers would please make room, we'll get started."

I was about to reply when Franklin stepped forward. "I think you need a warrant for that. Especially since Ms. Burlington-Duke is not present."

"Sir, this is a possible crime scene, and we can search the open areas of this lobby without a warrant," Officer Griffiths replied. A trifle embarrassed, Franklin acquiesced and went to stand beside Flora.

Zach and Jude moved forward to assist the men from the coroner's office with their burden, but their offer was courteously declined. Flora began to weep again and was comforted by Franklin, who made soothing noises while handing her tissue after tissue. As I stood aside with the agents, Griffiths asked them several questions about Marlette, but it was obvious they knew almost nothing about him. The other officer started to search the area around the sofa, peering behind the throw pillows and running his hands between the cushions.

Eventually, Franklin escorted Flora back to her office. Jude, Zach, and I stood around looking at one another, then at the policemen. One of them was on his hands and knees shining a flashlight under the couch, while the other was flipping through a notebook. It was as if we expected them to provide us with an explanation, to reason away the morning's tragedy. No one said anything for a while, and a sudden breeze wafted up as the gurney was taken outside. Downstairs, the door closed with a click, then almost immediately opened again. Heels tapped up the stairs.

"Oh my!" a genteel voice exclaimed. "Whatever has happened?"

An elegant woman stepped into the reception area. She was wearing an ivory pantsuit that looked like it was fresh from a boutique in Paris. With strappy gold sandals on her feet and a gold-threaded, multicolored scarf arranged artfully around her neck, she exuded an air of sophistication and drama. Her red hair was arranged into a complicated chignon at the nape of her neck, accentuating her incredible cheekbones. Who was this beauty? Could she be a movie star? If so, what was she doing here, in a literary agency in Inspiration Valley?

Standing—no, posing—at the agency's entrance, she took off her sunglasses. Green eyes the color of jade cast around the space, taking in all of us standing about like thoughtless zombies. Barely glancing at me, her gaze alighted on both Jude and Zach longer than necessary before she turned to Griffiths.

"Oh, officer," she gushed, approaching him. "Has something terrible happened here? I saw men outside with a gurney. Pray tell, who was under the sheet? Not . . . one of us. Tell me it wasn't . . ." Her hands fluttered at her heart, and she batted long eyelashes at him.

Griffiths blushed and cleared his throat. "I'm Officer Griffiths, ma'am. And you are . . . ?"

The woman stood a little straighter. "I am Luella Ardor, an agent here at Novel Idea. Please, what's happened?"

Ah, the romance agent. Jude and Zach stared at Luella as if they were under some kind of spell. I felt an odd twinge of jealousy.

"A man named Marlette was found dead on this couch." Griffiths's tone was solicitous. "Maybe you could tell me something about him."

Luella brought both hands to her cheeks. "Oh! Oh! Poor Marlette. Such a strange man. But rather a fixture around here." She sighed. "How did he die?" Her eyes widened as she looked at Griffiths.

"We won't know until the coroner submits his report, ma'am."

The stocky policeman suddenly appeared beside Luella and touched her elbow. "Are you all right, Ms. Ardor? Would you like to sit down? I know this must be a shock." He gently guided her to a chair.

"Why, thank you. You're just as sweet as a caramel apple in autumn." She smiled, small dimples appearing in her cheeks, and lowered herself into the seat.

Griffiths looked at me. "Maybe some water?" I pretended not to notice and shuffled the folders of queries on the coffee table.

"Oh, are you the new intern?" Luella suddenly seemed to realize I was in the room.

I introduced myself.

"Nice to meet you, Lila. Could you be a dear and get me a coffee? A skinny latte?"

"I don't do coffee," I answered pleasantly.

Luella's eyes widened, and she quickly looked away. "Eww, what is that?" She pointed to a spot on the floor near her chair.

We all directed our gaze to the place she indicated. Griffiths bent and picked up an object with his thumb and forefinger. "It's a dead bee."

"A bee?" I looked at Jude. Maybe Marlette had simply succumbed to an innocent bee sting.

Griffiths examined it closely. "They do fly indoors sometimes."

Luella perked up. "It could have been inside Marlette's flowers." She touched Griffiths's arm as if she wanted him to appreciate the brilliance of her deduction. "He brought in a bouquet of weeds every day."

Griffiths's eyes circled the room. "I see. And where might those flowers be now?"

"Jude threw them out," I quickly replied as I pulled a tissue out of my bag. "I can take that from you, Officer Griffiths."

"Thank you for being so helpful, Ms. Wilkins." He took the tissue with his free hand and then gave my fingers a brief squeeze, causing my pulse to skip a beat. "But I'll take care of this little insect."

He smiled, and our eyes met.

"Ahem." Luella coughed, causing Griffiths to break his keen gaze. "Can *I* help in any way, Officer?"

"Why, yes, Ms. Ardor." Griffiths pulled his notebook out of his pocket. "We'd like to ask you some questions."

She stood up and started toward the hall. "Let's do that

in my office, shall we?" she said, looking back at him over her shoulder with a flutter of false eyelashes.

Griffiths and the other cop were quick to follow her. Zach and Jude hustled behind them. I watched them all disappear down the corridor, the beauty queen and her entourage. Shaking my head, I looked at my stack of queries. Although it seemed somewhat disrespectful, I decided to attempt to focus on work. After all, I still had to prove myself at this job.

I eyed the couch. It would be irreverent, not to mention a bit creepy, to use as a backrest the piece of furniture on which a man had just died. Reluctantly, I gathered the files and wormed my way back over to the student desk. Ignoring my discomfort, I picked up the query at the top of the pile.

In my suspense mystery novel titled No Insurance Against Murder, *a woman is found dead in the office of the vice president of an insurence agency. Her cause of death is musterious, since there are no outward signs of physical truama, and no one in the Agency knows who she is.*

A chill tiptoed up my spine as the similarities between this poorly written query and the events of this morning crossed my mind. The paper fluttered out of my hand as I sat back and pondered. Marlette's death was mysterious. In fact, everything about him was mysterious. No one even knew his last name, and he'd climbed those stairs carrying wildflowers day after day. I, for one, wanted to know more.

If only I'd been able to read his query letter!

And then I remembered the wilting bouquet of flowers

Jude had been directed to throw in the Dumpster. There had been a piece of paper fastened around the flower stalks. The least I could do was fulfill the last wish of this tragic stranger.

I couldn't concentrate on the folder of query letters for another second. A man had just died a few feet from where I now worked. I was too rattled to read, but not to hunt down Marlette's final words.

I tossed my pencil aside and hustled down the stairs. Nothing was going to stop me from reading that query, even if it was too late to help the author. After all, that poor writer was already on his way to the morgue.

Chapter 4

I DON'T MAKE A HABIT OF RUNNING, ESPECIALLY DOWN stairs, but I moved my body as fast as it would go, my mind locked on the wildflower bouquet Bentley had told Jude to toss into the Dumpster.

When I reached the garbage receptacle, I groaned. It quickly became clear that Novel Idea shared a Dumpster with the coffee shop. The smell of rotten fruit and old coffee grounds mingled with even more repugnant odors, but I was determined to find that query letter.

Unfortunately, the top of the Dumpster was locked, leaving only the sliding doors open, through which all the trash had been shoved. As this opening was at eye level, I was able to view the most recent deposits. Though I saw several black garbage bags and a few flattened pieces of cardboard, there was no sign of the cluster of white flowers.

Looking around for something to stand on, I spied a plastic crate near the back door of Espresso Yourself. Balancing on top of the crate was a challenge. The pointy heels of my shoes keep slipping into the holes of the crate, and I had no choice but to grab onto the edge of the Dumpster's open door in order to maintain my footing.

This angle, however, allowed me to see into the darkened corners, and I was certain I saw a glimmer of white petals in the far left. There was no way I could reach it, so I eased myself off the crate, now in search of an object with which I could slide the bouquet back toward the front, but where was I going to find a rake or a broom in this tiny unloading area?

I knew I couldn't spend much more time down here. My first day on the job and I'd already left my desk unmanned without a word of warning. The truth was, I didn't know whom I could trust. A man had just died at Novel Idea by suspicious means, and I had to have answers.

Raising my chin in determination, I strode over to the back door of the coffee shop and pulled it open. I was a bit surprised to find the door unlocked. In Dunston, it would have been securely bolted, but I suppose the merchants of Inspiration didn't have to worry about break-ins. This realization gave me a warm feeling even though I felt like a trespasser as I entered a narrow hallway where the restroom and a tiny closet were located. In the closet, propped inside a yellow bucket, was a mop.

Eureka! For someone who never enjoyed having to use this particular domestic tool, I was quite pleased to see one now.

I admit to being rude and cowardly, but I didn't ask Makayla if I could borrow the mop. She'd find out about Marlette's passing soon enough, having undoubtedly noticed the paramedics taking his body away, and I'm sure she was aware of the police presence, but I didn't want to get caught up explaining what had happened. However, if I discovered any pertinent information about the unfortunate writer's death, I felt certain I could entrust my findings to Makayla.

Back at the trash bin, I flailed about with the mop handle, forcing the ragged flowers to inch toward me. When they abruptly stopped moving, I noticed that the string holding them together had gotten snagged on the ripped corner of a sign illustrating the refreshing purity of a glass of cold cranberry pomegranate tea. No matter how I batted at the bouquet with the mop, the flowers remained stubbornly attached to the torn sign.

"You won't get the better of me!" I shouted, my voice echoing against the metal walls. "I am *not* leaving without that query letter."

Kicking off my pumps, I wriggled my upper body into the opening and stretched my arms out as far as they would go. The flowers were a mere finger length away. I scooted my hips forward, grabbed onto the stems, and tipped forward.

"Oh no!" was all I had time to exclaim before my entire body came crashing down onto a bag containing foul-smelling milk cartons and banana peels. My weight caused the bag to burst open, and I found myself up to my elbows in a pile of spoiled food.

Muttering curses I'd never allow Trey to speak, I grabbed hold of the flowers and waded through garbage bags until I reached the sliding doors. Suddenly, the daylight was blocked and a face appeared in the opening.

I heard a high-pitched shriek, and then a woman exclaimed, "Lord have mercy! I thought you were the world's biggest rat! I admit we don't know each other all too well, but I never pegged you for a Dumpster diver." Makayla peered in at me, and I could see an amused smile directed my way.

"Just give me a hand, would you?" I pleaded.

Safely back on solid ground, I inspected the flowers. They were still tied together, but there was no sign of the query letter. I examined the stems around the base, which were so tightly bunched together that there was no way the piece of paper had haphazardly fallen out.

Someone had taken Marlette's query letter. Was it Jude? He was told to toss the flowers into the trash. But why would he do that today when Marlette had shown up month after month with a letter that no one had cared about?

Makayla was staring at me, hands on her narrow hips. "Girl! Are you gonna tell me what is going on at the crazy place you work? Here I am, fixing espressos and serving muffins, when I look out my window to see a body bag being loaded into an ambulance." She stopped speaking and scrutinized my face. "Talk about a tough first day! Are you doing okay?"

I nodded and gave her a succinct account of this morning's events. It already seemed like months ago that I'd first boarded the Inspiration Express. Maybe I should have stayed on the train. I could have feasted on a frosted cinnamon twist and sipped a cup of rich decaf as the industrial parks of Dunston were left behind and the locomotive burst through a tunnel into the lush, green paradise that was Inspiration Valley. I could have been lulled to sleep by the train's gentle rocking and remained onboard when everyone else disembarked. But I hadn't. I'd wanted an adventure, and now I was right smack in the middle of one.

"Well, you might feel fine, but you don't smell fine." Makayla wrinkled her nose in distaste.

She was right. "'There's small choice in rotten apples,'" I murmured unhappily, quoting Shakespeare's Hortensio. I possess an uncanny ability, which I've had since childhood, to recall random lines of text from my favorite literary works. In moments of intense emotion, I turn to the words of familiar authors to help me express my own feelings.

Makayla, instead of being impressed by tribute to the Bard, ignored my mutterings. "I'm gonna have to spray you with the deodorizer in the bathroom. Smells like a lemon ammonia cocktail, but it's better than a mighty powerful whiff of rotten cheese Danish and brown bananas."

Makayla wasn't kidding. She literally opened fire on me with an aluminum can of room deodorizer. She got my clothes, my shoes, my hair. I examined my reflection in the mirror and was pleased to find that I didn't have bits of trash stuck to my shoulder-length nut brown hair. I swiveled this way and that, thinking that I needed to wear a longer blouse over my pencil skirt in the future, for even though I was tall, I was curvy. Perhaps too curvy for such a snug skirt. No wonder men I didn't know were flirting with me! But now that I smelled like eau de Lysol, I doubted that even my coffee-colored eyes or Rubenesque figure would attract too many admirers. Heading back upstairs, I felt like a freshly disinfected hospital ward.

"Come find me at the end of the day, Ms. Pine-Sol!" Makayla called after me. "I'll fix you something special to make you feel better."

I paused on the landing. "Thank you, but I'm going to want something much stronger than coffee by the time *this* day is finally over."

Returning to my sad little desk and the stack of query letters, I half expected one of the other agents to rush into the lobby, demanding why I'd been absent for so long, but the office was eerily quiet.

I noticed the relaxing guitar music that had been playing earlier in the day had been turned off, but I was able to remedy the problem by flicking a wall switch located just inside the door of the electrical closet. A lovely melody ebbed from the overhead speakers, and the soothing harmonies created by flutes and cellos allowed me to concentrate on my work once more.

I read through thirty query letters, placed them all in the rejection folder, and then heard the sound of footsteps in the hall. For some reason, I felt compelled to hide the single flower I'd brought back with me. As my desk had no drawers and the tiny, delicate petals would be crushed in my purse, I slipped the bloom in between the pages of the first book I pulled from the shelves containing the works of Novel Idea clients. It was called *Can't Take the Heat*.

Luella Ardor strode into the lobby as though she were on a catwalk in Milan. Pausing at my desk, she flipped a strand of glossy hair over one shoulder and smiled at me. "That's by Calliope Sinclair, one of my most prolific authors. Borrow that book if you want, but be warned: You will *not* want to sleep alone after you've had a taste. Chapter three contains the most erotic sex scene I've ever come across. The heroine is in an elevator with two firemen and—"

"Thank you," I interrupted hastily. Truth be told, I was rather interested in hearing the rest of that sentence, but Franklin had suddenly appeared in the lobby, and I didn't want to be caught discussing a ménage à trois in his presence. I wanted his respect, and I suspected I'd earn it by acting like a professional and a former journalist, not like a tween swooning over a poster of a shirtless heartthrob.

Still, I couldn't help exchanging a secretive smile with Luella as I slid the book into my bag.

"I'm off to lunch," Franklin announced and then paused. "In the face of this morning's unfortunate incident, Bentley probably forgot to mention that you may take an hour for lunch whenever you'd like. The main switchboard number has been set to voicemail since the last intern left, so it might as well stay that way for another sixty minutes."

I looked back and forth between Franklin and Luella. "I'm expected to be the agency's receptionist as well?"

Luella waved an elegant hand at me. "Don't worry, darling. Our clients call us on our personal lines. The only calls you have to field will come from writers checking on their query status or members of the media who haven't pleased Bentley enough to be given her direct number." She fished a compact from her crocodile-skin clutch and examined her reflection. After licking her teeth with her tongue, she snapped the compact and smiled at me. "Honestly, the phone doesn't ring much. Though after this morning . . ." She turned to Franklin. "I think we'd better let it go to voicemail for the remainder of the day, don't you?"

Franklin nodded, recommended I try a sandwich shop on Lavender Lane called Catcher in the Rye, and disappeared downstairs. Luella followed on his heels, talking animatedly into a bejeweled cell phone as she walked.

One would imagine that having seen a dead man would ruin my appetite for the rest of the day, but judging from the growling coming from my lower belly, my body had made a quick recovery.

Catcher in the Rye was three blocks away, but the comforting aroma of baking bread was adrift on the breeze before I even stepped foot onto Lavender Lane. The café, which had both indoor and outdoor eating sections, was already crowded. As I tried to get my bearings, a man explained that I needed to order my food at the counter, pay for it, and wait to be assigned a name.

"I already have a name," I told him. "I don't get it."

"Big Ed'll call a fictional name when your sandwich is ready." The friendly local grinned at me. "Everyone's given a random name by the cashier. Big Ed is a creative fellow, you'll see. Enjoy!"

I had no time to make sense of that last bit, as I had the daunting task of selecting a sandwich from the dozens listed on an enormous chalkboard mounted above the cashier's station. I was tempted by the Van Gogh—turkey, sliced Brie, and apples with honey mustard on a French baguette—and by the Pavarotti—Genoa salami, prosciutto, provolone, and roasted red peppers on toasted Italian bread—but I went with the Hamlet, which was a tasty combination of Black Forest ham, sliced Havarti, tomatoes, and a Dijon mayo on rye.

After I'd ordered and paid, feeling guilty for choosing crinkle-cut potato chips instead of a side of sliced carrots or fruit salad, the cashier handed me a laminated card. "What's this?" I asked.

"Your name," the woman answered and called for the next person in line to step forward.

I smiled. I'd been given a card bearing the name and photograph of Eliza Doolittle. I loved *My Fair Lady*. Somehow, having been given this card made me stand with a more upright posture. With a slight tilt of the chin, I inexplicably felt more hopeful that I was capable of unraveling the mystery behind Marlette's demise.

"Who did you get?" I asked the man who'd been so helpful when I first entered the sandwich shop.

The man frowned unhappily. "One that I don't like. I always feel like a five-year-old child whenever Big Ed calls out this name and I have to step forward. For once, I'd like to get Sinbad the Sailor or James Bond. But no, I'm stuck with—"

"RUMPELSTILTSKIN!" the portly server behind the counter bellowed, and the man next to me slunk forward to collect his lunch.

"Better luck next time, Mr. Hodges!" Big Ed smiled merrily as the man tossed the card bearing his fairy tale identity in a basket. He then caught my eye. "And you must be Eliza Doolittle."

"I's very pleased ta meetchya, I'm sure," I said in my best Cockney accent and performed a small curtsy as Big Ed placed my order on the counter.

Big Ed threw his head back and roared, his second chin wobbling with mirth. In his late sixties, the owner and sandwich artist was completely bald with the exception of a crescent of gray hair hugging the base of his large head. "I sure like it when folks play along. Are you visiting our lovely town on this fine day?"

"No. I just started working at Novel Idea," I said with a hint of pride.

Reaching over the counter to give me a sympathetic pat on the hand, Big Ed said, "I heard what happened over there this morning. A terrible thing. Poor Marlette. He just drifted around this place like a tumbleweed, but he was a harmless old fool, despite what Flora might have told you."

Big Ed wrapped a tuna salad on whole wheat in a sheet of wax paper and shouted, "PIPPI LONGSTOCKING!"

An elderly woman wearing thick glasses shuffled up to the counter. "I *was* a redhead, once upon a time."

"And you're still as hot as a chili pepper." Big Ed winked as his customer accepted her sandwich with a delighted grin.

I liked Big Ed. Opening my bag of chips, I leaned against the counter as though I had all the time in the world to chat. "Was there animosity between Flora and Marlette?"

Big Ed spooned hot meatballs onto a hoagie. "I should think so. Flora called the cops on Marlette a few times. He liked to hang around the Wonderland Playground. It's where all the moms take their kids to play, and Flora thought it was creepy that Marlette would sit on a bench and watch them for hours on end." He topped the meatballs with shredded Romano cheese and garnished the mound with a sprinkle of fresh oregano.

"MICHELANGELO!"

A man wearing coveralls dotted with paint splatters appeared at the counter. "You're giving me too much credit, Big Ed. I just paint houses, my man."

"You never know, Bobby." Big Ed smiled and began to assemble another sandwich. Glancing at me, he continued his story. "Flora accused Marlette of acting like a pedophile. She tried to get the parents riled up to the point of having Marlette banned from the park as a public nuisance or something ridiculous like that."

He placed the next order on the counter. "WALT DISNEY!"

I was entirely focused on Big Ed's story, but the name made me raise my brows. I was surprised that Big Ed had chosen Mickey Mouse's creator to appear on one of his cards.

"What?" Big Ed gestured at the middle-aged woman collecting her sandwich as if he'd read my mind. "You don't consider Walt here an inspiration? He's one of the most inspirational people in history."

Crunching on a potato chip, I nodded in agreement. "Some of my happiest memories are of taking my son to Disney World, but back to Marlette. I only met him today, and I could tell he wasn't a child predator. Why did Flora go out of her way to try to get him banished from the park?"

Big Ed shrugged. "I'm not going to trash-talk your coworker, Eliza. Let's just say that Flora has an image of how things should be. Comes from reading nothing but kids' books, I guess, but her idea of a children's park did not include a vagrant, so she spent a great deal of time trying to make him disappear."

"She wanted the children's park to be like those green and lovely places from a Tasha Tudor or Beatrix Potter book," I murmured. "Talk about preserving one's fantasy."

Big Ed didn't answer, and I realized that I'd lingered at the counter long enough. After wishing him a good day, I found a shady spot on the patio, unwrapped my Hamlet, and pulled the romance novel entitled *Can't Take the Heat* from my bag.

I examined the pair of bare-chested firemen on the cover and hoped I'd have enough time to read through chapter three before my lunch hour was over.

THE FIFTIETH QUERY fluttered to the table. Another one for the rejection folder. Another form letter to mail out. I'd only placed three in the possibilities file. Stretching my back, I glanced in dismay at the two remaining piles, having placed the letters in stacks of twenty-five to better track my progress. It was almost six o'clock, and I didn't see any possible way to meet my quota of one hundred queries even though I'd already read and made comments on the two proposal packets for today. Would Bentley fire me for not having read all the queries?

"Hey, Lila, time to call it quits." Zach, who'd suddenly appeared in front of me, snapped his fingers and pointed to the stairs. "It's the weekend, baby!"

"But I haven't finished my quota."

He stared at the piles of paper. "Don't worry about that. Finish up at home. You don't want to be sitting in the office on a Friday night, do you?"

"No." And I had a mission before catching the seven o'clock train back to Dunston. Franklin had told me that the previous intern, Addison Eckhart, was now employed at the town's garden center. I wanted to talk to her about Marlette and his mysterious query letters. Having phoned the Secret Garden, I discovered that Addison would be working until eight tonight. "You're right. I can do these at home." I gathered up the remaining queries.

"Atta girl. See you Monday." He bounded down the stairs.

I tidied my workspace, hoping Bentley would see fit to give me a proper desk on Monday, and put the unread queries into my bag. I looked around. Should I just leave? Everyone except Franklin was already gone. I knocked on his door.

"I'm going now," I said, as it swung open.

Franklin looked up from his desk. "Sure, sure. Have a good weekend."

"Who locks up? And what if I get here on Monday before anyone else? Do you think I should have a key?"

"Well, the last person to leave usually locks the door, and we all have keys." He scratched his head. "Ask Bentley about that on Monday." He smiled. "Just don't get here before eight. That's when she arrives, and she's always the first."

Before heading out the door, I checked in my bag to make sure that Marlette's flower was still tucked between the pages of *Can't Take the Heat*.

The Secret Garden was on Sweetbay Road, just past the railway station. Walking along the cobblestoned High Street, I turned right at the fountain, making my way toward Walden Woods Circle. I loved walking past these charming cottages, left over from the town's Illumination days, when they served as spacious rental units for a contemplative retreat site. As part of Inspiration Valley's refurbishment, these cabins were renovated and sold as private homes. Painted in an assortment of pastel colors, their tiny gardens were enclosed with white picket fences, and although there was an element of sameness about the neighborhood, each home had its unique character.

My heart went aflutter when I saw a *For Sale* sign in front of a creamy yellow house with blue shutters. Its garden was filled with abundant hydrangea bushes ready to bloom, and the path leading toward the house was made up of stepping-stones in the shapes of leaves. I wondered if I could afford this endearing cottage and jotted down the phone number of Ruthie Watson, whose name was listed on the Sherlock Homes Realty sign in bold blue letters.

When the picket fences ended, I turned onto Sweetbay and found myself walking next to an old stone wall covered with trumpet vines. It led to the entrance of the Secret Garden, an arched double gate with pink and white roses climbing up trellises on either side. The wooden doors stood open, revealing pathways leading to various sections—trees, shrubs, garden plants, supplies. For a moment, I felt like

Frances Hodgson Burnett's heroine, Mary Lennox. Gazing around the blooming paradise, I whispered, "'She liked still more the feeling that when its beautiful old walls shut her in no one knew where she was. It seemed almost like being shut out of the world in some fairy place.'"

A man in denim overalls was watering plants but paused to wave as I passed by. Knowing that Addison worked in the gift shop, I headed straight there, even though I was intrigued by the many colors and species of flora outside.

A little bell jangled as I opened the door, and I was instantly surrounded by a plethora of floral scents.

A young woman stood behind the counter arranging irises in a vase as she chatted with a handsome man I immediately recognized as Carson Knight, the literary agency's charming author. Surprised to see him back from New York already, I hesitated, not wanting to interrupt the obvious camaraderie between Carson and the pretty garden center employee. She was petite and dainty and wore an apron printed with wildflowers, which she smoothed coquettishly before giving Carson a playful poke on the arm. He laughed, reached over the counter, gave the long, tawny braid that hung over her shoulder a brief, playful tug, and then exited through a side door.

By the time I drew up in front of the counter, the young woman was still grinning, wispy curls escaping around her face. Freckles dotted her nose, and her blue gray eyes sparkled as she looked away from the flowers to smile at me. "Can I help you?"

Placing my bag on the counter, I rooted around inside for *Can't Take the Heat*. "Yes, I have a flower I'd like you to identify. Are you Addison Eckhart?"

"I am. Do I know you?"

"No, not yet." My fingers finally closed around the book's spine, and as I pulled it free from the rest of my clutter, the bag fell, scattering a hairbrush, a packet of tissues, and query letters all over the floor. Muttering over my clumsiness, I dropped the book on the counter and bent down to retrieve all that had fallen.

"Let me help you," Addison said as she came around and proceeded to pick up papers. Rising, she straightened the pile she'd collected and glanced at the letter on top. "Do you work at Novel Idea?" She handed them to me. I felt like a giant standing beside her.

My cheeks flushed. I put the pages back into my bag. "As a matter of fact, I'm the new intern. I just started today. I'm Lila Wilkins."

"Is that why you're here?" She looked a little disgruntled. "I thought you wanted to ask me about a flower."

"I do." Pulling the single bloom from the pages of the book, I handed it to her. "Do you recognize this?"

She held the flattened, droopy thing that bore little resemblance to the pretty and delicate blossom it once was. "It's *Asclepias*, or as the average person would know it, white milkweed. You can find them in fields and by the roadside. Bees and butterflies love them. Most people associate milkweed with the silky white seedpods that fly all over the place, but the flower is very pretty, isn't it?" She handed it back to me. "Where did you get this one?"

"It was in a bouquet."

"A bouquet! Not many people would put . . . Wait a minute." She pointed at the ruined milkweed. "Marlette gave this to you, didn't he?"

I nodded.

"That man! He was *such* a nuisance." She went back to

her side of the counter and started vigorously snipping iris stems.

I leaned my forearms on the counter. "What do you mean?"

"Every day he'd show up at the office, and he'd always bring some kind of flowers, usually weeds, as an excuse to give us his query letter."

"Did you ever read his letter?"

"Are you kidding?" She scrunched her nose. "He was a loony. And he stank. I couldn't stand having him anywhere near me! I'd chase him out as soon as he showed up."

How could this beautiful creature not have an ounce of compassion for Marlette? "So you have no idea what his letter said? Or what his novel was about?"

She shook her head. "Nope."

"Poor man." I couldn't help my remonstrative tone. "He died at the office today."

Her dainty hands flitted to her throat. "How? What happened?"

"We don't really know. Jude Hudson thinks someone murdered Marlette, and—"

"Jude?" Her voice had an edge of panic. "Jude was involved?"

I touched her arm reassuringly. "We don't know who was involved. Jude saw something that made him believe it was murder. The police are investigating."

"I bet Jude accused Zach." She rearranged the irises in the vase, her expression grim and knowing. "Didn't he?"

Taken aback, I asked, "Why would Zach murder Marlette?"

"Well," she began, leaning in close, "about two months ago, just before I left, Zach almost signed Taylor Boone, you know that reality show teenager who became an actress? She was writing a tell-all about the life of a Hollywood glamour girl with lots of stories about parties, drugs, and sex. Zach was going to make a fortune on her deal."

I was puzzled. "So what did Marlette have to do with that?"

"When she came in to sign her contract with Zach, Marlette was in the lobby." Addison twirled the end of her braid. "I was having a particularly hard time getting rid of him that day. Taylor walked up the stairs, and there was Marlette, waiting at the top, like some dirty scarecrow. She screamed when she saw him, and Marlette tried to comfort her by putting his hand on her shoulder. Then she *really* freaked out. Zach came running and confronted Marlette, but Taylor took off and never came back."

"Oh my," I said and opened my eyes wide in encouragement.

Addison flipped her braid to her back. "Yeah, it was bad. Anyway, Zach never forgave Marlette. Every time he saw the bum after that, he'd mutter threats under his breath. Stuff like, 'I wish you were dead.' Not that Zach would hurt anyone. He just talks a big game." She shook her head emphatically. "At least I don't think he would."

The bell jangled behind us. A stooped man with a cane approached the counter. He removed his hat, revealing a full head of silver hair, and said in a distinguished voice, "Good evening. Is that my iris arrangement?"

"Yes, it is, Mr. Blake. I just need to put a ribbon around the vase." Addison pulled two lengths of blue and lavender ribbon from the spools behind her.

Mr. Blake turned to me. "I'm sorry to interrupt, but I need to bring this to my girlfriend in time for dinner. It's her seventy-fifth birthday, and irises are her favorite flower." He smiled. "She's expecting me at seven and doesn't take too kindly to me being late."

"Seven?" I looked at my watch. "I've got to catch the train! Addison, can we get together for coffee sometime? I'd like to hear more about your time at the agency."

She shrugged. "I guess so. You know where to find me."

"Thanks." I ran out through the Secret Garden gates just as the whistle of the Inspiration Valley Express blew in the distance. As exhausted as I was, I sprinted all the way to the station.

Chapter 5

IT WAS FRIDAY NIGHT. ALL ACROSS THE TOWN OF DUN-ston, people were preparing to celebrate the commencement of the weekend by going out to dinner, catching a movie, or attending a local baseball game.

Not me. I got in my pajamas and ate a comforting bowl of macaroni and cheese in front of the television while watching the Food Network. By ten I could barely keep my eyes open, and even six-foot cakes fashioned into the Seven Wonders of the World couldn't compete with my exhaustion. When I'd decided to walk to the Dunston train station that morning, I was in high spirits and had no way of knowing that I would disembark from the Inspiration Express feeling so exhausted that just having to carry my purse was almost too much to bear. I climbed the stairs and fell into bed, but not before experiencing another pang of annoyance that Trey had borrowed my car without permission.

My bed had never felt so good. I curled up on my side

and went right to sleep, but sometime after midnight I woke up, feeling thirsty. I drank from the water cup sitting precariously on a stack of paperbacks on the bedside table and drifted off again.

Fragmented images permeated my dreams. Marlette appeared, carrying a bouquet of white flowers. As he presented them to me, the blooms transformed into small birds. The creatures flew right at me, and I lifted my hands to shield my face, but they darted above my head, seeking escape through the windows in the reception area. Their bodies slammed against the glass, obscuring the light and covering Marlette's stricken face in shadow.

Someone was calling my name from the bottom of the stairs, but I was too busy trying to open the nearest window to reply. I was able to unlock the window with ease, but no matter how hard I pushed, it would not budge.

The birds became more and more agitated, striking at the glass with their beaks. The shouting from the first floor became louder and shriller, dominating the rest of the dream elements.

My brain struggled to comprehend that the sound was coming from my bedroom. The noise was not a part of my dream. My phone was ringing.

I wasn't wearing my contacts, so the numbers of the digital clock were a red blur, but I was conscious enough to know that it was too late at night or too early in the morning for a phone call.

As my fingers grasped the receiver, I could only think of two people. My mother. Trey.

"Hello?" My voice was raspy, fearful.

"Ms. Wilkins? This is Officer Griffiths. I'm sorry to bother you at this hour, but we have your son here at the station and, well, he's asked that you come down and pick him up."

It took a moment for his words to break through the fog, but by the time I turned on the table lamp, I was fully awake, my heart pounding against my rib cage. Panic made it nearly impossible to breathe, let alone speak. "What's happened?"

"Your son has been in an accident," Griffiths informed me gravely, and I drew in such a sharp breath that I almost missed the next thing he said. "He's not hurt. A few cuts and bruises, but that's all. There were three passengers in the vehicle with your son. They are also, luckily, uninjured." He paused. "However, the vehicle, which I understand is registered in your name, is totaled."

"Good Lord!" I exclaimed, my throat constricting again. "What did Trey do?"

Griffiths seemed reluctant to be the bearer of bad news but kept his voice steady as he described how my son had destroyed my only means of transportation. "It would appear that Trey and his friends got together at East Dunston High, drank some beer, and then decided to create an obstacle course on the football field. They broke into the shed containing the outdoor athletic equipment and helped themselves to the football team's blocking sleds, agility dummies, throwing nets, and a handful of orange cones. They then took turns driving the course at reckless speeds. During your son's turn, he lost control of the car and slammed into one of the metal supports beneath the bleachers. That section collapsed, effectively crushing the car. Fortunately, your son had already exited the vehicle when this occurred."

Closing my eyes, I said a silent prayer of thanks. My hands were shaking so badly that I had to hold the receiver in a white-knuckled grip, otherwise it would fall to the ground.

Trey! I cried his name to myself and exhaled loudly, but my relief was quickly replaced by fresh anxiety. I could easily picture the destruction created by Trey and his friends. I could see the pristine turf of the football field marred by muddy tire tracks and ruined equipment. And my car. My reliable little red Honda Civic. Flattened beneath pounds of steel bleachers. In the ten years I'd owned it, that trusty vehicle had never broken down, never failed to start, and never left me stranded. It pained me that such a dependable friend had met such a violent end.

All at once, the financial ramifications of Trey's tomfoolery hit me. "Oh, God. The school's going to sue me for damages. And my car! My insurance premium!" I wanted to howl in anger, but I knew Griffiths was only doing his job and didn't deserve to be the recipient of my wrath.

"Don't think about that now," Griffiths counseled. "What's important is that none of the kids were hurt. However, you'll need to come down to the station and sign some forms."

"But I don't have another means of transportation," I told him. "My mother has a pickup truck, but I can't call her at this time of night. Besides, she lives in Inspiration Valley." I allowed a bit of ire to rise to the surface. "Maybe Trey should spend some time in a cell until I can find a ride. It would give him a chance to think about what he's done."

Griffiths spoke softly. "If it makes you feel better, ma'am, your son is not being charged with driving under the influence. His Breathalyzer test showed him as not having alcohol in his system."

65

"Well, I guess I should be grateful for small miracles," I said with a sigh.

"Trey could face charges of trespassing and the destruction of public property." Griffiths sounded as though he regretted having to give me more bad news. "Ms. Wilkins, I'm not officially on duty right now, but when I can't sleep I often tune to the police scanner. When I heard what had happened at the high school, I called the station and learned that Trey was your son. Considering how we met earlier today, I know you've already had one hell of a day, so . . . I wanted to see if I could help in any way. For starters, I could pick you up and bring you to the station."

I felt a rush of gratitude toward Griffiths. I'd only met him this morning, and yet he was being so kind, so gentle with me. In my hour of need, this veritable stranger was stepping forward as my friend. If he'd been in the room with me at that moment, I would have thrown my arms around his neck and kissed him.

Instead, I thanked Griffiths and asked him to call me Lila henceforth. After I put the phone down, I sat on the edge of the bed and stared at the framed photograph of seven-year-old Trey on my dresser. He was dressed as a cowboy and wore a faux leather vest and red boots with silver plastic spurs.

Even then, his eyes glimmered with mischief.

A line from *The Tale of Peter Rabbit* flitted into my head. I picked up the photograph and murmured, "'But Peter, who was very naughty, ran straight away to Mr. McGregor's garden, and squeezed under the gate!'"

I touched my fingertip to the glass protecting the photo as though I was caressing my son's cute little face. "Oh,

Trey. I'm afraid you've lost more than a blue jacket with brass buttons this time."

TEN MINUTES LATER, a dark blue Ford Explorer pulled into my driveway. Officer Griffiths got out and opened the passenger door for me. Looking at his tired face and concerned eyes, I resisted the urge to sag against his broad chest in the hopes he'd wrap his arms around me. Instead, we drove to the Dunston Police Department in silence.

Inside the station, our footsteps echoed on the tiled floor. Vacillating between anger and anxiety, I searched for Trey. In the main area, two policemen at steel desks were typing on computers. Behind a counter sat a stern woman in uniform who looked up as we approached, holding out papers. Officer Griffiths handed me a pen and showed me where to sign, then pointed to one of four empty chairs set in a row against a wall.

"Wait here," he directed, giving my arm a quick squeeze. "I'll get Trey, and then I'll drive you both back home."

"Thank you," I said, disconcerted at how weak my voice sounded. Lowering myself into the plastic seat, I thought about what to say to Trey. His obstacle course would cost me a fortune. I'd never be able to afford that charming cottage on Walden Woods Circle now. In fact, I'd be lucky to have a dime left to my name once I'd covered the school's damages and paid Trey's court costs.

A bark of laughter disrupted my brooding, and I glanced up. The two officers were chuckling at something on a computer screen. Movement in the hall made me turn to see Officer Griffiths and Trey walking toward me. Trey shuffled with his head bent, a mop of shaggy hair obstructing his face. His UNC Tar Heels shirt was covered with dirt and grass stains. I rose from my seat, resisting the urge to hoist up his baggy jeans.

"Trey, what were you *thinking*?" Despite my resolve to stay calm, my voice blared loudly in the room.

He shrugged. "I dunno."

Officer Griffiths put his hand on Trey's shoulder. "Let's get you two home," he said, looking at me. "I'm sure you'd rather hash this out in private."

The drive was uncomfortably quiet. I wanted to blast Trey and had to bite my lip to stop my anger from pouring out. Instead, I aimed piercing looks in his direction. Officer Griffiths tactfully kept his eyes on the road and said nothing. Trey sat in the back, with his mouth pinched in what I hoped was remorse. The tension was palpable, and I think we were all greatly relieved when Griffiths pulled into our driveway.

Trey shot into the house before I even stepped out of the truck. Turning off the ignition, Office Griffiths opened his door. "Go easy on him," he said as he walked me up the front path. "He seems like a good kid. And at least he had the sense to not drink and drive."

I nodded, appreciating his voice of reason. "I'll try. Thank you so much for everything, Officer Griffiths."

"You're welcome. And please, Lila." He tilted his head. "I think we can dispense with the 'Officer Griffiths,' don't you? Call me Sean."

I nodded. "I'd better go in. Thanks again . . . Sean." His name tasted good on my lips, like I'd just sipped a fine glass of wine.

We shook hands, even though what I really wanted to do

was lean into him for support. The warmth of his fingers lingered on mine as I watched him back his truck out of the driveway. Taking a deep breath, I walked into the house.

Trey was lying on his bed, earbuds firmly inserted and eyes closed. Still dressed, one of his blue-jeaned legs rested on the other, a foot bobbing in time to the beat. Swallowing my irritation over seeing his shoes on the bed, I touched his shoulder. "Trey," I said loudly.

His eyes popped open. He yanked out the earbuds and sat up. "Mom." He stood, reached down, and hugged me. "I'm totally sorry. It was really stupid. I'll never do anything like that again."

This show of repentance derailed my planned reprimand, and for a moment I was at a loss for words. Perhaps sensing my retreat, he offered, "Do you need a drink or something? Wine, maybe?"

That did it. "No, I do *not* want a drink! Trey, you took the car without permission. What you did at the school was not only stupid and irresponsible, it caused a lot of damage. Someone could have been really hurt, even killed. What were you thinking?"

He shrugged. "Guess I wasn't."

"You could be charged with trespassing and the destruction of public property. We need to get a lawyer. You'll have to go to court." My heart was racing as these thoughts tumbled through my mind. I glared at him. "Not thinking isn't a defense."

"Aw, Mom, you know how it is. A couple of guys get together and there's beer involved, then things can get crazy." His eyes widened in an attempt at innocence. "Not me! I didn't have beer. *I* was the designated driver." Looking absurdly righteous, he continued, "We're young. We do stupid things. It's like a rite of passage or something. We can't help it."

He grinned, a mischievous twinkle in his brown eyes taking the place of contriteness. In that moment, I saw his father in his features—the pointed chin, tousled chestnut hair, and dark eyebrows.

"You can't absolve yourself because you're a teenager, Trey. There are consequences to your actions. They impact other people."

Shrugging, he picked at the apple-shaped hole in his jeans just above his right knee. "Nobody was hurt."

"Well, *I* was! First of all, I was terrified that something had happened to you. Secondly, because of your recklessness, my car's totaled. The school equipment and football field are seriously damaged. Who do you think is going to pay for all that?"

"Insurance?" he said, raising his eyebrows.

I glowered at him. "*I* have to pay, Trey. *I* have to find another vehicle to get me to work. *I* have to deal with the school's damages. My insurance premiums are going to skyrocket because of this." I sank down on the edge of the bed.

Trey sat beside me and put his arm around my shoulder. "You'll manage, Mom. You've got that new agency job. You're gonna make millions—"

"I'm just an intern." I pushed his arm away. "And you aren't getting off scot-free. You will get cracking and find a summer job, and you will hand over your paychecks to help cover the costs."

"But that's not fair!" he whined, his bravado faltering.

"Don't tell me about fair," I said, getting up and starting

for the door. "You made this mess, and now you're going to help me clean it up."

Trey sighed. "At least I learned something from all of this."

"What's that?" I asked, thankful that this disaster would have at least one positive outcome.

He leaned back on his elbows, grinning at the ceiling. "Hondas aren't so good at three sixties."

I TOSSED AND turned for what was left of the night. Trey and his transgressions, my financial worries, Marlette's murder, the pile of queries I'd brought home, the agents at Novel Idea: they were all tangled in angst-filled dreams.

When the sky finally lightened, I dragged myself out of bed, had a hot shower, and brewed a very strong pot of coffee. I needed to figure things out before Monday. Without a car, I'd have to take the train to work every morning, and that was too expensive. Moving to Inspiration Valley was the solution, of course; a prospect that had excited me Friday evening when I'd stood before the cottage for sale on Walden Woods Circle. After last night's fiasco, I knew I could never afford it.

As I was refilling my coffee mug, the phone rang.

"I flipped around in bed last night like a fritter in the fryer!" My mother greeted me dramatically. "What happened at work yesterday? I was right about somethin' bad comin', wasn't I? I got a real case of the shivers, like a spirit was standin' right behind me, breathin' down my neck!"

Sighing, I admitted that her prediction had been accurate. I'd expected her to be triumphant over the successful demonstration of her physic abilities, but she fell strangely despondent.

"Poor soul," she whispered. "He was all alone in this life."

I started. "You knew Marlette?"

"Not well enough to trade recipes, but the whole valley knew him, hon. He stood out, like a low-cut dress in church." I heard a shuffling sound in the background and knew Althea had her tarot cards in hand. "But you'll set things to rights, Lila. People can't just pluck a string from Fate's brilliant tapestry and not pay the price." She went on before I could interrupt. "I do believe you were gonna call and ask me somethin' this fine mornin'. The answer is yes, of course. You and Trey can live with me so you can fill up your piggy bank again. Maybe livin' in the country will keep that boy outta trouble!"

My jaw came unhinged. "How'd you know about Trey?"

A satisfied cackle emitted from the earpiece, and then I recalled that my mother was great friends with the police chief's wife. In fact, she was one of my mother's most loyal customers and often spread news of a juicy arrest before the most dogged journalist could get a jump on the story. I suspected the woman slept with a police scanner by her bed.

I didn't feel like further questioning Amazing Althea's sources, especially since her invitation was a godsend, so I simply said, "I *was* going to ask if we could spend the summer with you. I'm going to put this house up for sale, hope it sells right away, and pray that three months without mortgage payments, thanks to living with you, will keep my head above water." I stared at the papers on my kitchen table, which included bank statements, insurance policies, and the business card of a real estate agent I'd met while working at the *Dunston Herald*. "Between Trey's tuition bill, the house payment, and whatever I'll have to fork out in damages because of my son's unbelievable lack of judgment, I'll be lucky to have enough left over to buy a bicycle, let alone a car."

My mother clucked her tongue. "Trey's just helpin' you go green. Now tell your mama everythin' that happened last night. And don't forget the part about the good-lookin' man. I turned up the Lovers card in the Future position, and I want to know who this hot new number is. I can already tell he's got enough electricity to fuel a power station!"

I hedged the question, wanting to keep Sean to myself for a while, and went on to describe how I'd spent the midnight hour. When I was done, she offered to drive her vintage turquoise pickup into Dunston late on Sunday afternoon and bring Trey and me back to her place. Trey could look for a summer job in Inspiration Valley, and I wouldn't have to worry about commuting to Novel Idea come Monday.

"I love you, Mama." A rush of affection and gratitude flowed through me. Amazing Althea might be eccentric, but she was a bighearted woman who'd do anything for us. For the first time since I found Marlette's body, I felt like things might turn out okay.

I'd barely hung up the receiver when the phone rang again. "I'm still not going to answer your question about the Lovers!" I exclaimed, assuming the caller was my mother again.

"Oh? Which lovers?" a male voice quipped. "This is Sean, um, Officer Griffiths?"

Immediately, my exasperation disappeared and I smiled. "Oh, good morning."

"I wondered if you'd like to meet me for coffee," he said. "At Java the Hut? Say in half an hour?"

I stared at the empty mug in my hand. Any more caffeine in my veins and I'd be bouncing off the walls, but the thought of saying no didn't occur to me. "I'd love to," I replied, thinking fast. Trey wouldn't be awake for hours yet, and I'd still have the afternoon to read through my pile of queries.

Hurriedly changing out of my sweats, I fiddled with my hair and applied makeup. Under close scrutiny in the mirror, I looked pretty good, despite what I'd been through over the past twenty-four hours. I'd been told more than once that I bore a close resemblance to Marilyn Monroe when she was still Norma Jeane Baker, but that's only partially true. I'd kill for Norma Jeane's perfect lips or luminescent skin, but our smile was almost identical, and I definitely had Marilyn's curves.

Even with the additional primping, I managed to arrive at Java the Hut in thirty-two minutes. Sean was at the counter, looking attractively authoritative in his uniform.

"I took the liberty of ordering you a caramel latte," he said. "That's what you were drinking yesterday, wasn't it?"

In the midst of all the excitement at the agency, he'd noticed what kind of coffee I drank? This man was a keeper.

"Yes, thank you," I said, trying to conceal my astonishment. "It's my favorite."

We sat down at the corner table by the window. Across the street, the *Dunston Herald* building seemed to mock me. I looked away, preferring to meet Sean's guileless blue eyes.

"I have some news," he said. "I had a quick chat with the principal and a member of the school board's legal team.

They called an emergency meeting this morning to discuss the damage to their field." He grimaced. "Doesn't sound like a fun meeting, does it?"

"No," I said with a groan, thinking about how often Trey and I had met in the principal's office over the past few years. "Are they going to press charges?"

"Actually"—he paused, and his mouth stretched into a wide smile—"I pleaded your case. I mean, er, Trey's case. I assured them that his blood alcohol level showed that he hadn't been drinking and suggested his actions were not malicious. I tried to toss out the 'boys will be boys' excuse."

"He still needs to be held accountable." I felt strongly about that point, even though I wished it could all just go away.

"Oh, I agree. And so did the bigwigs at the meeting. But they've agreed to drop the charges against Trey if he helps with the cleanup."

Relief flowed through my veins. "Like community service?"

"Yes, but without an official court record. Of course, you'll be required to cover the costs of the damage. They're going to call you today to set up a meeting with you and Trey." He touched my hand. "But I wanted to tell you the good news right away."

His fingers were warm on mine. "Thank you, Sean." I shook my head. "I don't know what's going on with that boy."

"Could his father help with this? Sometimes a man has better rapport with . . . not that you don't . . ." He scratched his head. "I'm sorry, I didn't mean to overstep."

"No, you were right to ask," I assured him. "My ex isn't in the picture. I haven't laid eyes on Bill since I walked in on him in bed with Miss Tobacco Leaf. I was pregnant with Trey at the time."

"Hold on a sec, Lila. Miss *Tobacco Leaf*?"

My cheeks flushed. Even now, after all these years, the memory still affected me. "Bill was an advertising executive and was very involved in the community. His lifelong goal was to run for public office. As a result, he was often asked to judge contests. For years, he judged those creepy toddler pageants, and then he began to serve as a head judge for the Miss Tobacco Leaf pageant." I took a sip of coffee. "I guess he took his role as interviewer *very* seriously, because he brought one of the candidates home." I paused. I'd come to the part of the story that made me ball up my fists, even though I'd told it a dozen times by now.

"It's okay," Sean said gently, obviously sensing that I was struggling to continue. "The fool hurt you. That's all I need to know."

I held out my finger. "Just wait. You'll never hear a version of cheating spouse like this one. Let me earn my coffee." I toasted him with my cup. "Basically, I came home early from an assignment, kicked off my shoes, and headed upstairs to change out of my work clothes. There was Bill, lying naked on the bed. His wrists were handcuffed to the bedpost, and he wore a blindfold made of what looked like a pair of black lace panties."

Sean's eyes grew round. "Uh, oh."

"It gets better," I promised. "So I'm standing in my bedroom like a deer in a shotgun sight when this redhead with big hair and heavy makeup struts in from the bathroom. All she had on was her Miss Tobacco Leaf sash. It didn't cover much. She was *very* well endowed."

Sean squeezed my hand, but I could see that he was fighting back a grin.

"Go ahead, it *is* kind of funny." I smiled, too. Somehow, in Sean's presence, Bill's infidelity didn't sting as much. "But that's all in the past. Trey and I have been fine without him. My son will be going to college in the fall. I have a new job. We're doing okay."

"Speaking of your job, it seems like Bentley Burlington-Duke is a bit of a cold fish, taking off with a dead man in her office." He stroked his chin. "Somewhat suspicious, I might add."

Did he truly suspect that Bentley had anything to do with Marlette's demise? "Have the medical examiners established it was murder?" I asked. "I keep thinking about poor Marlette."

A look crossed his face that resembled a gate closing. "Lila, I know I just brought up the topic by commenting on your boss, but I can't discuss the case with you. If we're going to be friends"—his cheeks dimpled as he smiled—"then details about this case can't enter our conversation. Deal?"

I nodded.

"Unless I need to bring you in for questioning. *That* kind of conversation would be official," he added, a flicker of steel in his eyes.

I finished the rest of my coffee and grimaced. It had grown cold.

Chapter 6

I SPENT THE REST OF THE WEEKEND PACKING. AFTER telling Trey to load the things he couldn't live without from his room into suitcases, I carefully wrapped framed photographs and fragile knickknacks in newspaper. Upon leaving the café where I'd had coffee with Sean, I stopped by the UPS Store to pick up supplies and then, while eating lunch, read an informative article on the Internet about preparing one's house to be put on the market. The author recommended removing all personal items and clearing surface areas of clutter so prospective buyers could picture themselves putting their own possessions in the house. I followed this advice by boxing photos, books, and various keepsakes. I also emptied the closets of clothes, coats, and shoes, frowning at the scuffmarks on the walls and the dust bunnies that had been hiding behind my winter boots and galoshes.

Once I'd removed everything from the kitchen counters,

including my English cottage cookie jar, the ceramic canisters for flour, sugar, and tea, my rotating spice rack, and a pottery utensil jar, I took all the magnets off the refrigerator and tossed them into the garbage.

That afternoon I fielded a phone call from a member of the school board. We scheduled a meeting to discuss remuneration for the damages Trey inflicted on the football field, and I jotted the date and time in my day planner.

On Sunday, I vacuumed, dusted, and polished until my arms ached. Trey had just finished mowing the lawn and weeding the flowerbeds when my mother arrived. The rumble of her pickup's engine preceded the old truck. While Trey and I sat drinking sweet tea on the stoop, the 1970s C-10 came into view.

My mother had bought the truck for a song ten years ago and driven it straight from the used car lot to a detail shop in Raleigh where it had been painted a custom turquoise reminiscent of the waters off the coast of Fiji. She then slapped a magnetic sign to each door advertising her services as Amazing Althea, Inspiration Valley's famous psychic.

Now here she was, laying on the horn to announce her presence as though the sound and hue of her truck could somehow be missed. Trey began to mumble a torrent of complaints about how bored he'd be living in the sticks.

"She doesn't have cable or Internet access," he groused. "How am I going to check my email or download new tunes?"

I pointed at the nearest box and told him to carry it to the truck. "Maybe you'll land a summer job at a company that has Wi-Fi."

"Right." Trey rolled his eyes. "Like all the losers flipping burgers and delivering pizzas are booting up laptops during their breaks."

I was too tired to get into another argument with him, but my mother saved the day by throwing her arms around Trey and saying how happy she was that he'd be living under her roof. "It'll be like the sleepovers we used to have when you were a little tyke," she said, beaming. "Remember that time we painted the room with all those wacky creatures from *Where the Wild Things Are*? And then we pretended the bed was a boat and we had to catch Swedish fish for our supper? Oh, I'm tickled just thinkin' about those magical nights." She reached way up and ruffled his hair.

He immediately shook his long bangs back into place over his brows. "That was fun, Nana, but I'm not a kid anymore."

My mother studied him carefully. "No, you're not. You're caught in that place between boy and man. Can't decide whether you should be flexin' your wings or hidin' under the covers until the tough times pass on by. But bein' away from Dunston will do you a world of good. This town is as worn-out as my favorite pair of boots. You need to breathe fresh air and be around young folks who know exactly what they want, like those *interestin'* people up on Red Fox Mountain." She looked at me, her eyes alight with mischief. "That's where Marlette lived, you know."

That got my attention. As my mother and I carried boxes to the truck, I asked her if it was a long hike from her place to the co-op.

"Not at all, sug. Anytime I need to refill my spiritual well I take the path through the back woods leadin' right up the mountain. The co-op folks are lovely. We trade things fairly regular. I'll read their cards in exchange for goat's milk soap or one of their cute hemp shoppin' bags. Mighty strong, those bags. Can hold two bunches of bananas and three bottles of my leadin' man, Mr. Jim Beam."

I slid a heavy box onto the truck bed and wiped my slick forehead with my shirtsleeve. "And Marlette lived among these people?" I couldn't picture him coexisting with a bunch of goat farmers and weavers. He seemed too much of a recluse to enjoy the constant company I imagined would be prevalent at the Red Fox Mountain Co-op.

My mother shook her head. "No, honey. Word has it he had some run-down cabin near the creek. I don't know where, but I have a feelin' you're gonna find out."

Ignoring her twinkling eyes, I handed Trey the last of the boxes and settled onto the Chevy's bench seat with a weary sigh. Despite my fatigue, I watched my house recede in the rearview mirror with a stirring of hope. Sandwiched between my son and my mother, I knew that my little family could make it over this bump in the road. As my mother began singing along to Patsy Cline, Trey did his best to suppress a smile over her off-key notes. Suddenly, I was aware this was one of those moments when I should count my blessings, so as we left Dunston behind, that's exactly what I did.

This burst of optimism carried me all the way to Inspiration Valley, but when we passed the sign announcing the town limits, I realized that I needed to be at Novel Idea by nine the next morning. I didn't have a car, I hadn't finished reading my quota of query letters, and I'd have to spend Monday night meeting with both a real estate agent and the school board. Afterward, I'd have to haul more of my belongings to the shed behind my mother's house.

"Cheer up," my mother said, sensing my shift in mood.

"Least your life's more excitin' now. Shoot, I know ladies in the old folks' home who've got more goin' on than you've had for the last twenty years. Now you've got a mystery to unravel, a fascinatin' new job, and good-lookin' men droppin' from the sky like cherry blossoms in April. And don't argue, because I have a clear sense that you're workin' alongside a few fine specimens."

I considered her words as we bounced along the narrow gravel lane leading to her house. She lived in a refurbished tobacco barn three miles outside of town. Painted cardinal red, the façade was Shaker plain, but the inside more than made up for the exterior's simplicity.

To say that my mother was a pack rat was an understatement. Her definition of decorating was to bring home any object that she deemed interesting and to find a place for it somewhere. Anywhere. Her kitchen, for example, closely resembled the interior of a T.G.I. Friday's. Rusty signs, painted placards, framed movie posters, flags, pennants, and photographs all vied for space on the lavender walls. She even had an illuminated exit sign affixed to the ceiling and a working traffic signal perched on top of a massive open-shelf pine cupboard. I could only imagine what a real estate agent would say upon entering this room.

It was in this chaotic space that Althea met with her clients. She sat them down at the farm table, brewed a fresh pot of coffee or tea, and served them a slice of fresh-baked chocolate banana bread. I was convinced that my mother had a long list of clients because of her banana bread. If there was anything magical about my mother, it was that bread.

She'd been making it as long as I could remember. Some

of my earliest memories were of being hypnotized by her graceful movements in the kitchen baking this bread. Using slightly overripe bananas and chunks of rich chocolate, she folded them into the batter with such infinite gentleness, singing a soft lullaby all the while, that I used to fall asleep before the pan reached the oven.

While the bread baked, the entire house would be redolent with the scent of buttery dough, bananas, and chocolate. It was Althea's secret weapon, for no client could keep quiet about even their most intimate desires as they nibbled her bread and sipped her strong brew. While they savored each bite, Althea laid out their cards, already aware of what they wanted to hear.

I wasn't impervious to the smell, either. As soon as the three of us stepped into the kitchen, it settled around me like a shawl. I inhaled gratefully and noticed that Trey did as well.

Dropping my purse into a chair, I turned to my mother. "Let's walk up Red Fox Mountain right now."

Trey checked his watch and groaned, "It's almost dinnertime."

"Don't worry, sweet boy. We'll eat at the co-op. Grab that case of beer outta my fridge and we'll make ourselves a trade for a fine vegetarian feast."

"That's just great." Trey scowled but obeyed his grandmother.

My mother collected an exquisitely carved walking stick leaning against the porch post, and we set off. "The members of the Occaneechi tribe gave this to me," she said as we struck out through the field behind her house. "I helped one of their secrs get over a bad case of blocked vision."

"How nice," I said, casting a covert glance at the entwined snakes carved into her stick. They were so lifelike that I half expected them to wriggle right up the wood onto my mother's hand. I turned away, preferring to focus on the tall grass strewn with yellow buttercups and the benevolent shadow of the mountain rising before us.

We left the grassy path and stepped into a copse of trees, instantly cooled by the forest's canopy of summer leaves and needles. Birdcalls followed us as we strode deeper into the woods, and my cares slipped away as I inhaled the scents of tree sap, pine, and fecund soil. Trey stopped to investigate a clump of mushrooms, squatting on his heels to marvel at the size of the umbrella-shaped caps.

After another ten minutes of hiking steadily upward, the narrow path widened. It was apparent that someone had trimmed the sapling branches and stray vines from encroaching on the well-trodden trail, and we soon arrived, rather short of breath, at an arch made of willow branches secured by pieces of rope. A wooden sign hung down from the top of the arch. We passed beneath the words *Welcome to the Red Fox Mountain Co-op* and emerged into a wide and surprisingly flat clearing.

This plateau was circular shaped and had recently been mowed. Clippings still peppered the grass, and an old-fashioned push mower rested against a chain-link fence that dominated the left side of the clearing. On the other side of the fence, a herd of white goats with brown faces and floppy ears lifted their heads and bleated and then returned to the business of nibbling grain. In the distance, a large unpainted barn rose up behind the spacious goat paddock, and a cluster of small cabins were situated haphazardly to the right of the barn. A pretty woman seated on a crude stool weaving hemp into what appeared to be a hammock raised her hand in greeting. We waved back.

"What is this place?" Trey asked in wonder.

My mother gestured around the complex. "Back when the town was Illumination, this was a meditation and retreat spot. Folks used to hike up here to commune with nature. Most of the hard-core New Agers moved out when the money dried up like a creek bed in July, but some people who truly wanted to live a simpler kind of life founded this co-op. Here comes their leader now."

A man in his early thirties wearing a plain T-shirt, dust-covered cargo shorts, and leather sandals made his way toward us. "He looks like Jesus," whispered Trey, and I had to agree. With a beard and hair of dark brown that fell in soft waves to his shoulder, the man issued a generous smile that reached from his mouth to his lake blue eyes.

"Jasper." My mother held out both hands, and the young man gave them a hearty squeeze. "I brought my family to meet you."

Jasper studied us for a moment longer than was customarily polite, but then he offered his hand in sincere welcome. "Excuse my rudeness. We haven't had visitors for a while, and we've withdrawn even further from society over the last two days. An acquaintance passed away rather abruptly, and it's reminded us that the violence and chaos of town life could taint our little paradise."

I'd just opened my mouth to ask if the death Jasper referred to was Marlette's when my mother pinched my forearm—a signal that I should be quiet. "I was hopin' you'd show my grandson around. There's nothin' in Dunston like this slice of heaven, and I wanted him to see that folks can live a rich and fufillin' life off the land."

Looking extremely pleased by the request, Jasper waited for Trey to fall into step beside him as he led us toward one of the larger cabins. "This is where we dry and process our wild hemp plants that we then make into rope for bags and hammocks or twine for jewelry and key chains," he began. "We have crops growing all over this side of the mountain. Hemp plants and every kind of fruit and vegetable you can imagine. The soil up here is really fertile, and we get more rain than they do in the valley."

"Did you say hemp?" Trey looked around eagerly, and then his eyes widened in astonishment. "Wait. There's no electricity?"

Jasper shook his head, his wavy locks glistening in the waning light. "Except for the solar panels on all the roofs, we're a human-powered community." Smiling, he patted his flat stomach. "Keeps us fit." He then had us follow him to the dairy barn where the goat milk was bottled or made into cheese, soap, and lotion.

I was impressed by both the cleanliness of the workspaces and the genuine friendliness of the co-op's inhabitants. While Jasper invited Trey to sample a piece of goat cheese and my mother began to discuss our supper plans with a middle-aged man labeling the goat products with elegant calligraphy, a young woman entered the barn.

Upon seeing her gauzy white dress and flowing rivulets of golden hair, I had to blink hard to make sure that I wasn't envisioning a fantastical forest nymph. The girl was small, with childlike limbs and fair skin, but her blue eyes were large and framed by a sweep of long lashes. She walked *en pointe* like a ballerina, with an empty metal pail swinging by her side and a dreamy expression on her lovely face.

"Who is *that*?" Trey interrupted Jasper's discourse on

goat vaccinations, gazing at the fairylike young lady with utter rapture.

Grinning indulgently, Jasper beckoned for the girl to come closer. "This is Iris, my sister."

She gifted us with a shy smile, her gaze lingering on Trey. "Are you staying for supper?"

"Yeah," Trey answered immediately and puffed out his chest in a show of macho self-importance. "And we brought beer."

The evening meal was held outdoors on a grouping of picnic tables and blankets. Oil lamps and tiki torches were lit, more for atmosphere than for the light they cast since the sky had yet to darken, and a stream of men and women began carrying mismatched platters and bowls from their individual cabins to the tables. Grilled vegetable kabobs, spinach salad with strawberries and goat cheese, scalloped potatoes, fried goat cheese with sliced tomatoes and fresh pesto, and a berry medley were among the dishes on the communal buffet. As I filled my plate with the fresh, locally grown food, I began to appreciate the advantages of life in the co-op.

With its wholesomeness, proximity to nature, and close sense of community, the Red Fox Mountain Co-op was somewhat of a utopia. Thomas More's description of virtue as "living according to Nature" might well have suited these people, who "think that we are made by God for that end."

However idyllic life here seemed, I reminded myself that I'd come on a mission. I needed to find out where Marlette had lived. Somewhere inside his home might be a clue to his demise. Perhaps I'd find a copy of the book he'd written or an indication of why his very existence had become a threat that his murderer could not ignore.

Seeing Trey and Iris sitting alone on a picnic blanket, I

decided that it would be easier to worm information out of a girl close to my son's age than from Jasper or one of the older residents of Red Fox Mountain.

"I'm sorry to hear that your community is grieving for a lost acquaintance tonight," I said without preamble. "Was the person a close friend?"

Iris shook her head. "He wasn't a member of the co-op, but he shared the mountain with us. He lived in a cabin by the stream, and sometimes he'd write poems and tie them to the branches of a laurel bush for me to find. They were beautiful."

This tender gesture caused a lump to form in my throat. "So he was a writer?"

She shrugged, uncertain how to answer. "Not professionally. He just wrote things and put them in special places. He talked to himself and didn't take very good care of his things. Some people thought he was crazy, but I didn't. He was just really shy, but he was sweet, too."

"Was his name Marlette?" I asked gently.

She looked at me with unveiled distrust. "How'd you know?"

"I met him for the first time on Friday," I assured her hastily. "And I agree with your description. He seemed harmless and kind." I hesitated. "Listen, Iris. I know this is going to sound strange, but since I was with him at the end, I'd really like to visit his cabin." I held out my hands, indicating a feeling of helplessness. "I don't know how else to pay my respects, but if I could do something for him, like show some of his poetry to a literary agent on the off-chance it might get published, it would mean a great deal to me."

"How could you do that?" Iris wasn't easily convinced. "Do you know a literary agent?"

"My mom works for the Novel Idea agency," Trey stated

proudly, and I couldn't help but blush in the face of his boasting even though I knew he was only mentioning my new job to impress a pretty girl.

Iris considered my request. "All right, but we should go now, before it gets dark. Jasper doesn't like me to wander too far after sunset."

Walking through the woods in the dusky light was a little spooky, but Iris knew where she was going and forged confidently ahead along a narrow path. Well away from the co-op, but not so far that we couldn't hear the murmuring of voices in the still night, she stopped.

"This is the laurel bush I told you about," she said quietly as she stroked a branch. Despondently, she added, "No more poems." Her sadness made me want to hug her.

But Trey beat me to it. Gently touching her shoulder, he asked in a tender voice, "Are you okay?"

She nodded and pointed to the right. "Come on, it's this way."

Twigs cracked under our feet, and I furiously swatted at mosquitoes until we came to a small clearing, upon which stood a cabin. Actually, calling it a cabin was generous. In the shadowy light, it appeared more like an old toolshed.

"This is where he lived," Iris said as she pulled open the canvas flap covering the doorway. "Jasper offered to have some of our members build him a real cabin, but Marlette didn't want it. Said he only heard from his muse when he slept close to nature."

"Do you know if anyone's been inside since he died?" I asked.

Iris shook her head. "No one ever came here that I know about. Other than Jasper or me, that is. We used to bring him food."

I peered inside and was assaulted by a mixture of smells created by an odd blend of body odor, rotting wood, and hemp. It was not unlike Marlette's own stench, though not as overpowering. Trey moved back from the entry.

"Do you really want to go in there, Mom?" he asked, waving his hand in front of his face. "It reeks."

Scrunching my nose, I stepped through the opening but couldn't see very far inside the space. "Is there any kind of light in here?"

Iris thrust a small flashlight at me. "You can use this. I'll wait outside with Trey."

After giving her a nod of understanding, I shone the narrow beam into the interior, illuminating a cozy-looking refuge. Despite the smell, it was a tidy space, with bedding arranged neatly in one corner, a makeshift table in another with a wooden crate in place of a chair, a basket filled with clothes, and an old cabinet with missing doors and dangling hinges. Its shelves were jammed full. One held paperbacks, and the others contained a leather-covered journal with ragged paper edges, two chipped teacups, a dented saucepan, a tin can filled with pens, a ball of twine, numerous empty chip and cookie bags, and dried bouquets of flowers.

An ancient typewriter stood on top of the cabinet. I touched its dusty keys, remembering Marlette's pathetic questions about his query, and wondered if he had written anything significant using this decrepit machine. There was also a hand-carved walking stick resting against the table. To me, it seemed to be waiting for its owner to return, for Marlette to grasp its polished knob and set forth for the steepest, most secluded parts of the mountain.

I stood transfixed. The place was crude and simple, but

it had been special to Marlette. A sense of security and peace hovered in air filled with the dust motes. I found this sense of tranquility surprising, considering his lack of possessions and the fact that he had lived in what most people would consider a hovel.

"'His house was perfect,'" I whispered, borrowing from *The Hobbit*, "'whether you liked food, or sleep, or work, or story-telling, or singing, or just sitting and thinking, best.'" What had Marlette liked best? What invisible element remained in this crude shelter, giving it a coziness that seemed incongruous with its appearance?

My musings were interrupted by Jasper's voice calling in the night. "Iris! It's getting dark."

In unison, Iris and Trey stuck their heads inside the cabin and beckoned urgently.

"Ms. Wilkins?"

"Mom! We gotta go back."

My head swiveled to the entrance and then back into the dimness. "I'm coming." I redirected the flashlight beam to the cabinet. On impulse, I grabbed the journal and jammed it into the waistband of my jeans, untucking my shirt to conceal the bulge. I followed Iris and my son, glancing back once at Marlette's deteriorating cabin. It seemed as though it was aware that its owner would never return and was now willing to be claimed by the encroaching forest.

My sleep that night was deep and dreamless, thanks to my being exhausted from the day's packing and cleaning, settling into my mother's place, and all that followed at the Red Fox Co-op. Unfortunately, I'd set the alarm for five thirty to get a head start on my work, and its buzzing woke me all too soon.

At six twenty I stood at the door to Espresso Yourself

but was dismayed to read on its sign that it wouldn't open for another ten minutes. Through the window I could see Makayla behind the counter stocking the bakery case with muffins, so I tapped on the glass. She looked up and smiled, opening the door for me just as my mouth stretched into a big yawn.

"Girl, you look like you need a triple latte!" she exclaimed in a voice far too chipper for such an early hour. "Sit yourself down and I'll bring you one."

Gratefully, I lowered myself into the closest chair, dropping my bag full of unread queries onto the floor. I had intended to tackle them when we got back to my mother's last night, but by that point I couldn't find the energy to even take them out of the bag. Besides, I was far more interested in Marlette's journal, which I took to bed with me. I'd been just about to delve into it when my mother quietly opened my door. Jamming it under my pillow, I pretended to be snuggling in to sleep.

"I made you an infusion of lemon balm and chamomile, honey. I reckoned you needed somethin' to help you relax after your long and crazy day," she said and then plunked herself down at the foot of the bed. I sat up and took the cup she offered. I sipped while she chatted. Later, I had a vague sense of her weight leaving the bed, and then, nothing. The next thing I knew, my alarm was buzzing.

"Here you go, sugar," Makayla said as she handed me my coffee, and I realized that I was lucky to have two women plying me with drinks and comfort within the space of a few hours. "This'll put some sparkle in your step. What's up? Too much partying?"

I proceeded to give her a synopsis of my weekend. It was hard to believe all that had happened over the last three days.

"Girl, you are living some kind of exciting life!" She shook her head. "What's that boy of yours think about living in Inspiration Valley with his grandma?"

"He'll adjust." I shrugged. "It's only temporary until I find our own place here in town. He made a friend at the Red Fox Co-op last night, so that should help."

"You mean the coop?" Makayla laughed. "That's what we call it here. The hippie coop. All that hemp—there's a rumor they grow the kind you smoke, too."

My heart sank. I was trying to get Trey away from such temptations. "They seemed legit to me." I took a sip of my latte. It was delightfully strong. "I found Marlette's place just outside the co-op."

"Marlette? The homeless guy you think was murdered?"

I nodded. "He wasn't homeless. He had a house of his own . . . so to speak."

"With the way he looked and smelled, he might as well have been." Makayla's lovely face turned somber. "It's sad, but there are way too many folks just like him. The other day I read an article that said there are over twelve thousand homeless people in North Carolina alone. People tend to think that they're degenerates, but many of them are mentally ill or victims of abuse. And most people don't care what their story is. They just want them off the streets." She turned as a customer came through the door.

"But I care about Marlette." I stood. It was time to get to work. "I found a notebook of his . . . a journal of some sort . . . Hey! Do you want to get together for lunch so I can show it to you? We can examine it together to see if it contains anything that could help the police figure out why someone might have had reason to murder him."

She gave me a sympathetic smile. "Sure, I'll meet you

for a quick lunch, but the police aren't going to invest too much manpower in Marlette. Not after that big fire in Dunston last night."

"What fire?" I hadn't listened to the news since yesterday afternoon. For a brief second I missed being at the *Dunston Herald*.

"It was all over the TV and radio this morning." Makayla stepped behind the counter at which a short, stout man in a suit was patiently waiting to place an order. "Hold on a minute while I get Mr. Cahill his macchiato."

The man pulled out his wallet. "Thank you, Makayla," he said in a surprisingly deep voice, and then he turned to me. "I couldn't help overhearing, but I believe our beautiful barista was referring to the fire at Dover Import Warehouse where two night watchmen died of smoke inhalation." He put some bills on the counter. "WRAL News reported that the warehouse was insured with a multimillion-dollar policy, and since my firm insures that warehouse, I expect to have a very stressful day."

Makayla was right. The police weren't going to bother with the death of an insignificant someone like Marlette when big money was at stake. It would be up to me to solve his murder.

WHEN I REACHED the stairs leading to Novel Idea just after eight o'clock, Bentley Burlington-Duke was already on her way up, her heels tapping out a staccato on the marble steps. At the top she turned, her eyes widening at the sight of me.

"You decided to return, I see."

"Of course. I'm committed to this job." Careful not to

spill my second cup of coffee, I hoisted my bag as I entered the reception area after her.

"It's good to know that you're dedicated." She waved her hand at the stack of papers sticking out of my bag. "Did you manage to get through all those queries?"

"For the most part." A little white lie couldn't hurt, could it? "I still have a few more to get through."

"Well, carry on then." She strode toward her office. I hustled after her.

"Ms. Burlington-Duke? Could I have a bigger work-space?" I hated to ask, but it seemed that was the only way I'd move out of that silly student desk.

"Of course. Your office is right next to Flora's. It contains everything you need," she remarked while unlocking her door.

My own office! Soon I'd have a brass placard bearing my name, just like the rest of the agents. Striding past Flora's office, I paused in front of my door, envisioning where the nameplate would be, and turned the knob.

The doorway revealed a small, dim cube, not much bigger than a utility closet. A tiny square window aimed a shaft of light onto an old-fashioned wooden chair and a large desk that took up most of the room. On its surface stood a lamp, a phone, a cup holder filled with pens, and two stacked desk trays. One was heaped with papers. More queries, no doubt. In the middle of the desk sat a laptop. I guess I must really have passed muster with Burlington-Duke, since I now had a computer, too.

Switching on the lamp, I put my coffee down and slung my bag onto the desk. The office was tiny, but I could pretty it up, make it my own. However, that would have to wait. Right now, I had a pile of queries to read.

I sat down, causing the chair to creak, and reached into my bag for the file folder of queries. I pulled it out, and Marlette's journal slid onto the desk. I touched it and shifted my gaze from it to the queries, then back to the book. Picking it up, I slowly opened the cover.

Chapter 7

THE MOMENT I OPENED THE JOURNAL, A RUSH OF FOR-est scents—fir trees and wood smoke and a trace of damp earth—escaped from between the pages.

Right away, I could see that this book did not contain orderly diary entries or a cohesive fictional narrative. The first page didn't even have any writing. Instead, there was an exquisite pencil drawing of a cardinal perched on a birch branch. Mar-lette had also drawn a squirrel racing along the bottom of the page, an acorn awaiting him in the bottom right-hand corner.

"How wonderful," I breathed, feeling as though I'd just discovered a folio belonging to Beatrix Potter. However, the next page didn't feature mischievous rabbits, fastidious mice, or daft ducks, but what seemed like a textbook exam-ple of stream of consciousness.

No one knows what I've put into the story, and I won't let her ruin my chances of seeing it published. All the nights I worked until the sun rose, in shades of pink grapefruit and tangerine beyond the window of my cabin, yet even now she would stop at nothing to punish me, to seek revenge for the imagined injury. I notice the worried looks from the corner of the eye from my colleagues when they think I'm not watching, and I can hear the words swirling in their minds silently wondering, "Did he do what she claims? Is he crazy? Will he end up in some kind of institution?" But I am not crazy or mentally ill or unstable. I just prefer my own company and that of my characters. I have lived in their world for so long now, have mapped out their lives from the cradle to the grave, that I cannot believe that their story is of no value. I won't believe it. Everyone's life is worth something, a great many things. If only the people who used to believe in me could see that I am more than I appear. I will prove it to them all. I will not let some spoiled little girl like that manipulative she-devil Sue Ann take this away, too. I want her to bear witness when someone else reads it. I want her to see that she hasn't beat me. Notyetnotyetnotyetnotyet.

To hear Marlette's voice, speaking from a page covered by splotches of ink from a bleeding pen, strengthened my connection to him. A few days ago, I thought of him as the sad, neglected figure who'd died my first day on the job, but now that I'd seen his cabin and was holding his journal in my hands, my sense of Marlette as an individual had deepened. He was an eccentric recluse before his death, but there had clearly been someone important in his life at one point. Who was this Sue Ann? A wife? A girlfriend? Where was she now?

I was about to examine the next page when there was a tapping on my door.

"Come in!" I called brightly, relishing the fact that I had my own space in which to invite people.

It was Jude. He held up a white paper bag and flashed me a smile that made my toes curl. This man was James Bond handsome. Setting the bag on my desk, his warm brown eyes met mine, and neither of us spoke for a moment. Desire crackled between us, as though we were tied by an invisible wire made of lightning.

Shaking his head slightly, as though to chase off lustful thoughts, Jude gestured at the bag. "You had such a rough start at Novel Idea that I wanted today to be a fresh beginning for you. This is a raspberry crème croissant from the bakery in town, and if this doesn't give you the energy to burn through those queries, then I don't know what else can . . ." he trailed off, and again, the room felt close, the air weighted down with heat.

My skin felt prickly beneath my clothes. I tried to call up a picture of Sean's face to help me get a grip on reality, but it was impossible. I couldn't see anything but Jude.

"Thanks," I murmured, embarrassed by the huskiness of my voice. After all, this man, beautiful though he was, could be Marlette's murderer. He'd been the last one holding the bouquet and therefore had had plenty of time to pocket Marlette's query letter. Recalling this fact allowed me to draw in a full breath, breaking Jude's spell long enough for me to reach for the bakery bag and peer inside.

A rush of sumptuous aromas sprang from within. Plump, tart raspberries blended with soft cream cheese inside a pocket of warm, flaky dough nearly seduced me all over again, but I folded the bag closed and smiled at Jude. "Wow, thank you. I'm going to save that as a reward for finishing twenty-five query letters."

"Good for you." He leaned against the doorframe. "I'm more of an instant gratification kind of guy."

Lord help me. In another second I was going to have to fan my flushed cheeks with a file folder. Mercifully, Jude gave me a little wave and made to leave.

I couldn't let him go without asking him about the flowers, so I called his name. "This might sound strange," I said, "but there was a piece of paper attached to the bottom of Marlette's bouquet—the one you threw out on Friday. Do you know what it said?"

Jude shrugged, his expression betraying nothing. "I assumed it was another query letter. I haven't read any of them, but our interns have never seen a reason to pass Marlette's on to an agent, so I didn't bother looking at Friday's version. Besides, I was kind of preoccupied with Carson's deal."

"So the letter was still wrapped around the flower stems when you tossed the bouquet in the Dumpster?"

"Yeah." He cocked his head inquisitively. "Why?"

I feigned nonchalance. "I just wanted to read his query. Professional curiosity, I guess."

He nodded. "Hopefully you'll have a winner in your current pile or in the hundreds of emails that probably came in over the weekend."

"Ugh," I groaned, wondering if I'd ever catch up. "I'd better get to it, then."

The moment he was gone, the fuzzy feeling in my head evaporated, and I vowed not to be so affected by Jude's charms that I overlooked the very real possibility that he might be a killer. I didn't know him well enough to trust that he'd told me the truth, no matter how much I wanted to believe that he had nothing to do with Marlette's murder.

With the workday now in full swing, I couldn't afford to spend more time perusing Marlette's journal. I'd save that investigation for my lunch with Makayla.

Reaching for my query folder, I began to read. It didn't take long to place twenty in the rejection pile, and I noticed that these aspiring writers were following a similar trend. Of all twenty queries, nineteen writers had compared their work to that of a contemporary bestselling author. Within the first two or three sentences of those letters, I'd been assured that I was being given the opportunity to discover the next John Grisham, Nora Roberts, Stephanie Meyer, Stieg Larsson, and so on. Yet not one of the writers had illustrated a strong enough voice, plot, or hook to convince me that their novels were worthy of consideration.

By the time my coffee was finished, I'd read over thirty query letters and had placed only one in the possibilities folder. It was for a young adult fantasy novel about twins who traveled back in time to a variety of ancient cultures. The high school sophomores, who were academically gifted but not always popular, never knew when they were going to embark on a new journey. However, their inventiveness and ability to blend in with their surroundings always enabled them to survive long enough to return home. I figured that the success of Rick Riordan's Percy Jackson series had created an interest in ancient cultures and decided to bring the query to Flora while getting myself a second cup of coffee.

Her office was empty, but I found her in the break room. Her back was turned, and I could see that she was concentrating on pouring boiling water into a ceramic cup covered by a design of wild roses with one hand while steeping a tea bag with the other. She hummed all the while, and I paused at the threshold, smiling at the pleasant sound.

"Hi there," I said when she'd finished pouring. "That's a pretty song."

"It's 'In the Cool, Cool, Cool of the Evening.' Rosemary Clooney." Flora poured two sugar packets into her tea. "A little before your time."

Putting the query letter on the counter, I gave the stainless steel coffeepot a little shake. Empty. As I searched the cupboards for ground coffee and filters, Flora sat at the square table and sipped her tea.

"They're in the freezer, dear," she informed me.

Spying several one-pound bags of coffee bearing Espresso Yourself labels, I focused on prepping the coffee machine, set it to brew, and then took a chair opposite Flora. "I have a query letter to show you. I think it has potential."

Flora accepted the letter and read it on the spot. I pictured the author, a middle school teacher in nearby Chapel Hill, standing in front of her class and waiting to call on a student. Did she experience a slight tingle? Did her sixth sense whisper that the woman in charge of selling the children's books and young adult novels of this literary agency was, at this very moment, perusing her query? If she knew, would her palms go clammy? Would her hand tremble as she wrote vocabulary words on the dry-erase board? Would she suddenly have to sit down? I grinned to myself, imagining the teacher's delight should Flora send her an email asking for the first three chapters of her manuscript.

Setting the paper down, Flora sighed. "It has potential, but it's too big of a story for the young adult genre. If they only traveled to one culture per book, that would be doable, but three? Too ambitious, I'm afraid."

I was surprised by my disappointment. Trying not to sound defensive, I said, "Couldn't you ask her to rewrite the book so that it focused on a single ancient civilization? She could turn this idea into a three-book series. I bet she'd jump at the chance to make those changes."

Flora reached across the table and gave my hand a maternal pat. "You've got a good heart, honey, I can tell. But we get letters that are close to the target *all* the time. We're looking for the ones that hit the bull's-eye, that make our blood rush through our veins. When we read one of *those* letters, we hope and pray that we can get in touch with the author before some *other* agent does." She fluttered her eyelashes and looked up at the ceiling. "Ah, the sensation is heavenly—that connection you make when a writer pitches a saleable idea *and* has the talent to back it up. It makes all the tough days worthwhile."

I didn't ask what she meant by "tough." My first day on the job had been fairly traumatic already, and I wanted to concentrate on the positive aspects of becoming a literary agent. Still, Flora's statement reminded me that she had disliked the man who died in this office Friday morning.

According to Big Ed from Catcher in the Rye, the soft-spoken, apple-cheeked woman across from me had tried to render Marlette even more invisible than he already was by getting him banished from the community park. I had to know just how much she'd resented his presence in Inspiration Valley.

My attempt to speak was abruptly interrupted by a shrill beeping, an indication that twelve cups of freshly brewed coffee was waiting to be had. I pushed back my chair and filled the black-and-white *Dunston Herald* mug I'd brought from home, inhaling the tantalizing smell of the roasted arabica beans.

"It seems odd to be sitting at my desk, plowing through query letters as though nothing happened here on Friday," I began, idly stirring cream into my coffee. "I know you felt sorry about Marlette's death, and I don't mean to sound callous, but won't it be a relief that he won't be showing up all the time?" Pasting on an exaggerated grimace, I carried my mug to the table. "He was odd and raggedy and had a bit of an odor problem."

Flora took the bait immediately. "I *know*. Shameful! Some people should *not* be allowed to wander about willy-nilly, unbathed, muttering to themselves, scaring children and making their poor parents very, very nervous."

"Did he do that?" I opened my eyes wide.

Spluttering, Flora put down her cup hard enough to cause the tea to slosh over the rim and puddle on the saucer. "He most *certainly* did! Skulking around the park, hiding scraps of paper in the purple martin house, drinking from the water fountain shaped like a dolphin—which is supposed to be for the *children*—and touching things around the play area. I could just *imagine* all the germs he left in his wake!"

Cheeks pink with indignation, Flora dabbed at the liquid pooled on her saucer with a napkin. The level of hostility in her voice startled me. I'd never imagined this jolly, picture-book-loving matron could harbor such resentment for a fellow human down on his luck.

I wondered if Flora was capable of killing someone simply because she disliked having to bear witness to the unpleasant face of homelessness, but when she spoke next, the true nature of her repulsion became clear.

"Why would a person constantly creep about where children are playing unless that person was *sick*?" she hissed, not really addressing me any longer, but an invisible enemy only she could see.

That's when I remembered Big Ed telling me that Flora believed Marlette to be a pedophile. If she was convinced of this fact, it was no surprise that she viewed him with malice.

Deciding to test the depth of Flora's enmity toward Marlette, I said, "We have our share of homeless in Dunston as well. I don't think any of them are pedophiles, but I do wish those poor people could all get the help they need. Whether that means rehabilitation into society, medical care, or counseling, it bothers me that they're left to wander around like half-starved zombies." I hesitated. Was I laying it on too thick? "What do you think, Flora? Should these folks be rounded up and sent to a facility somewhere so the rest of us don't have to see them?"

Flora frowned, considering my question. Finally, she shook her head. "No, dear. A town should take care of its people. Inspiration Valley doesn't seem to have any programs in place for"—she struggled to find the least offensive word—"these lost souls. I don't hate them, Lila. Don't think that of me. I just don't want the children to be subjected to scary-looking adults. They have so little time in this life in which they can enjoy their innocence. That's why I do what I do." She gazed into the middle distance and smiled dreamily. "Beautiful picture books, faraway places, magic, adventure. That's what a childhood should be about. Not ugly things like war or abuse or homelessness."

I nodded, amazed that Flora could be so naïve at her age. Or perhaps it wasn't naïveté at all. Maybe Flora's innocence had been stolen from her and she lived her life trying to preserve it for other children. Her words made me think of Trey, and I suddenly wished that his childhood had been as untainted as Flora's vision. Doesn't every mother hope for that?

"Perhaps this author can create that for a young adult audience," I suggested softly, pushing the teacher's query letter closer to Flora's hand.

She picked it up and flashed me a quick smile. "Okay, Lila. I'll give her a chance." Humming again, Flora washed her teacup in the sink and left the room.

In my office, I sat down on my creaky old chair. Cradling my mug, I slowly swiveled around and replayed my conversation with Flora. She was a bit of an odd duck, but she was certainly no murderer.

I spun the chair back to face the desk, and my eyes fell on the laptop that I'd pushed aside to make room for the stack of queries. Jude had mentioned emails this morning, as had Bentley on Friday. How many might be sitting there waiting to be read? I turned the computer on and waited for it to boot up.

Twenty minutes later, having had to interrupt Bentley once to ask for my assigned password, I accessed the agency's main email account. Jude was right. There were hundreds of email queries in the inbox. Three hundred and seventy-two to be exact. And Bentley had forwarded me the day's two proposals to read through. The remaining hours of the morning flew by as I fielded phone calls and read query letters, discarding each one into a virtual rejection file.

Finally, I looked up from the screen and rubbed my eyes. I was blushing from the query I had just finished reading.

It was for a novel in the erotica genre about a sea captain who gets shipwrecked on an island populated by salacious women. Although the letter was well written, the author's graphic descriptions made me squirm in my seat. Not being familiar with erotica, I was uncertain if this query was atypical for the genre. It was addressed to Ms. Luella Ardor, and I wondered if I should pass it on to her. I hesitated a few minutes but eventually forwarded it to her email address.

My stomach growled, and glancing at the clock on the computer screen, I saw that it was already half past noon. Making sure Marlette's notebook was in my bag, I headed for Espresso Yourself.

In the café, I stepped behind a gray-haired lady in a pink velour pantsuit who was waiting at the counter. Makayla handed her a takeout cup and then saw me. "Grab that table in the corner," she said, smiling. "I'll bring you something."

Surprisingly for this time of day, the coffee shop was quiet. A woman in a flowered skirt sat at one table with a laptop in front of her, a man holding the hand of a little boy was on his way out, and the pink pantsuit lady was adding sugar to her coffee. I settled down at the table by the window and examined the book Makayla had set there to claim her seat. It was Muriel Barbery's *Elegance of the Hedgehog*. The thought of the warmhearted barista escaping to a bourgeois Paris apartment during her breaks made me smile. I pushed the novel to the edge of the table and pulled out Marlette's journal.

"Girl, I'm glad you're finally here. I was getting mighty peckish." Makayla placed two plates containing bagels spread with cream cheese on the table along with two coffee cups. "A latte and a whole grain bagel with spinach and artichoke cream cheese. It's our newest flavor. Hope that's okay."

"It's wonderful. Thanks." The cream cheese, which was streaked with dark green spinach and had little chunks of artichoke throughout, smelled heavenly. "What do I owe you?"

"Lunch is on me today. I needed an official cream cheese tester, and you're it." She took a bite and chewed. "Hm. Not bad."

I picked up my bagel and crunched into it. It was delicious. The salty artichoke blended with the piquant spinach bits just enough to compliment the creaminess of the cheese. "Oh, this is good. Tastes like that dip everyone serves at parties in a pumpernickel loaf." I took another bite. "I'm surprised you're not busier right now."

"We're not really a lunch place. Bagels are all we have to offer. Most people go to Catcher in the Rye for sandwiches. Me and Ed, we have a good arrangement. I give people their morning jolt, he stokes their fires at noon, and then I'm here for an afternoon pick-me-up." She waved her hand at the journal. "Is that Marlette's? I've been thinking about it all morning."

"Yes. It's like a folio of art and stream of consciousness writing. I've only read the first entry, but I flipped through enough pages to realize that it's no ordinary diary." I opened the journal, inhaling the scents of the forest. "Can you smell that?"

"I can. It's like being in the woods." Makayla pulled the journal closer and inspected the drawings. "Wow, he was a gifted artist. People would have paid good money for these drawings."

"I know." I turned the page. "Read the first entry. If we can figure out who this Sue Ann is, we might be able to uncover the mystery of Marlette. Do you think she's a wife or girlfriend? A daughter, maybe? Do you know if he had any family?"

Makayla shook her head. "I don't know a thing about him. Just that he flitted about town like a leaf and smelled like a box of overripe fruit. And that I saw him climbing the stairs up to Novel Idea practically every day." She bent her head down to examine the first page.

I sat quietly while she read. This café was perfectly situated for Makayla to take notice of the people visiting or working at the agency. Maybe she had insights on my suspects. "What about Jude? Or Zach? Do you know anything about them?"

Makayla's jungle green eyes went wide. "You think they could've had something to do with Marlette's death?"

I shrugged. "I'm not discounting any possibility at this point."

"All I know is that Zach gets jacked up on double espresso every morning, and Jude could charm the habit off a nun."

Between bites of our bagels and sips of coffee, we skimmed through the pages of Marlette's book, being careful not to drop crumbs on it. There were more pencil drawings of woodland creatures and sketches of flowers, including a very detailed one of the milkweed he'd given me on Friday. But most of the pages were filled with writing: Marlette's unfiltered thoughts penned in his scratchy penmanship and ink spots blotting the paper randomly.

"This is so hard to read," Makayla said, turning to a particularly dense and blotchy page. "His writing is so small, and the sentences run on and on. Whoa, check *this*!" She pivoted the book to face me.

A sketch of a girl stared out from the paper; she was a

pretty young teenager, her braided hair hung over her shoulders and her rosebud mouth puckered. At first glance she was the embodiment of youthful naïveté, but a subtle shrewdness glimmered in her eyes. Marlette had captured an expression of arrogance underlying her innocence, and the longer I looked at her, the more uncomfortable I became. Underneath the face he'd written two lines:

Sue Ann Sue Ann Sue Ann Sue Ann Sue Ann.
  I should never have let you in never never never.

"Oh my gosh, it's her. It's Sue Ann." I stared at the sketch. What did Marlette mean about letting her in? I felt a flutter of memory stir. Something about the face looked familiar, but I couldn't quite—

The café door was thrust open, severing my train of thought. Three men wearing suits entered, their boisterous laughter charging the atmosphere.

"I'll be right back," Makayla said as she went to take their orders.

I closed the notebook and put it back in my bag. While gathering together the debris from our lunch, I pondered Marlette's ramblings. Would they help us find his murderer? Was Sue Ann a key to the mystery? I tossed the trash into the bin and put the dishes on the corner of the counter. I didn't want to leave without saying good-bye to Makayla, so I stared out the window and waited for her to finish with her customers.

A woman with a twin stroller jogged past, and then a robust young man on a bicycle pulled up outside the pharmacy. A man hustled down the sidewalk, glancing furtively back at our building. As his head turned, I realized he was Franklin.

Makayla, having come to the window, watched with me as he made his way into the park and disappeared beyond the fountain.

"Now *there's* a man you might want to investigate," she said.

I looked at her incredulously. "Franklin? Why?"

"That man carries a secret like a Hollywood starlet toting a dog in a Chanel bag. Every day he heads out at lunchtime and is gone for *exactly* forty-five minutes. And he never reveals anything personal about himself, no matter what I ask him." She shook her head. "He looks over his shoulder too much, just like he did today."

I was bewildered. Franklin seemed like such a sweet, ordinary guy.

"Girl, you're gonna have to hand that over to the police." Makayla gestured at Marlette's journal, which was sticking out from inside my bag.

"I know." I clutched the straps tightly. "But you said yourself they're not going to spend much time on Marlette's murder. It seems a shame for them to have it and then just file it away."

"So make a copy for yourself. You've still got a few minutes before you get back to the grind, right?"

"Smart *and* gorgeous," I told her, waving good-bye.

The first thing I did when I got back upstairs was to follow Makayla's advice by making a photocopy of Marlette's journal. I stapled the pages together and stuck the bundle in the bottom of my bag. The original went into a large brown envelope with Sean Griffiths's name on the front.

I left the door to my office open, hoping to catch Franklin when he returned from lunch so I could casually ask him where he'd been. In the meantime, I dialed the cell phone number on Sean's card. Unfortunately, I only got through to voicemail.

Just as I was leaving a message, Franklin walked past without a glance in my direction. Shoot. A missed opportunity.

The rest of the afternoon flew by. I managed to get through both proposals and a good chunk of the email queries. I now had three letters in the possibilities folder, but I decided to give them a second read in the morning before passing them on to the appropriate agents.

Satisfied with a good day's work, I tidied my desk and prepared to leave. Flora popped her head in my open door on her way out.

"Toodle-loo, my dear. I hope you had a productive day."

"I did, thanks." I slung my bag over my shoulder and walked with her. "Did you have a chance to follow up on that query?"

"Indeed, I did. The author and I are having an email conversation." She smiled. "She was thrilled to hear from me and responded to my email within seconds. She is very receptive to my recommendations. I just love it when an author understands the need for flexibility."

I held the door open for her. "Well, it was kind of you to spend extra time on it."

"Oh, I think something good might come out of this." She touched my arm. "Thanks to you."

Basking in her praise, I watched Flora walk to the parking lot. Her vehemence this morning about the homeless seemed so contradictory to this round, kind lady to whom I just wished a good night.

Unbidden, three words popped into my head. Purple martin house. I suddenly remembered our conversation from this morning and what she'd said about Marlette, that he'd put bits of paper in the purple martin house at the children's park. Right then I decided to take a detour on my way home. I had just enough time to make a quick stop at the park before my Monday evening appointments. But I didn't want to sleuth alone, so I dashed back to Espresso Yourself to find Makayla locking up for the night.

"Would you like to do some investigating with me?" I asked her.

She grinned. "Free as a bird. What are we doing? Breaking into a bank vault? Getting our hands on secret files?" Glancing down at her fuchsia T-shirt and white jeans, she smirked. "I'm not dressed in my best cat burglar outfit."

I couldn't help but laugh. "Neither am I. Fortunately, we're going to a public place to see if Marlette hid something in plain sight. It won't take long. Follow me."

The playground was on Dogwood, north of the town center. It was fairly new with brightly colored wood and plastic climbing equipment set in pea gravel, a flock of bird-shaped spring riders, and swings. Benches surrounded the perimeter, close enough for parents to keep watch.

At each corner of the park stood a tall pole with a birdhouse on it. One was a pink replica of the Magnolia Bed and Breakfast across the street, including an intricate gingerbread trim and a little front porch. Another looked like a log cabin. A small Noah's ark stood at the top of the third pole, and on the fourth was a miniature white apartment house with three rows of three round holes on each side. That, I knew, was the purple martin house, having had one at my childhood home. How I loved nesting season, when the birdhouse was filled with chirping and the bustle of the mother bird flying in and out with food in her beak. I wondered if this house had any martins residing within. I needed to see if there was anything from Marlette inside, but I didn't want to risk disturbing a nest.

A bench stood close to the house, and I figured if I stood on the armrest I'd just be able to peer into the closest hole.

"Can I hold your hand while I climb up here?" I asked Makayla.

She nodded. "Sure. If anybody asks, I'll tell them you're practicing lines for a play."

"Good idea," I said. "Which play?"

Makayla shrugged. "How about *One Flew Over the Cuckoo's Nest*?"

Grinning, I paused for a moment to look around. Two little redheaded boys who appeared to be twins were taking turns climbing up a ladder and going down a slide with their mother standing nearby. A blond, curly-haired girl of about three with her thumb in her mouth sat on one of the spring rider birds—a big green hummingbird—staring at a jean-clad teenager talking on a cell phone. A boy of about seven was sitting on the ground in the corner by the Noah's ark birdhouse, making intricate roadways in the gravel for his collection of cars. His concentration on his task reminded me of Trey laying out the tracks for his Thomas the Tank Engine collection. Somehow, it didn't seem all that long ago.

I put down my bag, took off my shoes, grasped Makayla's hand, and climbed onto the bench. Standing on my toes, I stretched up and was able to see into the holes on one side.

There were bits of twigs and grass within, but nothing else. I twisted to look in the holes on another side.

"What are you doing?" a small voice inquired.

Startled, I lost my balance and only managed to land on my feet because of Makayla's firm grip. The boy stood by the bench, a yellow Corvette in his hand.

"Are you putting a note in there for the Flower Man?" he asked.

Makayla and I exchanged excited glances.

"Do you mean the man with the long gray beard and coat?" I pantomimed a beard growing from my own chin.

The boy nodded. "He picks flowers even though my mom says that's bad. And he hides notes in there." He pointed to the purple martin house.

"That's what I'm looking for now," I said. "Did you see him put one in there recently?"

"Aiden! Come here!" The mother with the twins started walking toward us.

"Aw, Mom, I'm just talking to the ladies." He rolled his eyes. "She always thinks somebody's gonna take me or try to give me candy."

Makayla smiled at him. "Sorry, I'm fresh out of chocolate-covered coffee beans at the moment."

Having reached us, his mother grabbed hold of her little boy's arm. "What have I told you about talking to strangers?"

I reached out my hand. "I'm Lila Wilkins, ma'am, and I didn't mean any harm." Makayla also introduced herself.

"Hello," the woman said, barely making eye contact. "Sorry to act overprotective, but we've seen our share of weirdos around here. Come with me, Aiden." She pulled him toward the entrance. "We have to go home for supper. Dylan, Daniel, time to go!"

"But *Mom*, I gotta get my cars!" Aiden yanked free and ran to his toys, hastily dumping them into a bucket. "Bye!" he shouted, waving at us.

Disappointed that I couldn't ask him, or his mother for that matter, more questions about Marlette, I climbed back on the bench and inspected the rest of the purple martin house. But there was nothing inside except for nesting materials. The twigs and fluff and grass that once kept helpless baby birds safe and warm now served no purpose and were merely debris.

I climbed down dispiritedly, reflecting on how the emptiness of the birdhouse resembled that of Marlette's little home in the woods.

"Don't worry," Makayla said, seeing I was in need of a pep talk. "Tomorrow's another day. Who knows what clues are just waiting to be found?"

"I hope there's at least one, because at this point I am striking out as a detective."

She took my arm in hers. "But you make a fabulous park bench acrobat."

This earned her a laugh, but as we left the park, I carried the image of the vacant birdhouse with me. More than ever, I was determined to find out what happened to Marlette and to deliver a measure of justice to the person known to the children as the Flower Man.

Chapter 8

AS THE WEEK PROGRESSED, MY DAYS AT A NOVEL IDEA began to take on a regular rhythm. I was grateful for this, since the past two weeks had contained more drama than I cared to replicate.

On Friday morning my mother drove me to work, the way she'd done the previous few days.

"This is a nice little routine we got goin', isn't it?" She said as she pulled up in front of Espresso Yourself. "Me takin' you to work, then stoppin' in town for what I need, and I get back home in time to get my banana bread in the oven and prepare for my first client."

"It works well for now. Thanks, Mom." I watched her drive off and headed into Espresso Yourself. There was a line at the counter, but Makayla greeted me as I walked through the door.

"I saw your mama's darling turquoise truck outside," she said, holding out a cup. "Here's your latte." She then lowered her voice to a conspiratorial whisper. "Much as I'd love to, I'm way too busy to look at any of Marlette's journal today. Got a nice little catering order to fill and inventory to do."

Each morning, if Makayla had time, we'd examine an intriguing piece of writing or drawing from Marlette's journal. I had taken the photocopies I'd made of the original and placed them in a three-ring binder. The cover featured a print of monarch butterflies and blue hummingbirds hovering over the uplifted face of a gold chrysanthemum. The nature theme reminded me of Marlette. Still, I missed the pine-scented pages and the texture of the dried flowers and scraps of paper he'd pasted into his diary.

"No worries. Next time," I said. "I have a pile of work to do, too."

I had just turned my computer on when a young police officer appeared at my door.

"Are you Lila Wilkins? I was told to pick up a book or journal from you."

"Oh, I thought Officer Griffiths was coming to get it." I tried not to show my disappointment. From my desk drawer I removed the envelope containing the enigmatic book and handed it to the policeman. He dropped it into an evidence bag, his movements conducted without the slightest hint of care. I held back a complaint about his indelicate treatment of Marlette's most precious possession.

But then I remembered that not everyone understands what it means to reveal one's most intimate thoughts through lines of writing or meticulously detailed sketches. Not everyone is aware of how many emotions can be tucked away in the cursive loops and curves of a proper name. They don't know how a few scant lines of pen or pencil can represent a childhood memory, a strange and wondrous dream, or a desperate hope for the future. These feelings and so many more existed in Marlette's journal, and though I studied it each night before bed, I'd made no further progress in extracting a tangible clue.

Marlette was never far from my thoughts, but I have to admit that I quickly became too busy to devote as much time to his journal as I'd have liked. The queries and proposals kept pouring in. The moment I felt I'd made headway on electronic queries, the mailman would jog up the stairs, whistling to announce his presence, and I'd end up with a sack load of letters. They'd populate the corner of my desk, their colorful stamps and return address labels staring at me hopefully, then accusingly, then angrily as the hours passed.

"This must be how the post office feels when the kids start mailing off their letters to the North Pole," I murmured as I scrutinized the dozens of paper cuts on my thumb and forefinger and resolved to pick up a letter opener over the weekend. Thank goodness I didn't have to lick the endless envelopes filled with rejection letters I mailed out each day. If it hadn't been for self-stick envelopes, I would have had to use a sponge.

At this point, it became clear that the final workday of the week would once again be the most memorable, as my first email of the morning read,

> *I received your form rejection letter yesterday. You couldn't take five minutes of your precious time to tell me why you were passing on such a unique idea? It took me five years to write this book, but you can't be bothered to give even a single sentence of feedback? I will be sure to tell all of my many writer friends to forget about querying your agency because you clearly don't recognize talent when you see it.*

That email was better than the one that came next, which was much more direct in its hostility:

Dear Ms. Wilkins,

Thanks for nothing, you stupid bitch.

Instinctively, I reached out to delete the message and then paused. I needed to add these two writers to my Agents Beware file. Shaking my head over their lack of professionalism, I printed out copies of their emails and stuffed them into my red file folder. Zach caught me frowning as I dropped the folder onto the surface of my desk.

"Zach Attack!" he shouted and leapt across the threshold, his arms outstretched as though he expected applause from a studio audience. "What gives, Pretty Woman? Writers behaving badly?"

I nodded and gave the folder a dismissive wave. "I'm immune to these kinds of snarky comments. I have a teenage son."

Zach laughed. "Cool. I'll have to take him to a hoops game this fall. Is he into sports?"

"Definitely. He's a huge Tar Heels fan." I gave Zach a grateful smile, but the exchange reminded me that the ebullient agent carried a strong grudge against Marlette for chasing off Taylor Boone. If she hadn't been repulsed by Marlette's appearance, Boone might just have become Zach's star client. The young agent had undoubtedly looked forward to a long and lucrative relationship with the reality show star until Marlette had spoiled his plans.

As I searched for a way to bring up the subject, Luella breezed down the hallway. She gave me the ghost of a grin and a wriggle of her fingers but turned a dazzling smile on Zach, trailing her pinkie seductively down his cheek. She then kissed the finger and placed the kiss on his lips before continuing to her office. Zach forgot all about me and drifted in Luella's perfume-scented wake, a dreamy look on his face.

Resolving to ask Zach to join me for lunch next week in order to grill him about Marlette, I got back to work. So far, I'd only found one interesting nonfiction query, and since I needed a break anyway, I walked it down to Franklin's office. I rapped lightly on his door and, when he didn't answer, opened it a crack. Franklin was seated at his desk, the back of his swivel chair to the door. He had a phone held to his ear and was murmuring softly to the person on the other end.

I knocked again, louder this time, and waited on the threshold. I didn't want to interrupt an intimate conversation, but Franklin swiveled around in his chair and slammed the phone into the cradle as though he'd been overheard saying something monstrous. His face was flushed, and his jaw clenched in what was either anger or embarrassment or both. I took an involuntary step into the hall, and Franklin tensed like a leopard preparing to spring.

"Excuse me," I said apologetically as I tried to suppress my trepidation at Franklin's extreme reaction. "I didn't mean to intrude." I raised the sheaf of paper in my right hand. "This seems like a promising query on decorating with vintage items. The author has run an antique mall for twenty-five years and recently expanded her business to include interior design. She's local," I continued, despite the fact that Franklin hadn't spoken a word. "I've been to her shop—a renovated tobacco warehouse that's been divided into various rooms. Each room has a theme, like an art deco living room or a 1950s kitchen, for example."

Franklin blinked and allowed his shoulders to relax. The pink left his cheeks, and the look of animal wariness disappeared from his eyes. He made a show of tidying his already neat desk and said, "Won't you sit down?"

After handing him the letter, I complied, but I was unable to sink back into the chair's soft leather. The tension that had left Franklin's body seemed to have entered mine like a parasite in search of a host.

Franklin Stafford was a man with a secret. I had seen it just now, that flash of guilt followed by a flicker of menace? Fear? I didn't know exactly what I'd observed, but I'd have to drum up enough courage to find out, since it could have something to do with Marlette.

As Franklin read the query, I considered how the days had passed without my managing to confront any of my coworkers other than Flora about their feelings toward Marlette, but the agents weren't readily accessible. Between their staff and client meetings and my succession of long phone conversations and various errands, there wasn't as much socializing as I'd imagined. The agents popped into one another's offices throughout the day—only Bentley remained closeted at the end of the hall for the entire week purportedly finessing Carson Knight's contract—and I exchanged small talk with all of them in the break room. But for the most part, we worked independently of one another.

I was used to this atmosphere from my years at the *Dunston Herald*, but we reporters operated in a large room divided by cubicles. The setup of Novel Idea created more privacy and yet did not prevent genuine camaraderie between the agents. I certainly saw what a close-knit group they were during Wednesday's staff meeting.

It started off with Bentley walking into the room with a tray of coffee and a bag of lemon ginger scones from Espresso Yourself.

"I thought you'd appreciate a little pick-me-up," she announced, placing them on the table. "For all your hard work this week."

"Woo hoo!" Zach exclaimed. "Did you get me a triple espresso?"

"Yes, Zach. I had Makayla make all of your favorites."

During the meeting, the agents shared which of their clients' manuscripts had received offers by editors or had been passed on and were now with another publishing house awaiting review.

When it was Luella's turn to speak, she announced smugly, "Do you recall Gillian Lea's new romantic suspense series? The one featuring shape-shifters?" She waited as those around the table nodded their heads. I recognized Gillian Lea as a successful romance writer but had not read any of her books. "The manuscript is in the midst of a major bidding war," Luella continued. "I aim for the winning publisher to end up paying the author an advance of seventy-five thousand dollars per book."

My jaw nearly came unhinged, but I tried not to show my surprise, as none of the other agents seemed awed by this number.

"Congratulations, Luella," Jude said, raising his coffee cup. The other agents followed suit.

At the end of the meeting, Bentley stood. "I'd like to note that Lila, our newest intern, has had a very promising beginning. Thank you, Lila."

"Yes, I concur," Flora said. "Lila is a wonderful addition to our little group."

And then we adjourned.

No one mentioned Marlette or the investigation. No one whispered the word "murder." It was as if the unusual man had never climbed the stairs with his wilted flowers and hopeful face.

I hadn't mentioned Marlette, either, and though I kept looking at the newspaper for an article on his death, the crime pages were still focused on the arson case in Dunston. More than once over the course of the week, I flirted with the idea of calling Sean, but something held me back.

By the time I'd finished my daily allotment of queries, proposal critiques, and mailings that Friday afternoon, I was ready for the weekend. My mother picked me up and drove me the short distance to Inspiration Valley's organic food store, How Green Was My Valley. It was my intention to whip up a tasty meal for Althea and Trey. My mother had generously offered to make supper every evening, but last night's lasagna had been so undercooked that I nearly chipped a tooth on a noodle. On Tuesday night, she'd grilled hamburgers until they resembled miniature manhole covers. Althea's talents in the kitchen were truly restricted to banana bread, coffee, and comfort.

In addition to bagfuls of fresh local produce, I picked up a copy of Charlaine Harris's latest Sookie Stackhouse novel. After a week's worth of query letters, I wanted to read something fun over the weekend.

"Have you heard from Trey?" my mother asked me after I'd loaded the groceries into a box in the truck bed.

"No." I shot her a confused glance. "I thought he was going to borrow the truck and continue his job hunt today."

My mother shook her head. "I never laid eyes on the boy this mornin'. His bed is as wrinkled as one of those Shar-Pei puppies, and it looks like a tornado blew in his window, lifted up all his clothes, and sent 'em flyin' to every corner of the room. Doesn't he know what folks use hangers for?"

"Sorry, Mama. He's always been untidy."

My mother snorted. "Kindergartners are *untidy*. That son of yours is a flat-out slob. But his room won't put me off my supper. I just don't like not knowin' where he is, and the cards say he's bein' drawn away from the familiar. Somethin' powerful has a hold on the boy, and I can't tell if it's a positive or negative influence. Things go all cloudy when I close my eyes and try to search him out."

Ignoring the psychic mumbo jumbo, I said, "He's probably hanging out at the Red Fox Co-op. You saw how he looked at Iris. Totally thunderstruck."

"Yeah, I saw. I just wonder how far he'll go to turn that girl's head," my mother murmured enigmatically.

With the exception of Makayla's remark about the co-op folks growing marijuana as one of their crops, I wasn't too concerned about Trey being up the mountain. The people there seemed charitable and kind, if not a little spellbound by Jasper. Trey would be home by nightfall. He didn't enjoy roughing it much.

Back at my mother's, I put the groceries away and then popped the cap off a bottle of beer. After my long week, the cool liquid slid down my throat like cold honey, and I sighed in contentment. Althea turned on a Johnny Cash CD, and the two of us belted out "Daddy Sang Bass" as I breaded chicken cutlets and fried them up in peanut oil. In true Paula Deen style, my fried chicken was seasoned with a splash of hot sauce, and I served it with slaw and buttered corn on the cob. I made enough for three, but Trey didn't show up for dinner. I hoped he was consuming more than beer with his new Red Fox friends.

The sky had turned a bruised blue and gray by the time my mother and I finished supper and began to clear the table.

"It's gonna rain," she said, raising her nose into the air like a dog catching a scent.

Leaving the dishes to soak, we went out to the back porch and settled into a pair of rockers. My mother was having Jim Beam over ice for dessert, and I was going to digest a bit before attacking the quart of mocha chip I'd stashed behind a large bag of peas in the freezer. We'd barely set the wooden rockers in motion when my cell phone rang. The number wasn't familiar, but I answered anyway.

"Lila?" Ginny Burroughs, my Dunston real estate agent, sounded agitated. Her strained voice immediately put me on alert.

"Good evening, Ginny. How are you?"

A pause. "Well, I was just coming over to your house to put the lockbox on—two agents are planning on showing it tomorrow—when I saw something . . . strange on your front door."

I waited for her to continue, but she clearly wanted me to ask what she meant, so I played along. "Strange?"

She hesitated, drawing in a deep, fortifying breath. "Lila, someone's spray-painted a red skull and crossbones on your white paint!"

"What?" I jerked upright in the seat.

"Bright as a cardinal, but not at all cheerful," she added for dramatic flair. "My husband wouldn't mind slapping a coat of paint over it for you, but I thought you should know in case you wanted to call the police. The vandal added some letters, too, but I can't make them out. For some reason, he painted those a shade of white. A black light might help you read them. Luckily, I've got one you can use."

After thanking Ginny and ending the call, I rubbed my throbbing temples and tried to stay calm.

"There's trouble at your house," Althea stated, but I knew she wanted details.

I eased myself out of the rocker. "Someone played graffiti artist on my front door. Can I borrow the truck? I need to get over there and deal with this tonight."

My mother scrutinized me, the corners of her mouth pinched in concern. "This wasn't some hip-hop gangster wannabe, Lila. Mark my words. It's a warnin'."

"Okay, Mama. Please call me if you see or hear from Trey." I gave her an indulgent smile and headed inside for the truck keys.

On the drive to Dunston I began to feel the effects of my full week. The last thing I wanted to do was meet Ginny at my half-empty house. I knew that the darkened windows and the silent rooms would depress me, the *For Sale* sign and vacant garage serving as reminders of my dismal financial situation. Why would anyone vandalize my house? I'd been friendly with all of my neighbors, and we hardly had gangs of spray-paint hooligans living in our backyards.

Ginny was waiting in her sleek Lexus convertible when I arrived, but the moment I rumbled up the street in Althea's turquoise truck, she raced to my door, black light in hand.

"I'll shine it for you," she offered. "You stand back a few feet. Maybe you can read the writing that way."

In the time it had taken me to drive from Inspiration Valley, the resourceful Realtor had managed to find an extension cord. The cord trailed out from inside my house like a long orange worm, still very visible in the shadows cast by the encroaching night and the gathering thunderclouds.

Ginny angled the black light so that when she switched it on, the front door was thrown into a wash of spectral purple light.

I gasped. The skull, which had gaping eye sockets and an openmouthed snarl, radiated hostility. Part of me had been expecting a cartoonish pirate skull, but there was nothing childish or playful about this drawing. My heart racing, I had to force myself to meet its menacing gaze. I knew it was irrational, but I felt a presence behind those eyes. A wickedness lingering from the vandal like a powerful perfume. However, my need to decipher the writing below the crossed bones won out over my trepidation, so I steeled myself and drew close to the door.

"S . . . T . . . O . . . P," I read aloud. "I think the next letter is an 'L' followed by—" I couldn't continue. I now knew what the words said. They gave me the chills and I stepped back, retreating from the warning, but it seemed to follow me.

STOP LOOKING STOP LOOKING STOP LOOKING

Ginny was still peering at the letters. "Oh! I see it now!" She repositioned the black light, propped it against the doorframe, and came to stand beside me. "Who is this message for? Vampire home buyers?"

I shook my head, dread tiptoeing up my spine and raising the fine hairs at the nape of my neck. "I believe it's meant as a threat, but not to a potential homeowner. To me."

"But what are you supposed to stop looking for?" she wondered.

I pretended to be too busy taking photographs of the vandalism with my cell phone to answer. This warning had to do with Marlette's death; I was sure of it. I had no proof, but I felt it in my bones. I put my hand on Ginny's arm, trying not to tremble. "If your husband would be willing to paint over this, I'd be really grateful, but I need to tell the police about it first."

Thanking her again, I promised to fill her in later, but all I wanted to do now was get back to Althea's, track down Trey, and take a very long, very hot bath.

As I headed into Inspiration Valley, lightning scored the sky and the rain began to slap against the windshield. As it formed a steady rhythm against the glass, it seemed to take on the voice of the skull and crossbones, whispering its warning through the water.

"*STOP LOOKING STOP LOOKING STOP LOOKING . . .*"

MY VERY LONG, very hot bath was not to be. My mother was pacing on the porch when I arrived, her features pinched with more worry.

She rushed out to greet me as I opened the truck door. "Lila, Trey still isn't home!" My mother stared at me wide-eyed, her wet hair clinging to her face. "I've got a real bad feelin'. The cards won't show me what's goin' on with him. I get nervous when they go quiet."

I grabbed her hand, and we dashed up the steps to the shelter of the porch. The rain pummeled the roof, battering my already frayed nerves. Seeing my mother's frantic expression, my anxiety intensified. Trey had never stayed out this long before. "Did he leave a message? He didn't call to say he wasn't coming home?" I couldn't help asking these questions, even though I knew the answers. My mother wouldn't be this worked up if she knew something I didn't.

"Not a word. If I wasn't already worried about you, I might be able to focus on where he is, but I'm right overwhelmed!" She clutched my arm. "We haven't seen him since yesterday, sug. It's time to call the police."

Her trepidation was serious if she was suggesting we turn to the police instead of relying on her special powers. I was torn, vacillating between thinking that something was truly wrong and believing that Trey was just being rebellious in the aftermath of his accident and our abrupt move. I hoped it was just rebellion. The other alternative, the possibility that something horrible had happened to him, was too frightening to consider, and I pushed the unwelcome thought firmly aside.

"Do you think the truck would make it up that dirt road? Maybe we should go to the Red Fox Co-op and look for him," I suggested, already fingering the truck keys. The last time I'd seen Trey was at supper the day before, when he stomped off in a huff at my insistence that he be more proactive in his job hunt. I'd been so wrapped up in my own concerns, I'd failed to pay attention to what might be going on with him, and in my guilt I wanted to find him myself and fix the problem.

"But we don't know for sure he's there. And drivin' up the mountain in the dark in this kind of rain . . . There are no lights up there. I don't like it." My mother wrapped her hands around mine. "He's been gone for twenty-four hours, Lila. That makes him an official missin' person. Let's get someone official to look into it."

I had to admit her idea was warranted. Any chagrin about my failings as a parent should not get in the way of finding Trey. If I contacted Sean I could also tell him about the vandalism. Abruptly, a disturbing thought invaded my mind, making my mouth go dry. What if Trey's disappearance was connected to the message on my front door?

It was not without reservations that I dialed Sean's cell phone, knowing I should phone the police station and not be taking advantage of my personal connection with Sean. But I figured I'd get faster results dealing directly with him. Besides, I wanted to see him, to be comforted by his air of authority and assurance.

When his phone began to ring, I almost hung up. Why was I disturbing him so late? He was probably off duty, enjoying his Friday night. Perhaps he wasn't alone. Perhaps he would think I was a silly, easily frightened woman. However, I didn't hang up. My son was missing, and I needed the help of someone I could trust.

"Sean Griffiths here."

His welcoming, rich voice broke through my doubts. "Sean? It's Lila Wilkins. I'm sorry to call so late—"

"No problem. What's up?" He sounded glad to hear from me. A cacophony of voices and laughter reverberated in the background.

"It's Trey. He hasn't been home since yesterday and we, that is, my mother and I, don't know where he is."

My mother poked me. "Tell him he's been missin' for twenty-four hours," she whispered loudly.

I waved my hand at her. "We want to report him as missing. Can I do that through you?"

"Usually you'd call the station to do that. Just a sec." His voice became muffled as he said something indistinguishable, presumably to someone in the room with him. "Tell you what, I'll come over and you can fill me in. You're staying at your mother's place, right?"

Relief streamed over me like raindrops. "Yes, thanks,

Sean. My mother is, um, her professional name is Amazing Althea, and her place is just south of town, at the end of Magnolia Lane."

"I know where she lives," he said. "See you in a bit. And Lila?"

"Yes?"

"Hang tight. Trey is probably fine."

THE VERY PRESENCE of Sean in the house helped to alleviate some of my mounting dread. His calm demeanor and the concern that shone out of his blue eyes instantly settled the panic that had taken hold of me. I was able to describe Trey's situation in a composed manner, even with my mother interrupting me in order to ply Sean with banana bread and coffee.

And yet, my heart raced when I'd finished talking and he put down his mug to reach over and touch my hand in reassurance.

"Trey wouldn't be the first seventeen-year-old to seek solace at the co-op." He flipped closed his notebook. "I'll take my truck and see if he's up there. Mind you, this time of night, things'll be pretty quiet on the mountain."

"They do sack out kinda early. Up with the sun, down with the sun," Althea concurred, nodding. "Officer Griffiths, I've never had a bit of trouble with the co-op folks, so if he's there, I'm right sure they aren't doin' anything wrong. I think there's another force at play in this case." She tapped her temple. "You keep that in mind, ya hear?"

"We'll see, ma'am. I'll let you know what I find out. And if Trey isn't there, then we'll decide on the next step."

I walked Sean out to the porch. The rain had stopped,

and the night was quiet. The scent of after-rain freshness hung in the air. "There's something else I need to tell you," I said as I pulled out my cell phone. "My house in Dunston was vandalized with what I believe is a threatening message." I showed him the photo I'd taken with my phone. "It was painted with glow-in-the-dark paint, so it only shows up at night. I think the person who did it doesn't know that I've moved out."

In the dim light of the porch, Sean's face darkened. "This is serious. What is it you're supposed to stop looking for?"

"I think it has to do with Marlette. I've been asking questions at work and looking around the places where Marlette used to go. Nothing that would interfere with the official police investigation," I hastily added when I saw a glint appear in Sean's eyes. "I think somebody wants me to stop." I closed the phone, not wishing to see the photo anymore. "Somebody doesn't want me to find out what really happened."

Sean expelled a loud sigh. "You have to report this, Lila. The Dunston police need to send a unit to your house. And you need to stop trying to do our job. Stop putting yourself in danger."

"But you said yourself the police aren't dedicating any manpower to Marlette's case. Nobody even came for the diary until today?"

He shrugged. "It's not high priority at the moment. The arson case has become our priority. See, someone was locked inside the building when the fire was set, and so now we're dealing with murder, arson, and insurance fraud all wrapped up in one case. It's got precedence, especially with all the media attention surrounding it. We'll figure out what happened to Marlette eventually. Heed the warning and stop poking around."

"But—"

He touched his finger to my lips. "Shh. You have enough to worry about." His touch seemed to burn me with a delicious warmth, and for a moment, I forgot why he was there. I was jarred back to reality when he dropped his arm and said, "I'd better go look for Trey." He started down the steps, then stopped and turned. "Try not to let too many people know you're living here. If the vandal is an unstable individual, we don't want him or her to be able to find you."

As I watched Sean walk to his car, my gaze fell on my mother's blue truck, looking in the darkness like an over-sized, shadowy creature of the deep. Tomorrow I would look for some mode of transportation that didn't scream *I live with a fortune teller*.

"Sean?" I called just as he was climbing into the car.

"Yes?"

"Is there a chance that Trey's disappearance is related to the vandalism?"

Even in the dark, I could see his frown. "No. I think Trey's just being seventeen. But you can't be too careful."

I hoped Sean was right about Trey, but I wasn't going to heed his advice about my investigation into Marlette's murder. Someone had to find justice for the poor man, and I seemed to be the only one trying to do that. My probing may have made the murderer nervous, and if that person thought a little spray paint was going to deter me, he or she was dead wrong. If anything, I was even more determined to find out the murderer's identity. I would just have to be more careful.

My mother joined me on the porch, and we both watched the red taillights of Sean's truck burn through the night.

"That man's got a fascinatin' aura, Lila. He could be trouble for you." She smiled enigmatically. "Then again, he could be just what you didn't know you needed." She handed me a cup of coffee. "No sense goin' to bed. It's gonna be a long night."

Chapter 9

ONCE AGAIN, ALTHEA WAS RIGHT. IT TURNED OUT TO BE a very long night.

When I heard the rumble of Sean's truck and saw the headlights twinkling like will-o'-the-wisps through the trees lining the mountain road, it was quarter past one in the morning.

My mother was asleep in her chair with her head rolled back and her mouth hanging open. She snored gently, a tumbler holding an inch of whiskey dangling precariously in her right hand.

I stood up, my body aching with stiffness from the rocker, and eased the glass from my mother's hand. The rain had stopped hours ago, leaving the air steamy and thick with moisture.

The lengthy wait had calmed me a bit. I assumed Trey must have been up at the co-op, because Sean was there for a long time. That meant my son was safe, but just as stubborn as always. Sean would have needed to sit down and talk some sense into my love-struck teenager before coercing him to come back home.

Being the kind of man I sensed he was, Sean probably spent the return trip gently scolding Trey for having worried his mother and grandmother. Hopefully, he also gave my son a few sound pieces of advice on how becoming an adult meant accepting one's responsibilities. In my mind, I could already hear Trey's words of contrition.

Of course I'd forgive him, wrapping my tired arms around his broad back. Then, after I'd thanked Sean effusively, we would go inside and get some much-needed sleep.

So when Sean's truck finally cleared the trees and drew alongside the porch close enough for me to see that the passenger seat was empty, I felt the knot of fear form in my belly again.

I covered my mouth with my hand as though I could hold back the question I was too scared to ask.

"Trey's okay," Sean said the moment he got out of the truck, and I drew in a deep breath. He hurried to my side. "Your son is all right. He was sitting around a campfire playing the guitar when I got there. He had an open beer can at his side, but he wasn't inebriated. He was well fed and relaxed and completely . . . happy."

As my body sagged in relief, Sean's description hit home. "Is that why he didn't come back with you? He's not happy here?"

Sean shifted uncomfortably, and I felt ashamed for putting him on the spot. He was a police officer, not a therapist, and he'd done me a huge favor by driving up the mountain in search of my son. "Sorry," I said. "I'm just tired. You must be exhausted, too. I know how much you have going on . . . professionally, I mean. Would you like to come in?"

He shook his head. "No, thanks. Let me tell you what Trey said, and then I'll be on my way. I've got an early start tomorrow."

Glancing at my mother, he grinned and sat down on the top porch step. "Trey wanted me to assure you that he isn't trying to upset anyone. He said he feels like he belongs with the people of Red Fox Mountain and he has something to contribute to their community."

"Like what?" I wondered aloud.

"Apparently, he's quite interested in their methods of organic farming. He's also, ah, quite fond of the goats. He spent all day tending to them and, well, he seemed very sincere about learning how to care for them and market their products."

I sunk down onto the step below Sean's and stared into the inky night. "Trey has an affinity for goats? Are you sure he's talking about goats and not Iris?"

Sean's eyes twinkled with mirth. "He also admitted that he wanted to impress the young lady, but Jasper made it perfectly clear that the co-op is not a place for the disingenuous or for freeloaders. People are welcome to visit, but they cannot stay indefinitely unless they contribute to the community. Tomorrow, Trey will begin the first day of his monthlong trial process. At the end of thirty days, if he still wants to stay, the community will vote on whether to accept him as one of their permanent members."

"Don't they need my consent? He's still a minor."

Pursing his lips, Sean considered my question. "I don't know, Lila. He's earned his high school diploma, so truancy doesn't enter the picture. You'd have to ask a lawyer. I'm no expert on this sort of thing, but if Trey likes living up there, he may apply for emancipated minor status."

"Good Lord!" I leaned back against the stair railing, stunned and speechless. A vision of Trey with long, matted hair, a dirt-smudged face, and threadbare clothes entered my mind. I pictured him feeding a carrot stick to a mangy goat with one hand while smoking a joint with the other. "I wonder if he'll even go to college now."

Sensing my consternation, Sean put a hand on my shoulder. "Don't worry, this is probably just a phase—something he needs to go through before he settles down into a more, ah, mainstream career."

I nodded, really wanting to believe him. "You're probably right. We're talking about a kid who breaks out in hives if he can't check Facebook twenty times a day. And whenever I really wanted to punish him, I just took away his video game system for a week." Laughing, I felt pretty confident that Trey would be back in front of Althea's only television set by Monday. "No DVDs, no text messages . . . Wait a minute, is there any kind of cell phone reception there? What if he needs to reach me? What if I *have* to talk to him?"

"It's spotty, but they do get a bar or two," Sean replied. "Don't bother to call if there's a thick cloud cover or a storm. You won't get through." The pressure on my shoulder increased. "It'll be okay, Lila. The folks in the co-op will treat him well, and he's in no danger."

I raised my brows. "There are rumors that those 'folks' grow pot as one of their staple crops."

Sean's hand slid away, and he stood up, as though I'd reminded him that he had unsolved crimes waiting and that he needed to get going. "People in town have been spreading that story since Red Fox was founded, but we've conducted at least three surprise investigations and never found so much as an illegal seed, let alone an entire crop. And Jasper has always been cooperative, gracious even, about these searches."

I got to my feet as well, amazed that my mother hadn't stirred a muscle throughout our entire exchange.

Thanking Sean profusely, I walked him to his truck, wishing those fifteen feet could stretch into a mile. Part of me wanted nothing more but to climb into bed and process Trey's impulsive decision, and part of me wanted to linger beneath the heavy indigo sky with Sean.

He turned before opening the driver's door, and for one breathless moment, I thought he might pull me to him. There was a hunger in his eyes that I knew was reflected in my own, and I desperately wanted to feel his mouth on mine, to get lost in an embrace that could make me forget about Trey and everything else outside the circle of his arms. But suddenly, my mother uttered a loud, guttural snort, and the glimmer in Sean's eyes morphed into a silent laugh.

"It's the whiskey," I whispered with a snigger.

As if to reinforce that our romantic moment had passed us by, it began to rain again.

Sean wiped a droplet from his forehead, promised to keep in touch, and hopped into the truck. I watched him drive off, waving until his red taillights disappeared around a bend in the road.

"Stupid rain!" I said, raising my voice. I hadn't even realized that I was angry. But I was.

I was angry at Trey for how helpless his decision made me feel. How could he leave and not even bother to write me a note telling me where he'd gone? I was bent out of shape that I hadn't worked harder on Marlette's behalf, and I was also annoyed that I didn't have enough gumption to lean in and kiss Sean. What was I waiting for?

"It just wasn't the time," Althea spoke, answering my question.

I swiveled, my fists in tight knots. "How long were you pretending to be asleep?"

"Since you took Mr. Beam outta my hand," she said, still groggy. "Some folks have teddy bears, some have sound machines, but I like to drop off holdin' my sweet-smellin' cup."

"No wonder you have to wash your sheets so much," I grumbled.

My mother roused herself and began to shuffle inside. "You'd best have a swig yourself. With the way your hormones are ragin', you won't get a second of shut-eye. G'night, darlin'."

I SLEPT LATER than I wanted to the next morning, but both my body and mind had really needed those extra hours of slumber. The house was quiet, and I assumed my mother had gone out for a walk, so I poured a cup of coffee and went up to Trey's room to think about my next course of action.

Sitting on the edge of his unmade bed, I felt like I was losing my son, like he was drifting down a fast-running stream and no matter what I did, I couldn't catch up to him. I couldn't reach him. He couldn't even hear me calling his name.

Of course he craved independence and the companionship of people his own age, but did he have to move to an isolated mountaintop to find contentment? Where had I gone wrong?

One thing I knew for sure: Trey was still my son, and I had every right to hike up to the co-op and demand he tell me face-to-face why he wanted to stay there. I put on a pair of cropped sweatpants and a tank top and stole a few loaves of banana bread from my mother's freezer. It was then that I spotted a note taped to the handle of the refrigerator. It read: *Give him some space, Lila.*

Apparently my mother didn't find the idea of her teenage grandson living with a troupe of goat herders as disconcerting as I did. Ignoring her advice, I headed outside for the narrow trail.

Thirty minutes later, I stopped at the co-op's entrance to catch my breath and spotted Trey shoveling goat droppings into a wheelbarrow. I could scarcely believe my eyes. He wouldn't even put the toilet seat down at home, and now he was voluntarily cleaning up malodorous animal poop.

When Trey saw me coming, he set down the shovel and gave me such a warm smile that my eyes grew misty. He *was* happy.

He jogged over to the edge of the enclosure and hopped the fence with the agility of a white-tailed deer. Everything about him seemed to be shining; he was completely aglow with a sense of purpose and belonging, and I had to admit that the co-op might actually be good for him.

"Mom! I was going to come down and see you after work," he said. Even his speech was clearer, more energized. He wasn't mumbling, and he looked me right in the eye. Amazing. "I'm *way* sorry I freaked you out by not telling you my plans." He gave me a coy grin. "But I figured it would be better for you to find out *after* I was already here. I guess that was kind of uncool."

"I'm your mother, Trey. I'll always want to know where

you are. You did scare me, but your apology is accepted." I patted his back and glanced around. The co-op was buzzing with activity, and somewhere off in the distance I could hear the sound of a violin being played. I felt more at ease standing here with Trey than I had for many weeks. "I can understand why you find this place so appealing."

Trey looked surprised. "You can?"

I laughed. "I was young once, too, you know." I handed him the banana bread. "Share this with your friends, work hard, and know that your family is right down the hill if you need us." I hesitated. Leaving Trey here was hard. "You're going to visit us, right? And call me when you can? And what about college? Is this just for the summer or . . . ?" I trailed off. It was too hard to give voice to my fear that he would one day announce his intentions to settle here permanently.

"Right now I'm just living in the moment, Mom. I want to see what it feels like to live like this before I rush off to college where my whole life will be one big, fat schedule." He looked pained by the idea. "But I promise to come over every few days. Take a shower, do some laundry, and have supper. How's that?" He gave me a hug. "And I'll do my own laundry, Mom. You've got your new job to focus on. It's time I took care of myself."

I nearly fainted. Trey was going to wash his *own* clothes?

Instead of swooning, I kissed my son on the cheek and let him get back to work. As I turned to leave, Iris appeared from a path leading into the forest. She sent Trey a dazzlingly beautiful smile and wished me a good morning.

"This *cannot* be coincidence!" Iris declared in her melodious voice as she strode over to me. "Ever since I brought you to Marlette's cabin I've been thinking about him, so I started wandering on the paths he liked best and visiting the places where he liked to sketch or just sit for a while. And I found something. Do you want to see it?"

"Absolutely."

Iris led the way, her lithe, ethereal figure barely making a sound as we moved out of the meadow and into the woods. This time, we headed away from Marlette's cabin, veering northwest instead.

"Where are we going?" I inquired in a hushed voice.

Without turning, she said, "It'll be more rewarding for you to experience it firsthand."

What an old soul. I was slightly awed by the girl's poise, by her certainty.

The air was refreshingly cool, and the summer foliage allowed only a dappling of light to reach the carpet of pine needles and twigs. Soon, the path disappeared, turning to the barest hint of a trail, and eventually we began to tread through a part of the forest that looked to my untrained eye as though it hadn't been disturbed in a long time. Iris didn't hesitate, however, and her certainty allayed my fears that we might be lost.

As we walked in companionable silence, I began to puzzle over the details of Marlette's daily routine. From what I'd heard, he would stop by Novel Idea, visit certain hidey-holes around Inspiration Valley, and then come back to the forest, probably to recover from being exposed to the noise and commotion of town.

"This is the place," Iris said, almost reverently.

We had arrived at a secluded meadow, a wide oval of grass filled with wildflowers. Scores of butterflies and bees flitted from blossom to blossom, and birdsong filled the air.

I could picture Marlette resting on the fallen elm, his diary on his lap, allowing the harmony of the scene to wash away unpleasant thoughts or memories.

Iris sat down on the grass and closed her eyes. I, too, felt an infusion of peace, an uplifting of my worn spirits, and a line from Thoreau whispered in my ear like the hum of dragonfly wings.

"'You must converse much with the field and woods, if you would imbibe such health into your mind and spirit as you covet for your body.'" I whispered it softly, as though trying to tell Marlette that I understood why he'd set himself apart from the rest of the world in search of a measure of tranquility on this mountain.

"Henry David Thoreau," Iris said, surprising me. "From one of his journals." She pointed at a birdhouse made from twigs and vines, so well camouflaged that I hadn't even noticed it hanging down from a branch just over my head. "I was right to bring you here."

I walked over to the birdhouse and then threw her a questioning look over my shoulder.

"It's hinged. The roof opens like a box top," she explained.

The house was mounted too high up for me to peer inside, so I carefully lifted the lid and reached my hand into the interior. My fingertips brushed what felt like a piece of paper. Standing on my tiptoes, I managed to retrieve the sheaf and bring it down to eye level.

A dried flower, one that I didn't recognize, had been glued to a square of thick cardstock. There was a sketch of a girl in the background, and Marlette had drawn her so that her hand reached up to cup the dried flower in her palm. Below the pen-and-ink drawing, in Marlette's unique scrawl, were the words, *Looks can be deceiving. Beauty is only skin-deep. Sue Ann. Sue Ann. Sue Ann.*

Her name repeated right up to the paper's edge, the "n" tilted, appearing as though it would fall from the page into space.

I'd seen the girl's face before in Marlette's journal. Those challenging eyes and sly smile were unmistakable. Who was this Sue Ann, and why had he hidden this image of her in the forest? I *had* to discover her identity and her connection to Marlette.

"Do you know her?" Iris asked, watching me closely.

I shook my head. "No, but I'd like to take this to the Secret Garden if that's okay. Maybe the flower is a clue. I'll see if they can identify it."

Iris nodded. "I don't think Marlette would mind. So many times, when I'd come across him in the woods, I felt like he wanted to tell me something. Something important." Her eyes held regret. "But he was afraid to. Or he didn't trust me. I don't know what held him back. Now I'll never know."

I held up the drawing. "Don't give up hope. If there are more of these to be found, I'll find them. And I won't allow him to be forgotten. I promise."

TREY KEPT HIS word and joined us for Sunday dinner. I made one of his favorite meals: barbecued baby back ribs, homemade mashed potatoes, and green beans cooked in bacon grease. While I worked some magic in the kitchen, Trey did his first load of laundry and tidied his room. My mother was delighted by his new show of cleanliness, but to me, his orderly room served as a reminder that he wasn't living with us anymore. It took all of my willpower not to beg him to come back home. The truth was I missed him. We'd shared a house for so many years that being in my mother's place without him felt lonesome.

Still, we had a lovely supper together. Trey regaled us with stories about the goats and boasted a bit about how Jasper was seriously considering Trey's ideas on rebranding the goat products to make them more marketable. We ate and talked until after nine o'clock, and then Trey pulled a battery-powered lantern out of his backpack and said he had to get going. I hugged him hard and then watched him give my mother a kiss.

"See ya Tuesday!" he shouted as he made his way up the hill.

I stared at his wide shoulders, my heart aching. Would he make the same journey at the end of the summer? Would he forgo a higher education in favor of a bohemian lifestyle? For once, I wished that Althea could peer into the future and put me at ease, but she had already told me that Trey needed to work things out up on the mountain and she didn't know how long that would take.

I waited until the glow from his lantern faded from view and then crawled into my bed with Marlette's journal. As I'd done many times that day, I compared the drawings of the girl with the scheming gaze.

Tomorrow would mean the start of another busy week, and I had lofty goals for the next five days. Not only did I plan to fulfill my quota of queries, but I was going to try to find all of Marlette's hidden niches and figure out once and for all which of my coworkers had a secret that could have led to murder.

And the first name on my list was Franklin Stafford.

*   *   *

I BIDED MY time at the office the next morning, efficiently reading and responding to queries and all the while keeping one eye on the hallway to see when Franklin left for lunch so I could follow him. I found myself yawning several times and tried not to dwell on the tediousness of my job. Sifting through a myriad of story proposals in the hopes of coming upon a gem brought to mind the work of a prospector who seeks the twinkling of gold in a mess of sand. Still, I accorded each query the attention it deserved, trying to put myself in the place of the hopeful writer who penned it. Thankfully, there were none that found their way into the Agents Beware file this time, but there were no shining jewels, either. Only one gave me pause, and I considered it for several minutes before setting it aside to read again at the end of the day. The query was for a novel about a woman who changes careers by leaving the corporate world to open a cupcake shop and becomes entangled in a murder investigation. I wasn't sure if it appealed to me because of the succulent recipes, because it was a good, well-written story, or both, so I decided to distance myself and revisit it later.

Stretching my back, I looked up at the ceiling. As if they'd been hovering above me like a cloud, thoughts about Marlette drifted into my mind. I considered what little I knew of the man. Someone out there must be more familiar with his history. He couldn't always have been the strange, unkempt individual who died in our office. And who was Sue Ann?

Completely distracted from my work, I proceeded to search the Internet, Googling Marlette, Sue Ann, homeless vagrants, anything I could conjure up that might lead to the smallest nugget of useful information. I discovered nothing. Staring into the hallway, I was trying to think of other search terms when Franklin suddenly walked past my door on the way to the exit. Remembering that his secretive lunchtime excursions made him one of my prime suspects, I slammed the laptop shut, grabbed my bag, and rushed out after him.

When he left the building, he started walking up High Street and through the park. Makayla was right. His movements were furtive and suspicious. He walked quickly, constantly looking around the streets and over his shoulder. He definitely acted like a man with something to hide. Maybe his secret bore a connection to Marlette.

I stayed in the shadows when I could, ducking in doorways and pretending to look at interesting things in the shop windows.

Franklin finally turned onto Walden Woods Circle, the street where my little dream house stood. Perfect. If he caught sight of me, I could just say I was looking at a house I was interested in buying.

We walked past the charming yellow house, and Franklin hustled up the walk of a tidy pink one with blue shutters. A piano-shaped sign was posted on the lawn. *Music Lessons*, it read, and it included a phone number. Could Franklin be taking piano lessons during his lunch hour? But why would he be secretive about that? I hid behind a wide tree trunk and stared at the house.

He did not go up to the front door but walked along the wraparound porch to an entrance near the back and let himself in. When he closed the door, I rushed over to the house and peered very discreetly in a side window, hoping I wasn't too visible from the street.

I found myself looking into a kitchen, all done up with

lacy curtains in the windows and a vase of flowers on the blue granite countertop. The table was set for two, with wineglasses and bright green cloth napkins folded under the forks. A plate of sandwiches sat in the center.

Repositioning myself so that I could just peer above the window frame, I saw Franklin, caught in the embrace of another man. They exchanged a tender kiss, smiled lovingly at each other, and then sat down at the table and proceeded to eat lunch.

That explained his furtive behavior! Franklin—prim, solemn, conservative Franklin—was gay. His suspicious behavior had nothing to do with Marlette's murder. He just didn't want anyone to see this side of his private life.

And I had just wasted part of my lunch hour on a wild-goose chase. I could have been looking for one of Marlette's hidey-holes. Instead, I was behaving like a Peeping Tom.

I strode off the property in exasperation. Sighing deeply, I stopped for just a minute in front of the cozy yellow house I coveted. If my home in Dunston ever sold, maybe I could scrape together enough money to buy this perfect place.

My stomach grumbled in complaint, so I headed in the direction of Lavender Lane in search of lunch.

The smell of baking bread inside Catcher in the Rye assaulted my senses the same way it had the first time I visited the sandwich shop. I breathed it in deeply, my mouth watering. Scanning the delectable menu, I chose the Mowgli, a curried chicken salad with mangoes and walnuts wrapped in whole wheat naan. This time I virtuously asked for carrot sticks as the side. Glancing at the card the cashier handed me, I had to smile over being assigned the name of Miss Marple. It seemed fitting, considering my bumbling attempts at figuring out the mystery of Marlette's murder.

Waiting for my name to be called, I stared out the window. Just to the left of the fire department was Mountain Road, leading to the Red Fox Co-op. I wondered how Trey was doing up there.

"MISS MARPLE!" Big Ed bellowed, disrupting my musings.

I reached for the bag he handed me, and in my best British accent, said, "Why, thank you, kind sir."

"Hey, you're the intern at Novel Idea, right? You were Eliza Doolittle last time. I never did catch your real name."

"Lila Wilkins. Pleased to officially meet you, Big Ed." I shook his hand.

"I was thinking about you folks at the agency and that poor soul, Marlette. You were asking about him last time. Just last night I remembered something kind of unique about him and was hoping you'd stop in so I could share it with you."

I felt a tingle of excitement. Sometimes, answers come out of thin air. "I'm still trying to figure out what happened to him. What was it you remembered?" I leaned closer to the counter.

Big Ed pointed outside. "See those birdhouses attached to the tops of the fence posts at the side of the grocery store?"

I craned my neck to look. Sure enough, there was a fence along the side of How Green Was My Valley, painted with a mural of a farm scene. Rolling hills, patchwork fields, cows, corn stalks. And, equally spaced, atop each fence post was a birdhouse shaped like a little red barn. There were six of them in total.

"Those are so cute." I turned back to Big Ed. "What do they have to do with Marlette?" As soon as I asked the question, I remembered the purple martin houses in the park and the birdhouse to which Iris had brought me on Saturday.

"He was always poking around in those birdhouses. I saw him stick stuff in them at times, too. Maybe he left something inside them. A clue." Eyeing the cheesesteak meat on the grill, he quickly added, "It may be that I just watch too many detective shows on TV and there's nothing to be found in those little houses, but you never know."

I couldn't wait to find out. Hurriedly, I thanked him and, holding tightly to my lunch, ran across the street.

The first three tiny barns held nothing except bits of twigs and grass. But when I reached my fingers into the hole of the fourth one, they brushed against something that felt like paper. Carefully, I pinched my fingers together until they caught the edge of the paper and eased it out of the hole.

What I held in my hand was a ragged, yellowed newspaper clipping. Pieces were torn from it—chewed off, it looked like—and in a few spots the ink was smudged. But I could make out the year, 1985, and the byline, Jan Vance. I knew Jan! She'd been a reporter at the *Dunston Herald* and my mentor when I first began my career as a journalist.

I smoothed out the shredded bit of paper as best I could and began reading. The account was disjointed because of all the holes and ink smears, but I could make out the gist of the story.

> *Parents of Woodside Creative Camp are up in arms in response to allegations of sexual . . . Marlette Robbins is a tenured professor at Crabtree University . . . a fifteen-year-old and . . . a man in his position entrusted with young . . . Professor Robbins denied the accusations, saying the young woman . . . Woodside fired Rob-*

bins and the university is . . . Charges have not been filed.

Wow. Marlette had been accused of demonstrating inappropriate conduct toward a fifteen-year-old girl at a summer camp? The idea shocked me. He'd seemed like such a gentle, unaggressive soul. Still, charges weren't filed, so maybe there was more to the story. At least now I had a last name for him. And a former profession. But clearly, I didn't have enough facts to understand everything about what had happened. I needed to talk to Jan Vance. As soon as I got back to the office, I planned to give her a call.

The aroma of curry teased my nostrils, and I suddenly remembered my lunch. Leaning against the fence, I bit into the naan wrap. It was scrumptious. The spicy curry, blending with the tartness of the mango and crunchiness of the nuts, was heavenly.

After swallowing my last bite, I tossed the trash into the bin, and then, just to be sure, I checked the last two birdhouses. They contained nothing, so I rushed back to the office.

Dialing Jan's number, I composed questions in my mind. My eyes traveled to the pile of queries on my desk. I had to admit that at the moment I felt more like an investigative reporter than a literary agent. Guilt at not focusing on my work started worming its way into my conscience, but before it gripped too tightly, my old mentor answered the phone.

"Jan Vance." Her voice barked through the receiver, conjuring up her no-nonsense personality as if she were in the room beside me.

"Hi, Jan. It's Lila Wilkins."

"Lila! Good to hear from you, girl." She laughed, her hoarse voice a result of years of chain-smoking.

"How's retirement? Finished your book yet?" When Jan retired a few years ago, she'd announced she was going to write a novel based on her experiences as a reporter. I hoped I'd get to read it one day.

"The book's coming along, slowly but surely. What are you up to these days? I heard the *Herald* is making do without your talents."

"That's true, but I found a new job pretty quickly at the Novel Idea Literary Agency."

"No kidding! Are you cold-calling for clients?"

I didn't know whether she was teasing or not. "Actually, no. Did you hear about the homeless man who was found murdered in our office? Marlette Robbins?"

"That was Marlette Robbins? I did a piece on him years ago, you know."

Pleased that she remembered him, I continued. "That's what I'm calling about. I'm trying to find out what happened back in eighty-five. Could you fill me in?"

"Sure. Let me think a minute." Through the receiver, I could hear her blow out and guessed she was smoking her umpteenth cigarette of the day. "Robbins was accused of molesting a fifteen-year-old girl in his counselor's cabin at some arts camp. The name escapes me. The girl had gone to him for help with her creative writing project, and apparently Robbins pushed her on the bed and tore off her shirt and bra. The girl ran out before he got any further. Had a ripped bra to prove it."

I shook my head, unable to visualize Marlette as a man who preyed on innocent teenagers. I felt queasy all of a sudden and could only manage to whisper, "What happened next?"

"Just so you know, I don't think he did it. From all

reports, that girl got her kicks by manipulating people. I never interviewed her. I wasn't even told her name, seeing how she was still a minor and her parents wanted to protect her identity. But by all accounts, Marlette Robbins was as straitlaced as they come, an impeccable Southern gentleman. Nobody could believe he was capable of such an act."

I felt anger on Marlette's behalf. "And yet he was fired!"

"Yeah. I don't know what that girl's motivation was, but she sure ruined his reputation, even though he was never officially charged."

The story chilled me, but I chitchatted a bit longer with Jan and then thanked her and hung up.

I sat back in my chair and wondered if the accusations against Marlette were true. Had I completely misjudged him? If he *was* capable of violence against women, perhaps he'd done something unforgivable to another woman, and in return, she'd made him pay the ultimate price.

But if Jan was right and he hadn't harmed that girl, then why had she accused him? What did she have against him?

A shiver shot up my spine. If the girl *had* told the truth, she'd never received justice. Maybe she had meted it out herself, twenty-five years later.

Chapter 10

I DIDN'T HAVE TIME THAT AFTERNOON TO PHONE Crabtree University's English Department to find out if any of the faculty remembered Marlette. Bentley called me into her office and, after telling me that she was pleased to see that I'd been fulfilling my daily quotas, informed me that she was increasing my workload.

"You're the first intern I actually expect to make it through the three month trial period," she said, looking at me over the rim of her reading glasses. This pair was coral-colored and matched her blouse and handbag perfectly. Her white slacks had a knife-sharp crease, and I marveled over the height of her silver heels. My boss was the most coiffed woman I'd ever known. I felt downright dowdy in her presence and vowed to make my wardrobe more chic when I became a full-fledged agent.

I smiled at her. "I'm determined to have my own clients one day."

"Good for you. We need a fresh dose of ambition around here. Therefore, you'll be pleased to learn that I've decided to award you more responsibility." She handed me several file folders. "A Novel Idea is going green. That means we'll no longer be mailing paper copies of royalty statements. Instead, each author will receive an electronic version sent via email. I'd like you to design a template for each of these publishers and then fill in the royalty information for the authors in those folders." Bentley tented her hands on the desk and stared at me intently. "Authors don't like us to be tardy when sending out their royalty statements. For some of our clients, royalty checks cover their everyday expenses. Do you understand what I'm saying?"

I nodded. "Trust me, I know all about the stress of unpaid bills." Picking up the folders, I stood up. "Do these take precedence over the queries and proposals?"

Bentley waved at me absently, her attention now focused on her computer screen. "I'm sure you'll be able to manage both. You seem like an extremely capable individual, Lila."

Recognizing this as a dismissal, I headed back to my office feeling a surge of pride. I had proved myself. I *was* going to be more than an intern by the end of the summer; I could feel it in my bones.

Between the queries, critiques, mailings, and creating the royalty statement templates, the rest of the workday flew by. I managed to leave a message for the current English Department Chair of Crabtree University, but no one returned my call that day or the following morning. I wondered if the professors kept regular office hours during the summer, but I didn't have the time to review the online course listings or figure out who would be on campus. I had to focus on the pile of royalty statements if Novel Idea's clients were to be paid before the end of the week.

Finally, late on Tuesday morning, I decided I could spare two minutes at the tail end of a coffee break to call the university's switchboard. Luckily, the operator transferred me to a helpful receptionist who informed me that the only member of the English Department who had taught at Crabtree during Marlette's tenure was giving a lecture called "Shakespeare's Soothsayers" that very evening. I was delighted to learn that nonstudents were welcome to attend and planned to ask my mother if she'd like to accompany me.

Feeling as though I'd made excellent headway at work and was on the cusp of learning something significant about Marlette's past, I decided to devote part of my lunch hour to continuing the investigation. Taking the drawing of Sue Ann that Iris had helped me find, I struck out for the Secret Garden, thinking that with all the walking I now did, I'd soon be in the best shape of my life.

As I left my office and headed for the stairs, my cell phone rang.

"Guess what?" exclaimed my real estate agent. "Someone's asked to see your house for the *third* time! I think they plan to make an offer."

"That would really be great," I said, stepping out the front door into the powerful midday sun. "I don't know how much longer I can ask my mother to drive me to work and back. I feel like a little kid. If this goes on, she's going to be packing my lunches and slipping notes into the brown bag like she did when I was a girl."

Ginny made a cooing noise. "Your mama sounds so sweet. Anyway, I just wanted to tell you some good news, considering the last time I called you it was to report that awful vandalism." She paused. "Did the police ever find out who did that?"

"Unfortunately, no."

"Well, I wouldn't worry about it. Water under the bridge," Ginny declared brightly. "Gotta run, but I'll be in touch."

During our brief conversation, my feet had automatically carried me to the fountain in the center of town. I sat down on the damp cement and fished a penny out of my purse.

"This wish is for my house to sell quickly," I told the closest muse. She ignored me, her marble gaze studiously fixed on the scroll in her hands. Examining the plaque at her feet, I said, "Clio, Muse of History, let me look back on this summer as a time filled with positive changes." Closing my eyes, I sent the offering into the shallow water and watched the coin wobble to the bottom. Impulsively, I reached out and touched Clio's wet cheek before heading off to the Secret Garden.

When I arrived at the nursery, I was met by the clamor of a large group of children. According to a sour-faced employee who had escaped outdoors to organize a shipment of petunias, a group of campers from the community center's nature camp was spending part of the day learning how to grow a vegetable garden. Each child had been given a small terra-cotta pot to paint and plastic bags containing seeds and potting soil. It made me smile to see the eager campers decorating their pots with jolly round tomato men and stick-figure bean ladies. Addison was busy showing the children how to bury their seeds in the dirt. It was clearly not the best time to ask her to identify another plant for me.

Glancing at my watch, I knew that my lunch hour was nearly half over. After all, I had to hoof it back to the office and grab something to eat from Espresso Yourself if I was going to survive the rest of the day, but it was difficult not to linger. The laughter and high-pitched voices of the kids carried me back to a time over ten years ago. Suddenly, I was transported to my kitchen in Dunston. There I was, an old apron tied around my waist, busy painting homemade wooden toolboxes with Trey's Cub Scout pack. I wondered what he was doing right now. Bathing a goat? Picking berries?

A voice interrupted my musing. "Can I help you?"

I surfaced from my reverie and noticed that a middle-aged man wearing a green apron was giving me an amused stare.

"Sorry, I zoned out for a minute there."

He grinned. "Happens to the best of us. You might want to pick up a ginger plant. Or maybe a potted rosemary or Siberian ginseng. All three are proven memory boosters."

"I just might." Removing Marlette's drawing from my purse, I unfolded it, surreptitiously reading the garden center employee's nametag at the same time. "Do you recognize this flower, Martin?"

He handled the sheaf of paper with care and scrutinized the dried plant for a long moment. "It's a peony. We don't have many bushes left in stock, as most folks planted theirs back in April. We'll get a bunch more in September, but let's see if we can find a match."

Following Martin to the flowering vines and shrubbery section, we examined several bushes. The tags wrapped around the stalks showed fuchsia blooms called Beautiful Señorita, a bright red variety called Barrington Belle, or Candy Heart, a delicate and pale pink.

"It looks like there's yellow paint on the inside petals of your pressed flower," Martin remarked, eyeing the page once again. "None of our plants have a corn yellow middle with white petals, but we sell a wonderful book on the flowering bushes of North Carolina. It has full-color plates."

Thanking the helpful gentleman, I spent twenty dollars on the book, even though I probably could have researched peony varieties on the Internet for free. Still, I didn't feel like I could keep visiting the garden center without buying something, and I didn't want to carry a Siberian ginseng plant all the way back to Novel Idea, so I purchased the reference book.

On the way out, I noticed a lemon yellow Vespa scooter parked by the front door. It had a black leather seat, chrome embellishments, and a small *For Sale* sign taped to the top case.

I forgot all about my mystery flower. I forgot all about work. Hesitating only for a moment, I ran my fingers along the seat, letting them trail upward, caressing the handlebars and coming to a rest on one of the side mirrors. I caught my reflection in the glass and had to laugh. I looked like a woman in love. If not love, it was certainly a serious crush.

Rushing back inside, I found Martin watering a display of cheerful marigolds. Their golden hue made my heart beat faster. I *had* to have that scooter!

"Could you tell me who owns the Vespa parked out front?"

"That's Addison's," Martin replied. "We call it Big Bird, she calls it Banana Split, and her folks call it risky. Lucky for our gal, her big brother just bought her a beautiful, brand-new Volvo and asked her to sell the scooter."

I'd name it Sunshine, I thought, envisioning myself driving the Vespa down the road leading to my mother's. In my fantasy, the rain-parched flowers growing in the grassy meadows along the street burst into bloom as I whipped past, a scarf trailing out behind me, the wind curving around my shiny black helmet. My arms and legs were bronzed by the sun, and I was wearing tight capri pants and a pair of high-heeled boots. Drivers didn't mind my reduced speed limit. In fact, they were simply happy to be able to catch a glimpse of the woman on the scooter who looked as though she should be motoring through the narrow lanes of Paris or Rome. Perhaps they'd think I was a movie star, hiding out in Inspiration Valley to recover from the stress of shooting my latest blockbuster.

"Ma'am? I think I lost you again," Martin teased.

I blushed, feeling foolish for getting caught in a second round of daydreaming. I wrote down my phone number and handed it to Martin. "Would you give this to Addison and tell her I am *very* interested in the scooter?"

He nodded, tucking the scrap of paper in his apron pocket. "Sure thing. Have a nice day."

I hurried out of the garden center and back to the center of town. By the time I entered the blessed air-conditioning inside Espresso Yourself, I was hot, sweaty, hungry, and thirsty.

Makayla glanced up from the milk she was steaming, saw me sag against the counter, and laughed. "Don't you know better than to run around in the midday heat? Sit on down. I know just what you need."

Moments later, I was served an iced cappuccino, which tasted utterly divine. I took several refreshing sips and then uttered a gratified sigh. "You're a little like my mother, Makayla. Both of you seem to have a gift when it comes to knowing what people really need. Now how about lunch? Any bagels left?"

Makayla shook her head. "I've got nothing but sugary treats, and those are just going to make you thirsty all over again." She examined the gardening book poking out of my purse. "You working on a green thumb?"

"No. I'm hoping to discover a clue." I quickly showed her the drawing and the newspaper article.

She scanned over the lines and then stared at Marlette's portrait of Sue Ann. "Tell me she doesn't give you the creeps," Makayla said with a frown. "Those eyes . . . another picture showing those smug, hostile eyes. This girl probably got up every morning and set about planning to mess up somebody's day. I've seen that look before. She thinks she's better than everyone. Thinks she's owed something. Is only happy when another person is full of grief."

"I keep wondering if this girl is Sue Ann and if Sue Ann is the person who accused Marlette of molestation. This isn't the first drawing he made of her. So far, I've found two of them. She *must* have been significant to him."

Makayla's frown deepened. "Not in a good way, either. This girl haunted him."

We both fixed our gazes on Sue Ann's defiant eyes.

"I've got to get back to work!" I exclaimed, suddenly noting the time. I grabbed my takeout cup, thanked Makayla, and trotted up the stairs.

It was unlikely that anyone was keeping track of my whereabouts, but I needed this job. I wanted this job. And I had no desire to lose it because I was abusing my lunch hour.

By two o'clock, I was so hungry that I went rooting through the refrigerator in the break room. I was just pulling the tin foil from a casserole dish when Jude entered the room. I started guiltily and shoved the dish behind my back.

"It's not that bad," he said with a smile. "I've actually been told that my five-cheese, creamy tomato pasta casserole could bring about world peace."

He cooks, too! Not only was the man gorgeous, funny, and successful, but he knew his way around the kitchen as well? Again, I felt a surge of heat warm my body, and I swallowed hard, suddenly aching with thirst again. "I was so busy doing errands during my lunch break that I didn't actually get a chance to eat."

In two strides, Jude was next to me. He took the casserole from my hands and gently pushed me toward the table. "Please be seated, milady. I would be honored to serve you my humble fare." Giving me a deep, rakish bow, which earned him a laugh, Jude scooped pasta into a bowl and placed it in the microwave. Each of his gestures was theatrical to the point of being ridiculous, and I giggled like a teenage girl on a first date right until the moment I tasted my first bite of casserole.

My eyes went wide as the blend of cheeses and creamy tomato sauce coated my tongue. I shoveled in several forkfuls before finally pausing to compliment him on the delicious fare. Surely a man who cooked with such artistry couldn't be a murderer!

Jude bowed again and then walked behind my chair and bent over, his lips an inch away from my ear. "Dessert is in my office," he murmured. "Stop by anytime."

With his breath on my neck and the woody scent of his cologne tingeing the air, I nearly lost muscle control and dropped my fork. I could feel my heart thudding in my chest, and I closed my eyes, picturing Jude's full lips, his arms yanking me against his chest in a rough, passionate embrace, his hands moving under my blouse, feeling my hot skin against his fingertips.

I blushed again, recalling how recently I'd had the same fantasy sequence with Sean as the leading man. I was going to have to either rein in my crazed hormones or actually kiss one of these men. And clearly Sean was the better choice. After all, he wasn't on my list of possible suspects.

After I'd eaten, I attacked the query pile, amazed that over a dozen had come via email between twelve and one. Just how many aspiring writers were out there?

Ten queries fell flat before I ripped open an envelope and unfolded a query that gave me chills. Not only was it compelling, but the opening lines made me think of Marlette.

A murderer is preying on the itinerant population of downtown San Diego. Each morning, beneath a mound of bloodstained rags or inside a decrepit cardboard box, another body is discovered. The victims, murdered by strangulation, have all been given the fresh tattoo of a poppy flower. Seeing the glaring red bloom, Detective Jones Connelly refuses to subscribe to the department's theory that the killer is a deranged sociopath who believes he is helping the community by clearing the streets of "riffraff."

One of the oldest cops on the force, Connelly remembers a cold case in which a little girl was stolen from her bed in the dead of night. Her body was found two days later in the city center park. She'd been strangulated by her own jump rope.

Connelly remembers the case all too well. He still sees the crime scene photos whenever he closes his eyes.

He sees the bruises on the small neck, the torn night-gown, and the carpet of poppy blossoms the killer laid out on the grass for his victim.

He remembers, because the little girl was his sister.

The author's words carried a strong sense of grief and regret. I could tell that Connelly was the epitome of a troubled police officer and that the writer had likely developed a complex, three-dimensional character. This query deserved to be put in front of an agent's eyes.

I worked steadily for the rest of the afternoon, but the query about the Poppy Killer continued to silently call to me from the corner of my desk. I'd been putting off delivering it to Jude because I didn't know what he meant by saying that dessert was in his office. I did know that we generated enough heat between us to send this query letter up in flames.

Jude was on the phone when I knocked on his door, his feet propped up on the desk, his arms cushioning the back of his head so he could lean as far back in his chair as he dared. He waved me in and then told the caller, "You know you're the most beautiful flower in the garden."

Replacing the receiver, he dropped his feet and gave me a dazzling smile. "Do you have a treasure for me?"

"I believe so," I answered and handed him the query, an absurd rush of jealousy flooding through me. Who was his beautiful flower? I shook my head, trying to chase off such unprofessional thoughts. It was gratifying to watch Jude place the paper on his desk blotter, smooth it flat, and begin to read the contents without delay. When he was done, he rubbed his sensuous lips with a fingertip and gazed at some point in the middle distance. He remained in this pose for several seconds and then touched the letter.

"It has promise," he said. "The author makes you want to read more. That's the real challenge of a query. If you don't make the reader yearn for more, you've failed. Let's hope that this guy's first three chapters are as strong as this paragraph." Grinning, he gestured for me to come closer to his desk. "Want to see one of my dirty little secrets."

It was impossible not to respond to those dimples. I edged closer as he whipped his bottom drawer open. Peering inside, I saw that it was filled with an assortment of candy bars.

"Does your dentist know?" I asked in a conspiratorial whisper.

He scooted his chair toward me and cupped his hands as though he wanted to whisper the answer in my ear. I pivoted my head, inviting him to move even closer, and forgot to breathe.

When Jude didn't speak, I turned my face back to him and found that my mouth was inches away from his. Without thinking, because if I had been thinking, I would have remembered that Jude might be Marlette's killer, I parted my lips and closed my eyes, waiting for him to make his move.

And he did. Oh my, his kiss obliterated my ability to have a single rational thought. All I knew were his lips, brushing against mine as gentle as the flutter of a butterfly wing, and the warm wetness of his mouth when he kissed me again, harder and longer this time. Then, to my body's delight, his fingers dug into the flesh at the nape of my neck and moved tantalizingly down my spine. I put my arm around his back, wanting nothing more than to rip off the buttons on his shirt and touch his naked skin.

Suddenly, his phone rang and we broke apart, grinning foolishly, our lips swollen from kissing. Jude's cheeks were flushed, and he looked unbelievably sexy. As he reached for his phone, I smoothed my hair and let out a nervous little laugh that sounded more like a hiccup.

"Stay," Jude murmured huskily, his eyes shining with desire.

I swallowed. "I can't. There's this lecture tonight . . ." I edged away from him, trying not to be swayed by the sweep of his dark eyelashes or the feel of his mouth on mine. What was I doing? He was a potential womanizer, murder suspect, and my coworker!

"At least take a Butterfinger then," he said with a wink. I grabbed one and hurried out of his office, marveling at how normal his voice sounded when he answered his phone. His calmness unsettled me, and I knew that I'd just made a mistake. No matter how good kissing Jude had felt, I would not be repeating the experience.

Back in my office, I shut down my computer and collected the book I'd bought at the Secret Garden. I pulled a compact from my purse and examined my face.

"You've got to stay focused, Lila," I scolded my reflection. "You have a murderer to catch."

ENTERING THE LECTURE hall filled me with an excitement for which I was unprepared. The atmosphere created by the chattering groups of students carrying books and laptops sent me right back to my own college days. I remembered those four years fondly, cherishing the sense of fun, freedom, and endless possibility. I breathed in deeply, trying to soak in the feeling. Would Trey have this experience, too? For his sake, I certainly hoped so.

My mother nudged my arm. "Let's take those two seats at the end of the row. That way we can scoot out early if this is about as thrillin' as watchin' grass grow."

"We won't be leaving early, Mama," I warned her as we sat down. "I need to talk to Professor Walters after the lecture." I pulled up the writing tablet from the side of the chair and placed my bag on it, suddenly remembering how awkward it was to take notes on the right-side tablet. When I was in college, we left-handed students would covet the limited number of left-side desks in the lecture halls.

"I wonder what he's gonna say about Shakespeare's Soothsayers," my mother mused. "While ole Willie Boy gave us our due respect, people in these fancy schools tend to look down their noses at our kind."

I was prevented from responding by the arrival of a very thin and extremely tall man with a shock of white hair. Standing at the lectern, he shuffled his papers, cleared his throat, and directed his gaze around the room. His gold-rimmed glasses glittered in the light as he scanned the audience. Gradually, the buzz of conversation died down.

"'Beware the Ides of March!'"Professor Walters pronounced loudly. The few remaining voices were silenced. "'A plague o' both your houses!'" Putting his hands behind his back, he walked to the front of the podium and paced. "Do you recognize those prophecies? Do you know who spoke them?" A few people raised their hands. The professor ignored the eager students and continued. "Besides the obvious foreshadowing, what is the impact of prophecy in Shakespeare's plays? And how significant is it that my opening quote was spoken as a warning by the soothsayer in *Julius Caesar* and the second as a threat by Mercutio to Romeo?" He paused. "That is what we will discuss tonight."

I felt a nugget of pride that I had recognized both quotes. Yet as the professor continued, another memory from my time at college surfaced. The droning of a lecture provided the perfect opportunity for me to drift into a daydream. I had to admit that my best doodles were drawn during my economics classes. Tonight, though, Professor Walters's voice didn't inspire any creative graphics; instead my thoughts centered on the group of men that vied for attention in my brain: Marlette, Jude, Sean, Trey.

A snore from my mother brought me back to the present, and I nudged her just as the professor announced, "My next lecture will be on the role of Death—that's with a capital 'D'—in Shakespeare. See if you can prophesize what I will say about that!" He grinned at his own joke.

"That's one I'll be sure to miss," my mother announced as she gathered herself to stand.

"Mama, I need to talk to him. Do you want to wait here?" Anxious to catch Professor Walters before he left, I was poised to dash.

"Naw, sug, you go on ahead. I'll wait for you in the truck. I've got an emergency flask in the glove box."

I needn't have rushed. A circle of students surrounded Walters as he tried to make his way out the door. I dug into my purse and pulled out an old press card from the *Dunston Herald*, hoping it would legitimize my questions about Marlette. I bided my time until the last coed had left, and then I approached the professor.

He looked at me through his glasses, his gray eyes looking tired. "And what can I do for you, my dear? Do you also want an extension on your essay?"

"Oh no. I'm not a student." At the raising of his eyebrows, I quickly added, "But I thoroughly enjoyed your lecture. It felt good to be thinking about Shakespeare again."

He smiled. "I'm glad I was able to inspire you. Now, if you'll excuse me, I must go. These old bones don't handle the late hours so well anymore."

"Could I ask you a few questions first? I won't take up too much time." I handed him my *Dunston Herald* card. "I'm looking into the death of a former colleague of yours. Marlette Robbins?"

"Ah yes, Marlette. He was in the news recently. Such an unfortunate situation. I believe he was murdered, wasn't he?" The professor seemed genuinely aggrieved by the idea.

"He was. He was living as sort of an outcast in Inspiration Valley, and I'm trying to discover how a man who was an accomplished academic could fall into vagrancy." I omitted the detail of Marlette's cabin on Red Fox Mountain. "Homelessness is such a prevalent issue these days; we should help those who have to face such a dire circumstance."

"I couldn't agree more." He shook his head. "In Marlette's case, well, he found himself in a compromising situation. His reputation was smeared, the academic community lost all respect for him, and he chose to withdraw from society. I completely lost track of him and had no idea he was homeless. If I had . . ." his voice trailed off, and he cleared his throat. "Do you mind if I sit down?"

Pulling out a chair for him, I watched him position his long legs as he sat down heavily. In a quiet voice, I asked,

"What event precipitated such a significant change?" My reporter tentacles were quivering. I felt like I was on the verge of a breakthrough.

"Marlette was a good man. He volunteered every summer at that camp, running a creative writing workshop for talented teens." He chuckled slightly. "I used to tease him about risking his life in the woods. He had a severe allergy to bee stings, you know." My fingers tingled at this revelation. It would explain Marlette's bloated face and hands. The professor shook his head. "Little did I know it would destroy life as he'd known it in a way we never imagined. One year, a young girl—she was fifteen, I believe—flirted continuously with him, always seeking him out for extra help, carrying herself in a . . . suggestive manner. He called me from the camp one night in search of advice on how to handle her. He was wondering how to tactfully reject her without damaging her ego. 'Distance yourself immediately, Marlette!' I warned him." Professor Walters sighed.

I hung on his every word. "Did he? Keep his distance?"

"He didn't listen to me, of course. The next thing we knew, the police were at his door, the girl was traumatized, and Marlette was branded as a sexual predator." He looked up at me, his eyes glistening. "Every professor's nightmare. The camp fired him. The university revoked his tenure, and we never heard from him again."

This account matched the story in the tattered article I'd found in the barn birdhouse as well as what my reporter friend had told me. I felt queasy as I was once again faced with the possibility that Marlette had committed a violent crime against an innocent youth. "Do you know who the girl was?"

He shook his head. "We never were privy to the details.

She was a minor, after all. Even Marlette wouldn't reveal her identity. But I *know* he was innocent. He would not have done anything inappropriate. Couldn't have. It just wasn't in his nature."

The professor's confidence eased my disquiet somewhat. This man's opinion matched that of my mentor, Jan Vance, as well as my own initial impression of Marlette. We believed in his innocence. We believed that he was too kind-hearted and good to have caused harm to a helpless teenage girl.

I touched Professor Walters's arm. "You were his friend, weren't you—not just a colleague?"

He nodded. "The last thing we talked about before everything went wrong was his book. He was writing a suspense thriller or some such thing. I guess he lost the impetus for that, too."

My heart skipped in anticipation at this hint about Marlette's query. "I'll keep looking into it, Professor. Maybe we'll discover that he did finish his novel."

Slowly, Walters got to his feet. "And now I must go home. Can I keep your card?" He held it up. "In case I think of anything else?"

"Yes, but wait. My phone number has changed." I took back the card and crossed out the *Dunston Herald* number, writing my cell phone number beneath it. I didn't want him to call my old place of work and find out I'd been fired. Returning it to him, I said, "And thank you so much for your time. I'll let you know if I learn anything important about your friend."

He shuffled out the door with much less energy than when he'd entered. I hoped that my questions hadn't burdened him with the weight of bad memories.

Reflecting on the conversation on my way out to the truck, I felt disappointed that I hadn't really found out any new information. Other than the snippet about Marlette's novel, of course. At least I now knew the genre. And it felt good to hear that other people believed in Marlette's innocence. Maybe it had been worthwhile to sit through the Shakespeare lecture after all!

I saw that my mother was in the driver's seat, so I climbed into the passenger side of the turquoise truck. My mother's head was pressed against the steering wheel, and from the steady rise and fall of her chest I could tell that she was fast asleep.

The dim light from the streetlamp shone on a book propped open on her lap. I slid it free and realized it was the flower book I'd purchased at the Secret Garden. Marlette's sketch with the dried flower slipped out from between the pages, and I placed it on the dashboard before scrutinizing the open page.

In vivid white, yellow, and green was a photo of the flower from Marlette's sketch. I had looked at that drawing so often, the flower was etched in my mind, but I glanced at the sketch on the dashboard just to be sure. Large white petals with a round cluster of yellow stamen at the center— an exact replica.

I pressed the overhead light, and my mother stirred beneath its soft glow. Stretching, she yawned loudly. "I was just gettin' lost in a lovely dream involvin' Robert Redford and a large chocolate cake," she scolded as she turned the key in the ignition. "And don't worry, I'm not drinkin' and drivin'. That damn flask was empty."

Turning back to the book, I read the caption: *Paeonia lactiflora (Luella Shaylor Peony)*. My fingers started to tremble at the significance of this discovery. The flower from Marlette's diary had betrayed a secret. It had given away the name under which Sue Ann was now living.

My mother looked over her shoulder as she reversed the truck. She then paused before shifting gears in order to turn off the overhead light. In the darkness of the cab she murmured, "This is quite a pickle you're in, darlin'. Sue Ann's your coworker."

"Yes," I said in stunned agreement. "Sue Ann is Luella Ardor."

Chapter 11

"WAIT A MINUTE. HOW DO YOU KNOW THAT SUE ANN and the woman I work with are the same person?" I asked my mother once I'd digested the possible connection between the face in the drawing and the name of the flower Marlette had glued to the bottom of the page.

Althea gave a nonchalant shrug. "It's what I do, remember? I just feel my way around these things." Without taking her eyes from the road, she reached over and touched the book on my lap. "The second I saw that peony, I got electric tingles from my fingertips to my toes. I don't get those every day, I'll have you know."

Though the connection she'd voiced rang true, echoing my own thoughts, I still felt the need to play devil's advocate. The only way I could process this shocking turn of events was to look at it from all angles.

If Sue Ann really was Luella Ardor, then Marlette had been visiting the workplace of the very woman who'd cost him his reputation and livelihood so many years ago. Surely, she must have recognized him. And he undoubtedly realized that the sexy and sophisticated literary agent who routinely ignored his presence was the girl who'd forever changed his life. Otherwise, why would he have pasted the peony on his sketch of her?

I shook my head. "Too many assumptions. I'm assuming Marlette was falsely accused. I'm assuming that Sue Ann is Luella Ardor. And now I'm jumping to the conclusion that she knew Marlette, was possibly threatened by him, and therefore was motivated to kill him." I leaned back against the seat and closed my eyes, hoping the rhythmic sound of the road passing beneath the tires would help clear my mind.

"You've gotta chase after these wild thoughts, honey," my mother said softly. "They're leadin' you somewhere, even if it's not where you wanna go. They're like wily little foxes and you're the hound. The trail is gonna zig and it's gonna zag, but in the end, you'll catch your fox."

I prayed that she was right, because the significance of what I was doing suddenly hit home.

In the beginning, I'd gotten involved to make sure that Marlette's death wouldn't go unnoticed, but I never realized how deeply it would affect me. Since he had collapsed in our reception area, his story had permeated every day of my life. And even though I'd been viewing my coworkers as possible suspects from the beginning, the strength of the connection between Luella and Marlette now lent my investigation more weight. Accusing a coworker of murder was a far cry from running around town and discussing theories with Makayla. And to be honest, I was frightened of what I'd gotten myself into. If Luella could commit such a cold-blooded act once, then what was to stop her from doing it again?

My dreams that night were colored in shades of black and red. Sue Ann's dark eyes stared at me from Marlette's drawing until they transformed into sinister birds with pointed beaks and daggerlike black feathers. The two over-sized crows multiplied into a flock and chased me through the woods near Marlette's cabin. Their crazed caws and the roar of their wings were terrifying. They were hunting me.

When I burst into the cabin in search of shelter, I found only a dirty sleeping bag on the floor. There was fresh blood on the fabric, and a person was zipped up inside. With trembling fingers, I touched the zipper pull and then hastily drew back in revulsion. I was kneeling in a slick puddle of crimson. My dream self, though sickened by the sight of so much blood, had just reached for the zipper again when one of the giant crows crashed through the cabin's window. It slammed against the wall, hard enough to break a real bird's neck, but this one merely shook out his knife-sharp feathers and began to caw triumphantly. In a stream of black, the rest of the flock started to pour in through the window, their hungry, malicious eyes locked on me. I screamed myself awake.

Lying there, damp with sweat, I wished I'd taken my mother's advice and tossed back a shot of warm whiskey before bed.

"You need a solid eight hours if you're gonna figure out if that Luella woman hurt Marlette," she'd told me, offering her bottle of Jim Beam. "If what I saw in those eyes in the picture he drew of her is a reflection of the real girl, then she's got a soul as twisted as a pretzel. You'd best mind your step."

I'd declined the whiskey, changed into my pajamas, and wished that Trey were down the hall playing a game on his computer. I felt adrift, as though my family and my career anchored me to reality and now, the rope tethering me to them both had been abruptly severed. My son was gone, my mother's psychic abilities weren't adept enough to assuage my fear, and one of my coworkers might be a murderer.

Then again, she might not. How on earth was I going to incriminate Luella Ardor without losing my job?

"I need to be certain she's Sue Ann for starters," I'd murmured drowsily into my pillow. It didn't take long before I'd slid into the dream, into the place of nightmares where the crows had been waiting for me.

ALTHEA HAD NO more wisdom to impart as she drove me to Novel Idea the following morning. My head throbbed, I had bags under my eyes, and copious amounts of my mother's bitter coffee had failed to dispel the images of my nightmare.

I couldn't wait to order Makayla's biggest, most potent espresso drink, but when I stepped into Espresso Yourself, she immediately waved me out of line, indicating that I should wait by the pick-up counter.

A man grumbled about my cutting ahead, but Makayla smiled at him with such radiance that he immediately apologized.

"Don't give it another thought, Mr. Peterson. We all get a little crabby without a caffeinated kick in the pants. Why don't you treat yourself and have a croissant with your coffee? You look like you could do with something flaky and buttery. I'll even pop it in the microwave for you so it's nice and warm."

Mr. Peterson nodded gratefully. "The wife's got me on fiber bars for breakfast. They're not very satisfying."

"I reckon not," Makayla said and winked at me.

I shifted impatiently while she whittled down the line. Finally, there was only one customer left, a woman who had no idea what to order. She squinted at the chalkboard over Makayla's head and began to read every line aloud. Makayla told the indecisive woman to take her time and then seized the opportunity to make me a cinnamon dolce latte. After she placed my drink on the counter and I paid her, she handed me a takeout bag.

"But I didn't—" I began to protest.

"Order any food," she quickly interrupted and then lowered her voice. "Girl, this is no chocolate chip scone. I was jawing with a customer yesterday after you left, and after we both agreed that the last James Patterson book wasn't his best, we got to talking about Marlette. This gentleman, one of my regular customers, spends an awful lot of time hanging out at the bookstore, and he told me about another of Marlette's hiding places. So this morning before I came to work, before the birds were even up and singing, I decided to see if anything was inside."

Wishing she hadn't mentioned birds, I glanced down at the bag. "And you found something."

She beamed. "Broke a nail prying out a loose brick in the alley side of the bookstore's wall, thank you very much. But if it helps you"—her smile disappeared and her lovely green eyes grew serious—"and it helps put this whole sad mystery to rest, then it's worth an acrylic tip."

I wanted to reach over the counter and hug her, but at that moment the woman studying the menu came to a decision and started calling out an extremely complicated order without bothering to see whether Makayla was ready.

"Thank you," I mouthed and, leaving my coffee on the

counter for the time being, headed for the restroom. I didn't dare examine the find in my office and didn't want to chance having another agent enter the coffee shop and spy whatever it was that Makayla had removed from a hollow behind a loose brick.

I locked myself in a stall, hung my purse on the hook, and opened the brown bag. I pulled out a transparent photo sleeve and held it to the light. Inside was an eight-by-ten image of a group of teenagers seated in a row of chairs. The students were all wearing shorts and T-shirts bearing the Woodside Creative Camp logo (a paintbrush, pen, and the masks of comedy and tragedy over a roaring campfire), while the three adults in the photo wore polo shirts embroidered with the same crest. The hairstyles of both the campers and counselors were dated. The men had pronounced sideburns, and both they and the boys had shaggy, unkempt hair while the females wore theirs long, straight, and parted down the middle. The room where they'd gathered looked like a rustic lodge and featured an enormous stone hearth and handwoven rag rugs on the floor.

My eyes were immediately drawn to the girl seated in the middle of the group of campers. After seeing Marlette's drawings, I'd recognize her anywhere. Sue Ann's dark, calculating gaze was unmistakable, but the way she held her body was also familiar. With one hand placed saucily on her hip and her bust pushed forward, she was striking a pose I'd seen Luella perform a dozen times, especially when a man was present.

Scrutinizing the adults, who stood at the end of the rows of campers, I picked out Marlette with more difficulty. Though his hair was as bushy and wild as it had been the day he died, the man captured in this photograph seemed utterly carefree. With one foot up on a rock, Marlette had his chin propped on his hand and his elbow resting on his elevated thigh as he gave the photographer an easy smile. The other adults, a woman and an older man, had been caught laughing out loud, and I wondered if Marlette had said something amusing a second before the photographer snapped this picture.

I scanned over the faded text below the picture. Their names were listed. Professor Marlette Robbins. Sue Ann Grey.

It wasn't like me to be confrontational. In fact, I did my best to avoid conflict and to keep the peace. But after seeing an image of Marlette's younger self—a man who seemed so normal, so grounded and self-assured—my anger flared. I knew it made more sense to wait and show the photo to Sean, but when I recalled Marlette's pathetic appearance and confused eyes on the day he died, I had to act. It was impulsive and aggressive and totally out of character, but I decided to confront Luella now.

"Let's see how she'll react to a little trip down memory lane," I whispered to the fresh faces in my hands and then carefully put the photograph back in the bag. On the way out of the coffee shop, I grabbed my latte, waved at Makayla, and marched upstairs.

I'd barely made a copy of the photograph, placed it inside a transparent sleeve, and then settled into my desk chair when Zach burst into my office. "Zach Attack!" he shouted, and I was so startled that I nearly overturned my coffee cup.

"Can you stop doing that, Zach?" I glowered at him. "*Most* people knock."

"Whoa, sorry! The Zach knows how important the morning cuppa Joe is! I was just stopping by to tell you that I scored two extra tickets to the Dunston Bulls baseball game. I thought your son might like them." He plunked an envelope on my desk. "Great seats, right behind the dugout. Zach *loves* the stadium dogs with chili and cheese. Tell your kid to get at least three. That way he won't miss any action taking a second trip to the concession stand."

I felt horrible for just having snapped at my exuberant coworker. "You are too sweet, Zach. Thank you so much."

Before I could indulge in a rosy vision of Trey and I bonding over baseball, Zach did a drumroll on my doorframe. "Step lively, über-intern! We've got a staff meeting in five!" He spread out the fingers of his right hand to emphasize the point.

Examining my day planner, I found no mention of a meeting in its pages. "Did I miss a memo or something?" I asked Zach.

He shook his head. "Boss Lady has big news. She only calls us in for these kinds of meetings if there's a reason to start opening bottles of Cristal or a reason to get out a jumbo-sized pack of tissues and cry your eyes out. Trust me, I got no vibes from Bentley either way." A movement down the hall caught his eye. "Ah, remember how I said we had five minutes? Make that zero." He cupped his hand into a big O and then gestured for me to follow him to the conference room.

Bentley was seated at the head of the table like a queen waiting to grant an audience to her subjects. She'd paired a cobalt blouse with a charcoal gray skirt suit. Multiple strands of irregular pearls hung as low as the second button on her jacket, and there was an enormous pearl and diamond ring on her right hand.

"All right, people," she began, giving each of her employees an intense stare as if we weren't already giving her our undivided attention. Satisfied, she put on her reading glasses and examined the notes she'd made on a legal pad.

"I have some news," she said, her eyes twinkling with pleasure. "A Novel Idea and the Inspiration Valley Community Center will be joining forces in order to produce the very first Central Carolina Writers' Conference."

The agents broke out in spontaneous applause and immediately began to exchange animated small talk about the event. I happened to have sat down directly across from Luella, and despite the energy created by Bentley's announcement, I couldn't take my eyes off her.

In this room, in these circumstances, it was difficult to see the girl known as Sue Ann in my coworker, a woman who nodded agreeably to the list of tasks Bentley began to assign. After scribbling a few items on her to-do list, Luella touched the back of Zach's hand as he complained about the date of the conference.

"But college basketball starts that weekend," he protested in his quietest voice, which was still several decibels above normal. "And it's Halloween! Inspiration Valley has the best costume parties!"

Luella smiled prettily at him. "Just think of the *fresh* talent you could discover. And of *all* the good-looking women who'll be simply dying to attend your panel. The Great Zach Cohen, in the flesh. I bet *your* workshops will sell out the fastest."

The boisterous young agent puffed up like a peacock. Grinning, Luella turned to talk to Franklin while Zach stared into space, his eyes glazing over. He was undoubtedly indulging in a fantasy in which dozens of adoring fans pleaded with him to read their manuscripts, offering him a host of pleasures in exchange for a few minutes of his time.

Watching Luella work her charms on Zach provoked me into reaching in my purse for the Woodside Creative Camp photograph I'd copied seconds before the meeting. Tearing a sheet from my notepad, I wrote, *Do you remember when this picture was taken, Sue Ann?* I then signed my name, because I wanted it to be perfectly clear to Luella that I knew her real identity. I was hoping for a telling reaction, but I also wanted her to see that I was the aggressor and wasn't afraid of her. That wasn't entirely true, but I was going to do my best not to show any fear.

Sticking the note in the transparent sleeve on top of the photo, I waited until Bentley's attention was diverted by Jude's suggestion to bring in a big name to serve as the conference's keynote speaker. While the pair debated over which author would draw the largest crowd, I pushed the photo sleeve across the slick surface of the conference table.

Luella raised a quizzical, pencil-drawn brow at me, as though we were in school and were in danger of being caught passing notes discussing a cute boy in our class. She read what I'd written and blanched. Digging her French-manicured nails into the photo sleeve, she whisked my note out of the way and stared at the image of her younger self. And Marlette.

Her lips formed a tight red line of anger as she crumpled the pages between her hands. She glared at me, her green-eyed stare filled with loathing. If her eyes had the power to burn, she would have happily reduced me to a pile of ash. I realized two things at that moment: one, Luella wore colored contacts; and two, I had just made an enemy of Luella, a potential murderer.

I'd expected her to be shocked, to appear guilty or even hostile, but the raw hatred on her face was terrifying. I was the one person who could expose her, who could call the police and explain how Luella and Marlette were connected. She would become their chief suspect at once, and I'd shown her my hand without giving it a second thought.

But was she guilty of murdering Marlette? What would her motive have been? Her false accusation of so many years ago wouldn't threaten her career as a literary agent, would it?

"*Hel-lo?*" Bentley gave an impatient wave of her hands. "Earth to Lila?"

"Sorry," I said quickly, relieved to have a reason to escape the intensity of Luella's stare. "Could you repeat the question?"

Bentley sighed in exasperation while Flora leaned toward me and whispered, "She wants to know if you'd like to be the moderator for a panel on writing fiction queries."

"Yes, of course!" I declared as I saw movement from across the table out of the corner of my eye. Luella had risen to her feet, still glowering at me.

"We're not done," Bentley informed her briskly, but Luella's expression instantly changed to one of agony.

Clutching her stomach, she murmured miserably, "Please excuse me! I'm going to be sick!" and rushed from the room. She'd barely reached the hall before Jude sprang from his chair and dashed after her.

"What the hell is going on?" Bentley tossed her pen down in disgust. "This is *not* how my meetings are run!" She examined her watch and folded her arms across her chest in irritation. "I need to call an editor soon anyway, so why don't we adjourn until everyone is *healthy* enough and *focused* enough"—Bentley cast a steely glance in my direction—"to continue."

The agents remained seated until Bentley breezed out, at which point they began twittering excitedly about the conference. I joined in long enough to prove my enthusiasm for the event and then went after Luella. Her perfumed office was empty, so I checked Jude's next. It was also unoccupied. I hurriedly checked the bathroom, the kitchen, and the reception area, and it was then that I heard voices on the stairs.

"Luella, my beautiful flower, talk to me!" Jude's tone was pleading.

"Just leave me alone!" she cried above the sharp refrain of her heels striking the tiled floor in the lobby below. Seconds later, I heard the heavier treads of Jude's loafers echoing up the stairwell as he descended after her. Within seconds, both agents were gone.

I hesitated. Chasing after Luella without proof that she'd harmed Marlette might be a waste of time. It could also be dangerous. I needed to find a substantial piece of evidence and then hand it over to Sean. Heading back to my desk, I decided to go about business as usual, but when all the other agents left on their lunch breaks, I would stay behind in order to search Luella's office.

It would have taken a stellar query letter to capture my attention that morning, and I have to admit that not a single one ended up in the possibilities folder. At noon, I wasted a precious fifteen minutes buying yogurt, strawberries, and a granola bar at the grocery store, but I was back at Novel Idea with plenty of time to spare.

I dumped the food on my desk and checked to be certain that the agency was truly empty. It was. Even Flora, who usually brought lunch from home, had gone out today. Bentley always left for nearly two hours to dine at a restaurant in Inspiration Valley or Dunston, but I poked my head in her office just to make sure.

The place was deserted, and Luella's office was unlocked. It was now or never.

I turned the knob and pushed open her door. The cloying scent of roses infused with jasmine that was Luella's perfume assaulted my nostrils, and I warily ventured inside, feeling uneasy about entering the workspace of a possible murderer. But the suspicion that Luella had taken the life of another person for her own selfish reasons propelled me forward, and soon I stood behind her desk, looking around, trying to think of where to start.

Straight ahead, two ornately carved mahogany bookcases lined the wall. In the corner, atop a colorful Persian rug, a round Duncan Phyfe coffee table was encircled by two wing chairs upholstered in the same pink floral fabric as the drapes that graced the window. The file cabinet was crafted from wood and etched with intricate designs. Luella's computer sat upon a magnificent antique mahogany desk with two drawers and an inlaid leather top. It reminded me of a photograph I'd seen in a magazine of Agatha Christie's writing table that had been sold at an auction last year.

I pulled at the drawer on the left. It didn't move and was obviously locked. No matter how hard I tried, I couldn't make it budge. The second drawer slid open easily, and I sneezed as a hodgepodge of scents wafted out. A disorganized assortment of makeup containers and bottles and potpourri sachets were mixed in with a jumble of pens, paper clips, and other stationery items. Nothing of significance there.

Cocking my head to make sure there was no sound in the hall, I left the desk and quickly scanned the bookshelves. The books lined up in neat rows were romance novels, their spines depicting bare-chested, muscular men and bodacious maidens swooning, or women falling out of their dresses in the arms of brawny buccaneers. Many of the authors were big-name romance writers, and I was awed at Luella's stable of clients.

I riffled through the files, carefully opening each drawer and trying not to disturb anything. Contracts for authors, catalogues from publishers, brochures for various conferences, references for editors—nothing that pointed to any kind of involvement with Marlette.

Turning my gaze back to the desk, my eyes fell on Luella's desktop computer. I hadn't found anything among her things, but surely there would be a clue or connection to Marlette on her computer. I quickly stuck my head out the door to ensure that no one had returned from lunch, as I was beginning to feel a bit concerned over how much time had passed. The hall was silent.

Booting up the computer, I was dismayed to see that it was password protected. I sat back in frustration. Would my one chance to explore her hard drive be stymied from the start? I racked my brain to think of possibilities for her password, but I didn't know her well enough to come up with any viable solutions.

I started with the first words that came to mind—*Sue Ann Grey, Woodside, Marlette*—but even as I typed them, I realized she wouldn't want to remind herself of her past every time she logged onto her computer. I keyed in *romance, money, men*, and other words that made me think of her, but nothing would unlock the computer.

Idly, I wondered what Luella's perfume was called and rummaged through the desk drawer, sneezing twice. A small glass bottle in the shape of a woman's torso emitted Luella's overpowering scent and had the name *Goddess of the Hunt* inscribed on it. I smiled ruefully, thinking of Luella's perfume as a metaphor for how she saw herself.

Hurriedly I typed in *goddess* and was thrilled to find that it worked. I quickly scanned through the document files and her emails but found no reference to anything relating to Marlette's murder.

Checking the history file on her Internet browser yielded better results. I found several links to web pages about bee sting allergies and anaphylactic shock. My pulse quickened as I typed and clicked. One page in particular contained a detailed article on how anaphylactic shock can cause death. Luella had also visited herbal medicine sites that sold bee venom capsules.

Apparently, bee venom used in a therapeutic manner can alleviate arthritic and joint pain. However, at the bottom of the page was a warning stating that bee venom should under no circumstances be ingested by individuals with any kind of bee allergy. My fingers trembled over the keys as I recalled Marlette's bloated fingers and puffed face when he lay dead on the couch.

Sitting back, I went over the sequence of that tragic morning—finding Marlette, Franklin administering CPR, Jude suggesting someone had committed murder, Carson Knight pointing out that Marlette's death looked like an allergic reaction. Luella hadn't arrived at the office until after the police, so how could she possibly have injected Marlette with bee venom?

Then I remembered that she was the one who pointed to

the dead bee on the floor, making the suggestion it had come in with the flowers.

It was as if a jolt of espresso hit my brain. I didn't know how or when, and wasn't completely certain of the why, but with an Althea-like certainty, I knew that Luella had done the cruel deed and then dropped a bee on the floor in an attempt at misdirection.

I heard voices in the distance. They jarred me out of my ruminations, and I quickly turned off the computer. By the time footsteps sounded on the stairs, I had scurried to my office, where I opened the yogurt and stuck a spoonful into my mouth.

Feigning interest in the queries on my desk as I ate, I kept track of the agents returning to the office. I waved to Franklin, called hello to Flora, smiled at Jude, and raised a strawberry to Zach. I wasn't sure what I would do when Luella walked past my door, and I realized I should phone Sean and tell him what I knew, but I was too keyed up at the moment and needed to calm down in order to speak to him rationally.

My attention was drawn to a disturbance in the reception area, and I went to investigate, thankful for the distraction. A very short, stout woman with a cloud of wild dark curls and round tortoiseshell glasses stood with hands on hips, looking vexed. In her magenta pantsuit, she seemed the antithesis of Bentley, who towered over her and was gesticulating with one hand, her diamond bracelets glittering in the light.

"I'm sure she's just running a bit late. We'll track her down, Calliope. Never fear. I'll get someone to bring you a coffee while you wait."

"I don't want a coffee!" the woman named Calliope

replied in an angry voice, gesticulating dramatically. "I had an appointment with Luella that should have started fifteen minutes ago. I am *wasting* precious writing time."

As she turned toward the stairs, Bentley touched her lightly on the shoulder. "Please, don't do anything rash, Calliope. Think of the years you've been with us. Luella ran an errand to the pharmacy and is likely on her way back as we speak. Just wait a little longer while we get ahold of her."

A man's figure dashing up the stairs caused both women, and me, to stop and stare in that direction. Jude burst onto the landing, his smile searing away the tension in the room. My heart did a little skip.

"Calliope, Lady of the Midas Pen," he said, bowing slightly and holding out a small gold box. "I believe your favorite truffles are raspberry and champagne." He gave her a beautiful smile. "When I heard you were coming to the office, I rushed out to get some just for you."

Calliope blushed and twittered. "Oh, thank you, Jude. I'm *so* flattered you remembered." Taking the box, she turned to Bentley. "All right, I'll give Luella the benefit of the doubt. This *is* the first time she hasn't been prompt. I'll wait a *little* longer." She sat primly on the sofa, the very one upon which Marlette had expired. I was thankful it had been cleaned. Calliope glanced up at Jude, blushing again, before focusing on her chocolates.

Jude winked at Bentley, and she grinned deviously in response. I couldn't believe she'd used Jude's sex appeal to pacify Calliope. And if he was already back in the office, where was Luella?

Clearing my throat, I approached her. "Is there anything I can do?"

"Oh, Lila, thank goodness you're here." Bentley grabbed

my elbow and steered me toward the hallway, where she said in a low voice, "I need you to drive over to Luella's house and see if she's there. She's not answering her home phone or her cell." Quickly looking back at the woman sitting on the couch, she whispered, "Calliope is a *very* important client, and she's here to discuss the details of a contract for three more books in her bestselling Passionate Plantation series. She's been threatening to change to a New York agency whose name I *will* not mention because they apparently know how to wine and dine their clients to Calliope's high standards. But we cannot lose her! She is one of our most lucrative clients. You *must* find Luella."

"Where does she live?" I stammered, my thoughts darting about as I considered having to face Luella on her own turf after making her my enemy. "I don't have a car."

"Take mine." Bentley thrust a set of keys in my face. "She lives in Dunston, on Persimmon Avenue, number eighteen. Hurry!"

Caught up in Bentley's urgency, I scampered down the stairs and to the parking lot before I realized I didn't know what car Bentley drove. One of the keys had the BMW logo on it, so I scanned the cars and found the lone Beemer on the lot—a silver Z4. Climbing into the driver's seat, I wondered what Trey would think of his mother sitting behind the wheel of this sleek machine.

My mind didn't stay on Trey for long. As I drove to Dunston, I kept going over the reasons I believed Luella might be guilty of murdering Marlette. I wondered why she hadn't returned to work, knowing she wasn't really sick when she rushed out of the office this morning. I was both afraid and determined to meet her face-to-face.

Driving on Dunston's main street felt so familiar, yet it

seemed so long since I'd been there. Life had changed for me, and this town had become a part of my past, not my future.

I knew how to find Persimmon Avenue because Trey had attended a playgroup in the area when he was a toddler. I found number eighteen without any problem and sat in the car staring at the cream-colored clapboard Victorian house. Its wide front porch had wild rose vines climbing over the railings all the way up to the gingerbread trim. A flagstone walkway led to the porch steps, and at one end of the spacious porch, a large oak cast a cool shadow on the house.

Taking a deep breath, I stepped out of the car.

My knock echoed inside the house, and I tried to still my nerves. No one else involved in the investigation knew Luella's true identity, and if something happened to me . . . I backed down the stairs and took my cell phone out of my bag. Sean's voicemail answered after four interminable rings, and I whispered a harried message, indicating where I was and for him to please call me. Hoping I didn't sound too hysterical, I added, "I might be in a dangerous situation here." I then snapped the phone shut and climbed back up the stairs.

Knocking a second time generated no response. Steeling myself, I turned the knob and was surprised to find it unlocked.

"Luella?" I stuck my head inside and called out, louder this time, "Luella? Are you home?"

The house was silent. I stepped inside, leaving the door open behind me, just in case I should need to make a hasty retreat. In the closed hallway, I was glad for the daylight streaming inside.

My first impression was that of polished wood. Yellow

pine with a rich patina formed the floor, trimmed the door-ways, and made up the wainscoting in the hall. The living room was furnished just like Luella's office at Novel Idea, with beautiful antique furniture, a Persian carpet, and flow-ery upholstered chairs and sofa.

The kitchen featured bright red appliances, yellow cabi-nets, and a blue granite countertop, splashing the room with color. Everything sparkled, and nothing seemed out of place.

I continued along the hall. The first door revealed a study with a desk and book-filled shelves. The second room, a bathroom, was decorated in retro colors, with black-and-white tiles and green fixtures. A guest room was calming in sedate blues and grays. All the rooms were clean and tidy, as if they had recently been cleaned. I found it difficult to reconcile the woman who owned this neat, comfortable home with the monster Luella had become in my mind.

At the last door I paused, for no reason that I could fathom; I just knew that I would find something amiss. I opened the door and looked inside.

A scream escaped from my throat, sounding too loud and strangely foreign as it reverberated down the empty hall. I leaned against the doorframe and struggled to breathe. My mind did not want to accept what my eyes were seeing.

There was Luella, laid out on the bed like Sleeping Beauty, her dress tidily arranged, her hands crossed over her breast. Her abundant hair was fanned out almost lov-ingly, draping across the plump pillow. And on the pillow was a large red bloodstain.

Slowly, I approached and picked up her cold hand. I could find no pulse at her wrist.

Luella was dead.

As I struggled to take the phone out of my purse with

shaking hands, a movement outside the window caught my eye. I turned and looked. There, on a branch of the large oak tree, sat a crow. He cocked his head and cast his beady eyes at me as I stood there, frozen in shock.

I stared back at him, reluctant to return my gaze to Luella's waxen face. As if to mock my helplessness, he spread his wings and took flight, leaving me alone with the dead.

Chapter 12

I DON'T REMEMBER CALLING THE POLICE.

I vaguely recall the sound of sirens, but they seemed to remain at a distance, never coming close enough to break through the fog enveloping my senses.

I don't know how long I'd been sitting there when the first officers on the scene found me huddled on the front porch steps, my arms crossed protectively over my chest.

A policewoman touched me gently on the back of my hand and, keeping constant physical contact with me, knelt down and spoke to me in a calm, even voice. "Ma'am? Did you place the 911 call? Are you Lila Wilkins?"

Her eyes were beautiful in the afternoon sunlight, like honey melting in a cup of hot tea. I saw kindness in the young woman's face, but I also noticed the slight twitch of her fingers. She was on edge, and I guessed she was experiencing the same surge of adrenaline I'd felt tiptoeing through Luella's house.

I wondered if this woman in blue, this girl with the honey-hued eyes, would catch her breath when she entered the back bedroom. Would she pause on the threshold and think of Sleeping Beauty? Would she wonder why the red-haired beauty lying lifeless on the bed would never wake from her slumber? Would this officer burn with anger on Luella's behalf or become steel cold with a determination to solve the mystery behind the crime? Would she be haunted by the sight, as I was sure to be?

"Ma'am?" Her voice was soft but more persistent this time.

I swallowed, trying to moisten my throat enough to push the words out. "Yes, I called you. The woman inside is my coworker. Her name's Luella Ardor and . . ." I looked away from the officer's lovely eyes and stared up into the canopy of tree branches reaching toward the roof. "And she's dead. Someone killed her. Someone killed her because of me."

That was all I managed to say to the policewoman. She asked me more questions, but I had nothing more to add. I went numb while the world around me broke open into a thousand different sounds.

Radios crackled, car doors slammed, commands were shouted in and outside the house, footsteps clumped up and down the steps and across the groaning porch. I stared at the parade of policemen and technicians without seeing. The image of Luella was still burned into my mind, like a Polaroid photograph that kept developing over and over again.

At some point, a blanket was placed around my shoulders and a strong hand squeezed my arm. The pressure allowed me to return to the moment, and I looked up to find Sean gazing down at me, his face pinched with concern.

"Lila," he murmured and pushed a metal thermos cup into my hands. "Drink this."

I cradled the cup, welcoming the feel of its heat against my palms, and then drank. Sean had spiked black coffee with a shot of whiskey, and the bitterness surprised me, jarring me from my numb state and filling my throat and belly with a warm burn. It was exactly what I needed.

"More," he directed, pushing the cup back to my lips.

As I complied, he watched me, his handsome, intelligent eyes intense with worry.

"I'm better now," I assured him, feeling the whiskey's dull fire and the comforting weight of the blanket on my shoulders drawing me forth from a state of shock.

Sean sat quietly next to me until I was ready to explain what I was doing at Luella's house. I began by telling him about Sue Ann Grey and how she'd forever changed Marlette's life so many years ago. I went on to describe how I'd let Luella know that I'd discovered her secret identity and how that was the last time I saw her alive. I recounted how I'd searched her office and described the bee venom websites on her Internet search history. My voice faltered as it struck me that while I was trying to find proof that she was a murderer, Luella herself was falling victim to violence. I shuddered.

Sean squeezed my hand and nodded. "I shouldn't be telling you this, and it's not yet conclusive," he said, "but the coroner is fairly certain that Marlette died from anaphylactic shock brought on by bee venom, probably administered by injection. It appears from your sleuthing that Luella might have been instrumental in that."

By the time I had reached the point in the narrative in which Bentley told me to drive to Dunston in search of

Luella, two burly men wearing coveralls appeared at the front door.

"Sir," they said, clearly addressing Sean. "We're ready to bring her out." They sent a fleeting glance in my direction, and their message was clear. Luella's body was on the gurney behind them, and they were concerned about my witnessing the transfer of her sheeted form to the van marked *CORONER*.

A flash of a similar scene, in which Marlette's was the body on the gurney, made me want to escape the sight of another covered form being wheeled by as I watched, feeling guilt ridden and helpless.

There was a wicker chair with a floral cushion on the side of the wraparound porch. I pointed to it and told Sean, "I'll wait for you there." He responded with an empathetic nod.

Sitting on the edge of the chair, I glanced at the slightly raised window next to me. The view inside the house was obscured by a set of frilly lace curtains, but voices escaped through the opening.

"Looks like the victim was struck in the back of the head while she was leaning over to get an object from the nightstand," stated a man in a low, emotionless tone. "She fell where she was, leaving a blood smear on the side of the comforter. The assailant then moved her onto the bed." He paused. "I can't say for certain until I get her back to the lab, but I'd guess she was still alive at this point and her attacker finished the job by smothering her with a pillow. We've got it bagged, but there are shallow rips on one side as though the victim bit through the fabric."

I swallowed hard, wishing I could block out the horrible image, but I saw Luella, crippled by the blow to her head, shocked and reeling with pain, fighting for air with the last of her strength. I lowered my head in my hands and fixed my eyes on the ghost marks in the wood grain of the porch floor, but I couldn't block out the words that continued to seep out the window.

"This is what the vic was likely trying to retrieve from the nightstand. Don't see one of these every day."

A silence. "A pearl-handled lady's pistol. Antique. Recently cleaned." Sean's admiration for the weapon was evident in his voice. "And loaded."

"Yes, sir. Looks like the victim knew her assailant was a threat and so she was preparing to arm herself, but he struck her with this angel sculpture before she could get to her gun."

I heard the rustling of a bag and imagined Sean examining the weapon that had been brought down on Luella's head with enough force to drive her to her knees, to create the wound that resulted in the red stain on her white cotton pillowcase. I couldn't stop seeing that red, which was even brighter and more electric than Luella's hair, lovingly fanned out in a vain attempt to hide a terrible and irreversible deed.

"That's not an angel." This from the policewoman with the kind eyes. "Looks like Eros, the God of Love. See how he's holding a bow and arrow? I think it's a copy of the Eros fountain in Piccadilly Circus. In London," she added for good measure. "Makes sense, considering what Ms. Ardor did for a living. Her whole library is loaded with romance novels. Many of them are dedicated to her."

"Nice work, Officer Burke," Sean told her, and then their voices became fainter as they moved out of the room.

I drew the blanket Sean had given me tighter about my shoulders. How I could be chilled in the middle of a Southern summer afternoon was beyond reason, but so was everything else that had happened today.

It seemed like the police would have little difficulty proving how Luella had died, but there were two significant questions remaining. Who had killed her? And why?

I still didn't understand why she'd felt threatened by Marlette after all this time. Nothing made sense. If anyone should have been seeking revenge, that person was Marlette. And yet he had retreated from the world, only emerging to seek representation for his novel.

"That *must* be the key!" I whispered to potted ferns and the languid air. "Jude lied to me. He took the query letter off the bouquet before tossing it in the Dumpster. I bet he was helping Luella because he was probably her lover. Did they plan Marlette's murder together?" I exhaled as a dreadful realization washed over me. "Could Jude also be Luella's killer? But why?"

Suddenly, I wanted to get far away from this place. I knew Sean would need me to make an official statement, but I couldn't relate my account again. Not right now. I had to be alone. I desperately craved quiet and wished I could simply turn around and start climbing the trail winding up Red Fox Mountain. I wanted to sit silently in Marlette's hidden meadow until the world made sense again.

The more I pictured the sunlit woods, the more I needed to be there. It was not just a passing desire. Dunston was no place for me to recover from the shock. I had to get back to Inspiration Valley, and I told this to the honey-eyed policewoman, who had returned to the driveway and was watching the coroner's van drive off.

"I've already given Officer Griffiths my statement," I explained and passed her the blanket Sean had placed on my shoulders. "I need to bring my boss's car back, but I promise to drop by the station before the end of the day."

"I suppose that would be all right," the pretty officer said. "It's been quite an ordeal for you. We know how to contact you if we need to."

Before driving off in Bentley's BMW, I dialed the number to her direct line.

When Bentley answered, I did my best to keep my voice from shaking. "I have really bad news. Luella's been . . . murdered." I had to push the word out. "And I was the one who found her. The police are at her house. I'm going to take the rest of the day off."

Bentley wanted details, and I explained what I could before telling her I'd park her car in front of the agency and leave the keys in her mailbox. Knowing I didn't have it in me to face my coworkers, I did just that and quietly left the building.

I stood on the sidewalk, wondering exactly what I could do to escape from the chaos swirling within me, and I had a sudden image of the yellow scooter parked outside the Secret Garden. At that moment, I wanted nothing more than to put on the black helmet, become invisible to the world, and drive until I ran out of gas.

Clutching to this vision, I set off for the Secret Garden.

Addison was sitting on one of the little stone benches in the outdoor décor and statuary area, chasing a bag of corn chips with a jumbo-sized bottle of Mountain Dew. She smiled as I approached.

"Hey! I heard you might wanna buy my scooter." She offered to share her snack, but I shook my head.

"I'll pass on the chips, thanks, but I am interested in the scooter."

She pulled a Hello Kitty key chain out of her apron pocket. "Take it for a spin. As long as you want. If you like it, I'll give you a really good deal. No one else has been lining up to buy it, and I need cash to pay the insurance bill on the Volvo. My brother bought me a gorgeous Duke blue wagon and offered to pay for the insurance, too, but I've got my pride."

"What a gift," I said, thinking that the price tag of a new Volvo station wagon was well over thirty thousand dollars. "Your brother sounds very generous."

"He is. He's actually my half brother, but he's the only good thing that came out of my mom marrying again after my dad died. I'd never tell my brother this, but his father's kind of a jerk." Addison's eyes grew glazed, and she looked away. "*Gary* didn't buy my brother a thing," she said, pronouncing her stepfather's name with a hiss. "As a kid, he had no toys, no new clothes, nothing. Then *Gary* marries my mom and buys me everything under the sun to impress *her*. Guess it worked, because she's still with him."

I couldn't think of much to say in response, so I nodded in mock understanding.

Addison gave me a self-effacing grin. "Sorry. Too much info. Here." She held out the key chain. "Seriously, keep it until closing time."

I closed my fingers around the keys. This was exactly what I had hoped would happen. "Great. When do you get off work?"

Addison pulled a face. "My shift ends at six. If you want the scooter, I'll sign the title over to you the second I hang up this apron for the day." She told me her asking price and, after glancing at her watch, said she needed to hop on a register before her manager returned from his break.

In the parking lot, I put on Addison's helmet, released the kickstand, and turned on the engine. I'd had a scooter during my college days and hoped I could operate this sleek, chic Vespa GTS with the same ease.

I needn't have worried. Unlike my old scooter, which required manual shifting by moving the gear switch on the left handlebar, this Vespa was a variable automatic, so I only had to worry about accelerating with the right handlebar and braking by squeezing the brake levers like on a bicycle. Within minutes, I was racing through the streets of Inspiration Valley, the yellow scooter zipping through the open air like a goldfinch released from its cage. By the time I hit the road leading to Althea's house, the tension I'd been holding between my shoulder blades began to dissolve and my spirits lifted.

As I passed by fields of buttercups and grazing cows, I knew that I was going to blow the remainder of my savings on the Vespa. I hadn't felt this carefree for a long, long time, and damn it, I was due for a measure of happiness.

Pulling up in front of my mother's house, I couldn't help but grin to see her standing on her front porch, hands on her hips, shaking her head with disapproval.

"Aren't you a bit long in the tooth for that kind of toy?" she asked. "You look like you're ridin' SpongeBob, for cryin' out loud. And what are you gonna do when it rains?"

I put down the kickstand, took off the helmet, and shrugged. "Wear a raincoat, I guess. Listen, Mama, I can't depend on you to chauffeur me around. I'm already living in your house rent-free. I've got to start working my way back to an independent state."

My mother put her hand over her heart. "You were *meant* to stay here a spell, to figure out what you want from this life. Same goes for Trey." She frowned at the scooter. "But if you're tryin' to look like a teenager, you're gonna have to stuff yourself into those god-awful skinny jeans. No more banana bread for you."

"I'll skip the bread today, but I could sure use some coffee. Something horrible has happened." Hugging the helmet against my abdomen, I drank in my mother's familiar face and didn't bother to control the tremor in my speech. "I need to . . . I think it would help to talk about it."

She beamed. "That's how we women deal with stuff. We spit it all out, kind of like a hairball, and then we clean up the mess and move on. Come on inside, sugar."

In the bright and cozy kitchen, I told her about Luella. When I was through, Althea's main concern was that she had failed to foresee my coworker's demise in one of her visions.

"I can't understand it," she said, pacing back and forth between the stove and the table. "I should have had a feeling, a sense of darkness rollin' in, but I got no vibes at all." She shook her head, nonplussed. "There's only one explanation."

"What's that?" I asked, keeping the skepticism from my voice.

Althea looked past me toward the window and the mountain above us, her eyes glazing. "The person who did this didn't mean to do it. It just happened, takin' the killer totally by surprise."

"I wish you could just tell me who it was," I murmured glumly. "How can I go back into work tomorrow? One of my coworkers might be a murderer!"

My mother put her hand on top of mine. "No one's gonna hurt you. I've seen your palm enough times to know that you're gonna live a long life and—" She stopped abruptly and cocked her head to the side like an inquisitive parrot. "Trey's comin'."

I followed her gaze but saw no one on the path leading from the mountain to the field. Shrugging, I took out my cell phone and, cringing at the thought of how annoyed Sean probably was, settled into a chair in the living room and listened to my messages.

The first voicemail heralded wonderful news from my real estate agent. A young couple had made an offer on my house in Dunston. I listened eagerly to the amount of the bid and Ginny's suggestion that I make a counteroffer. I decided to call her back only after I phoned Sean to tell him that I'd be arriving at the station as soon as possible.

He had left me three messages, and it was clear by his clipped speech that he wasn't pleased with me. I was just about to dial his number when Trey came in through the kitchen door and shouted, "Hel-loooo!"

It was a balm to hear the undisguised cheerfulness in his voice. I hurried into the next room and gave my son a hug. His strong arms enfolded me, giving my weary body a brief squeeze before he shyly let me go. He hadn't embraced me like that for years, and I had to look away so he wouldn't see that I'd teared up.

"Don't mind her," my mother said, landing a noisy kiss on Trey's cheek. "She's had a real rough day. Why don't you take her mind off things by tellin' us what mischief you've been up to?"

Trey raised his brows in feigned offense. "For once, I'm cool with living by the rules. I mean, I'm working like crazy, but I don't feel like anyone's holding me back . . ." He let the words hang in the air. "I dunno. I can just be myself at the co-op." He turned a pair of shining eyes on me. "And Mom! I went into town with Iris today to sell some of the goat products to the grocery store, and they totally loved my new package designs!"

"That's great, honey." I smiled at him. I wanted nothing more than to focus on my son's optimism and vitality, but Luella's pallid face and posed body rose up in my mind like a fishing bobber breaking through the surface of the water.

"Yeah, Iris even let me do the negotiating while she left to do some other errands in town. We traded a whole bunch of our products for things we can't make. You know, razors, toilet paper, that kind of stuff. The manager at How Green Was My Valley said I drove a hard bargain." Trey's cheeks were flushed with pride.

My mother punched him on the arm. "Atta boy! You've got your grandma's horse-tradin' skills, don't you?"

"Where did Iris run off to while you were haggling?" I wondered aloud.

Trey shrugged. "I think she went to sell wood to the pottery center. She's strong enough to unload it from the truck by herself. I know she doesn't look it, but I've watched her chop through seriously huge logs faster than half the men on the mountain." His eyes were flashing with admiration.

"Wow," I said. "So she sold all the wood?"

With a frown, Trey shook his head. "No. It was still in the truck when we left. Guess she got busy with other stuff."

I recalled the mixture of hurt and anger in Iris's eyes when she talked about Marlette's death and wondered if she knew of the connection between him and Luella.

Trey shrugged again and continued. "Anyway, Iris and I met up for coffee at that place below your office around one She was acting weird and said she was going through a serious caffeine withdrawal. I was gonna see if you wanted to hang out with us for a bit, but I smelled like goat and, well, I figured you'd be embarrassed."

"Never," I assured him firmly. "I'm proud of you, Trey."

He grinned and then announced that he had laundry to do. I promised to be back in time to cook him something wonderful and hurried outside, hopped on the scooter, and drove into town, stopping at the ATM before parking in front of the Secret Garden.

Thirty minutes later, with the scooter's title safely in my purse, I returned to my mother's house and finally called Sean.

His voice blasted out of the phone as soon as he answered. "Lila, where on earth did you go? Why did you leave the scene? Are you all right?" I wondered how he knew it was me calling before I'd even said anything, but then I realized he must have my number programmed into his cell phone, generating my name on his call display. That thought warmed my heart.

"I'm sorry, Sean. I really needed to get away from there. And I had to return Bentley's car," I added lamely.

He sighed loudly into the phone. "Lila, you reported the murder, and we don't even have your official statement. You should have come to the station so we could record it." His voice softened a little. "At least you're safe and you sound as though you've recovered."

"I'm safe enough, but I don't feel very normal." It was obvious he was upset, but I could also sense that he'd been worried about me. "I know I shouldn't have left, but I had to get away from the image of Luella in her bed . . ." I trailed off, not wanting that picture to appear in my mind again. "Did you find anything that might point to who did it?"

"Nothing concrete. There was an item on her credit card statement from the bee venom company, so your instincts were right. It looks as though she was probably involved in Marlette's murder, but we still don't know what her motive might have been for wanting him dead."

Feeling validated that my investigations had proved correct, I was nonetheless mystified about more than just the motive. "There's something else I can't figure out," I said. "How could Luella have injected Marlette with the bee venom when she arrived at the office *after* he was already dead?"

"I can answer that. With the arson case put to rest, we were finally able to interview the employees of the businesses near Novel Idea. The clerk at the pharmacy across the street . . . Let's see . . ." I could hear him flipping through his notebook. "Here it is. Brenda Wagner. That morning while she was sweeping the stoop, she saw you go into Espresso Yourself from the agency. She noticed you because she'd never seen you before and wondered what you were doing at the agency."

I tried to remember seeing Brenda, but I must have been too focused on my new surroundings.

"Shortly after you went into the coffee shop," Sean continued, "she saw Luella arrive at Novel Idea, and then Marlette. Apparently he'd been following Ms. Ardor, because he entered the lobby right behind her. Luella hurried out of the main door again a few minutes later. You were still in the coffee shop looking at a book with Makayla—Ms. Wagner is *very* observant—anyway, while you and Makayla were discussing literature, Luella disappeared down the street. Ms. Wagner didn't see Marlette leave, and the next thing she knew, the police had arrived."

"Wow. We lucked out with that witness."

"We?" Sean teased. "I didn't realize you were a member of the police force." He cleared his throat and went on. "The timing of Marlette's reaction to the bee venom in conjunction with his time of death fits right into that window of Ms. Wagner's observations. Luella probably injected poor Marlette as soon as he arrived in the reception area."

"She must have known about his bee allergy from camp!" I exclaimed, wondering how long Luella had been carrying the venom and syringe in her purse, waiting for just the right opportunity. Had she also had the dead bee at the ready? It was a creepy thought. "Did you find out anything else?"

"There were fingerprints in the house that didn't belong to Luella. The techs are coming to Novel Idea to fingerprint all the agents in search of a match. Including you, I'm afraid. We need to eliminate yours from the mix."

"But I'm not at the office right now. I'm at my mother's." Being in my mother's house was like hiding in a safe cocoon. I was disinclined to leave the warmth and calm of her home so soon, and I wasn't ready to face my coworkers.

"Lila, I need you to meet us at the agency. This way, we can get everyone's statements and prints at the same time." Clearly, this wasn't a request.

"All right," I agreed reluctantly.

I thought of Jude running after Luella when she left the office this morning. My cheeks flushed as I remembered our passionate kiss, and I tossed my head to shake away that recollection. "Sean, you might want to look closely at Jude. I think there was something going on between him and Luella. And I know of another possible suspect."

"You do, do you? Why don't you leave the investigating to the professionals, Lila?" Exasperation was evident in

Sean's voice. Hoping I wasn't ruining my chances with him, I forged ahead.

"Iris, from the Red Fox Co-op. She came into town with Trey today and disappeared for a while. When she returned, Trey said she was acting weird."

"Pretty, waiflike Iris?" Sean sounded incredulous. "Why would she want to harm Luella?"

"She was truly upset about what happened to Marlette. Angry, too. And if she discovered that Luella was his killer, she might have confronted her. 'Pretty' Iris is also quite strong. She might be wiry, but my son swears she can wield a heavy ax as though it were a Wiffle ball bat." Even as I said all this, I found it difficult to envision Iris partaking of the violent act that produced the results I witnessed earlier today. Still, I never would have expected Luella to be capable of killing Marlette, either.

"Okay, I'll look into it. I have to go, but I'll meet you at the agency. When I see you, I'd also like your input on something we found at Luella's house."

So he did value my opinion! "Okay, I'll be at my desk," I answered, deciding I'd do my utmost to avoid my co-workers.

"And Lila?"

Hoping he would say something that would indicate our connection was still a possibility, I replied quickly. "Yes?"

"Don't talk about this case to anyone."

RETURNING TO THE office was less stressful than I expected since all the agents were working behind closed doors. I quietly snuck into my own office, shutting the door without alerting anyone, and didn't budge from my chair until the police arrived. Only then did I step into the reception area.

Sean smiled ruefully when he saw me. Glancing around the room, he said, "I'm sorry about all of this, Lila. Not what you signed up for when you took this job, is it?"

Finding it difficult to come up with a response, I showed the techs to the staff kitchen so they could set up their fingerprint equipment. Then I led Sean to Bentley's door.

"You get printed first," he told me. "After that, Officer Burke will take your statement in your office while I interview the others. When you're done, wait for me. I need to show you something."

"Lila, is that you?" Bentley called in response to Sean's knock.

We stepped in. "This is Officer Griffiths," I said. "He's here to talk to you about Luella's murder. Sean—I mean, Officer Griffiths—this is Ms. Bentley Burlington-Duke, my boss." I hustled out of the line of fire and headed for the break room to be fingerprinted.

Back at my desk, Officer Burke with the honey-colored eyes thankfully kept me distracted enough so that I couldn't hear what was happening around the rest of the office. I didn't relish repeating everything I'd already told Sean, and I found it especially difficult to describe my experience in Luella's house. Still, the process kept me occupied, and Officer Burke was polite and efficient, taking notes as I spoke into a recording device positioned on my desk.

When I finished, I did my best to smile. "And that's all I have to say." I felt drained of all energy like a deflated balloon hanging limp on a string.

Officer Burke closed her notebook and stood. "Thank

you, Ms. Wilkins. I'll type this up, and then you can come into the station and sign it."

I walked her to the door. "I'll stop by first thing tomorrow," I said, closing it tiredly behind her.

Returning to my chair, I rested my chin in my hands and stared at the pile of query letters and proposals on the desk. I was far behind in my work but felt no inclination to read any of them. I wondered what happened to Calliope and how long she'd waited before giving up on Luella. Briefly, I ruminated over who would handle Luella's long list of clients.

Feeling agitated, I went to my window and stared at the street. My yellow scooter sat by the curb, and I smiled, remembering my mother's reference to it as Sponge Bob. I longed to hop on it again, fly through town to my mother's, and cook dinner for Trey. How irate would Sean be if I just left?

I decided to settle for a cup of decaf instead, but before I could venture past my desk, there was a knock on the door and Sean entered.

"Officer Burke said you were very thorough with your statement, Lila. Well done."

"Thank you," I said as I lowered myself into my chair. "What do you have to show me? I'm exhausted and dying to go home."

"Of course you are. You've had quite a day." Sympathy shone out of his blue eyes, and he smiled slightly. Opening his black leather folder, he pulled out a pink sheet of paper sealed in a plastic evidence bag. "What do you make of this? We found it at Luella's." He handed the bag to me. The page contained a list, written in Luella's handwriting:

Birdhouses in kids' park.

Birdhouses (barns) on market fence.

Loose brick in bookstore wall.

Hollow in live oak.

My weariness fell away as my mind zipped back and forth to the places listed like a motorist tracing a complicated route on a map. "These are Marlette's hiding spots! Luella must have followed him in order to find them. How else could she know all of these specific locations? She probably checked them regularly to make sure he didn't leave any hidden clues that would give away her real identity." I paused briefly as a sense of relief flowed through me that Luella hadn't known about the secluded meadow in the woods. "People told me they'd seen Marlette hiding things in the birdhouses at the park. I found an old article in one of the barn birdhouses." I ran my fingers through my hair. "And Makayla removed an old photo from the brick wall behind the bookstore."

"I'd like to see those." Sean rubbed his chin pensively. "So Marlette might have left some kind of clue in the live oak at the center of town?"

"Maybe." I grabbed my purse. "I think we need to find out."

"Whoa! *I've* got to get back to the station and process all these interviews and fingerprints. And *you*"—he touched my arm—"need to get home. I'll send an officer to investigate the tree when we're done here."

I covered his hand with mine. "Please, Sean. This will only take a few minutes."

After a long pause, he nodded. I followed him out of the office and watched him exchange a few words with Officer Burke. She glanced at her watch and then got into the cruiser but didn't start the engine.

Sean and I started up High Street toward the live oak tree. I had a very strong feeling that we would find something important there.

What if, in its hollow, Marlette had hidden a copy of his elusive query letter? Even though I'd never laid eyes on it, that letter forever altered my first day of work at Novel Idea and was still affecting my daily existence.

I felt that somehow, discovering Marlette's letter would finally put to end the unanswered questions and horrible violence that had infected the literary agency like a fast-moving and deadly virus.

Chapter 13

THE LIVE OAK WAS A MAGNIFICENT, IF SLIGHTLY FRIGHT-ening, tree. It towered above the tight beds of flowering vinca and a neat square of wrought iron park benches, its ancient branches hanging low to the ground, grown too heavy to remain in the air any longer. The waning light filtered through the clusters of elongated branches, painting the grass with crooked shadows.

It was probably my imagination, but in the silence between night and day I felt as though I'd stepped back in time. With most of the town's businesses closed, the square and its environs were deserted and it was all too easy to picture this tree as it once stood hundreds of years ago—the monarch of a rolling field, as wide and endless as the sea.

Approaching the scarred and time-ravished trunk with reverence, I instantly felt a connection to Marlette. I pictured him seeking refuge here, beneath the umbrella of ancient branches. It felt a little like being tucked away inside a warm cave of brown and green, the last flickers of light mimicking a campfire.

Yet, as the sun retreated fully from the sky to make way for evening, I felt vulnerable and pessimistic about my task. My feelings must have shown on my face, because Sean gave me an encouraging smile and said, "Let's make the most of what daylight we have left. Trust your instincts, Lila. Maybe there really is something here."

The oak was pocked with dozens of knots and niches. Some of them rose far above my reach, and I wondered how Marlette could have found a place that no one else would be inclined to probe with curious fingertips.

While Sean examined the trunk, I decided to focus on the thickest branches. Prodding the wood, I investigated any depression large enough to contain a note. Normally, I would have enjoyed this exercise. I loved being outdoors, and the feel of the rough bark beneath my hands was a pleasant one. However, the shadows began to stretch and lengthen all around me, and even though Sean was only a few feet away, the silence became more of a presence. The bantering of birds was replaced by the shriller calls of bats, zigzagging in between the leaves in search of mosquitoes.

By the time I had searched the limbs above my head, my arms were so sore that I didn't feel like raising them again. My head ached and I wanted to give up. The impulse to forget about this task, to go home and change into my pajamas, flounce on my mother's couch, and drink an entire bottle of red wine, was almost too strong to resist. I was tempted to dull the sharp edges of this day with lots of alcohol, and yet, I couldn't turn away from this tree until I found Marlette's hiding place. Sean seemed just as determined.

"I know Burke is going to think I'm crazy," he said, "and

she's probably seconds away from calling me back to the car, but I have the strangest feeling that there's something here. You must be rubbing off on me."

I felt a rush of gratitude toward him. "Thanks for helping me. I knew it was a long shot but—"

Suddenly, I noticed a deeper shadow in a V where one of the thickest branches sprouted from the trunk. It seemed the perfect place for a nest or a concealed niche, and standing on tiptoe, I reached my tired arm over my head and blindly felt around the space with my fingertips. Two of my fingers sunk lower into the wood and brushed against material that felt oddly like wrinkled plastic.

My exhaustion was usurped by excitement. Pinching the object tightly, I eased it from the crevice and drew it down to eye level. It was a sheet of white paper folded into a square and swaddled in plastic wrap. I gave it a brief glance in the fading light and recognized Marlette's angular scrawl. There was also a large chunk of plastic and paper missing from one corner, and I groaned, picturing a squirrel nibbling at the edges.

I paused in the hazy blue twilight for only a moment and then handed it to Sean, who'd drawn on a pair of gloves the instant he saw me retrieve the prize from the niche. I knew that I'd just passed him a potentially significant piece of evidence, but I had a right to see what it was.

"Can you open it? Please?" My voice was soft and plaintive. "I won't touch it, but I need to know what's inside."

Two people had been murdered, and I needed to know why. This was no passing curiosity; my intentions had grown well beyond a concerned citizen seeking justice. I had a powerful new motive for inserting myself into the investigation. Self-preservation. It was only a matter of time before the killer became aware of my involvement. I wouldn't stand idly by while my mother or Trey became targets, and there was no way in hell I was going to give someone a chance to smother me with my own pillow!

"It's too dark," Sean argued.

Pulling a penlight from my purse, I turned it on and waited. Sean grinned. "I should have known you'd have come prepared."

Gently, he unfolded the piece of paper and held it out in front of his chest so we could both see it clearly.

My heart leapt in my chest as soon as I began to read. Without a doubt, I had found Marlette's query letter. I didn't need to be a seasoned literary agent to know that his idea was extremely marketable.

Marlette had created a character by the name of Knox Singleton. A tenured classics professor at Princeton University, Singleton was a renowned scholar and lecturer. He was also a member of a secret society formed to protect obscure and possibly dangerous texts rescued from the flames that burned the Ancient Library of Alexandria to the ground. In just a few lines, Singleton and the members of the illustrious Alexandria League leapt from the page, their passions and eccentricities immediately captivating my interest. Despite my surroundings, I was whisked off to covert meetings in wood-paneled reading rooms across the globe, eavesdropping in fascination as these intellectuals in bow ties and polished loafers formed a reckless plan to recapture a Babylonian scroll providing a magical formula for a substance that, recreated using modern chemicals, could be used as a weapon of mass destruction.

When I reached the final paragraph, I knew that this imaginative idea and well-written letter was a viable query and could indicate a very successful manuscript. Cursing whatever small creature had chewed off the section in which the thriller's title had been written, I reread the query in its entirety.

"What fool would turn this down?" I demanded, looking at Sean but not really expecting him to answer. The sound of my voice was muffled by the dense canopy and the impeding darkness. But I knew. It was time to let Sean get on with his work. Touching his arm, I thanked him for sharing the letter's contents with me. He nodded, his eyes distant, and carefully refolded the letter. He then walked me to my scooter, assured me that he'd be in touch, and hurried off to where Officer Burke waited behind the steering wheel of the police cruiser.

I zoomed away, my mind filled with images from Marlette's query letter. I barely remember driving to my mother's house. I found her in the kitchen when I dragged myself inside.

"There you are," she said with an affectionate smile. "No need to fret about makin' your son dinner. I told him you'd had a hell of a day and gave him a rain check for another night. Everythin' you need is waiting in your bathroom."

I was about to argue that what I needed most was a glass of wine, when she shooed me up the stairs using the damp end of a dish towel.

"I'm going, I'm going!" I growled, leaning heavily against the banister for support.

An inviting aroma of rose water drifted out from the bathroom, and when I opened the closed door, I was met by the sight of a full bubble bath and a large glass of wine resting on one of the tub's porcelain corners. As I squatted down to test the water, I noticed my pajamas hanging from a hook alongside an oversized towel. Not only was the bathwater hot, but my mother had also put my towel in the dryer. It still smelled of fabric softener and was warm to the touch.

"You really *are* amazing, Althea," I whispered. I wasn't even aware that tears were running down my face until I slipped off my shirt and the fabric became damp from moisture wetting my cheeks.

Sinking into the water's embrace, I closed my eyes. I'd reached that state of overtiredness where the mind darts from one thought to another but can't settle on a fixed image. So much had happened during the day that I couldn't stop the tumble of flashbacks, but eventually, I came back to the thing I most wanted to think about, and that was Marlette's query letter.

Lost in a brief fantasy in which I stood by Knox Singleton as he rolled out an ancient scroll in a dimly lit reading room, I drank my wine and exhaled as the smoky plum flavors of the merlot coaxed my shoulders to relax even lower into the tub.

"The question is," I addressed my toes, which protruded through a layer of rose-scented bubbles, "was the idea so good that someone would kill to call it their own?"

I emptied my wineglass and then looked around for the bottle, but my mother knew what I needed, and it wasn't alcohol. It was sleep. A long and restful night's sleep.

Draining the tub, I put on my pajamas, brushed my teeth, and collapsed into bed. I wondered if I should call Trey and warn him of Iris's possible involvement, but I decided that Sean would question the girl before the night was through. I also had a powerful feeling that the two deaths were tied to Marlette's thriller and had nothing to do with Iris. Someone in the publishing world had wanted his book so badly that they'd been willing to kill for it.

"But where is it?" I murmured groggily into the pillow. "Where *is* Marlette's book?"

THE RINGING OF my alarm woke me from a dreamless slumber, and I shut it off with a slow-moving hand and turned my face toward the window. The morning light made the thin, cream-colored curtains look like parchment paper, and I lay back against the pillow and pictured Makayla removing a tray of fresh-baked scones from the oven.

Despite all that had happened yesterday, I was incredibly hungry. I hadn't eaten last night, and after ten hours of rest, I felt revitalized and ready to tackle whatever challenges awaited me. But not without a hearty breakfast first.

When I got downstairs, I saw that my mother's wooden walking stick was not in its customary place by the kitchen door and knew that she had chosen to exercise early in order to avoid the oppressive heat Inspiration Valley expected today. I couldn't help but smile at the thought of my mother swiping at the tall grass with her stick, warning snoozing copperheads that she was about to invade their territory.

Like her, I wanted to begin my day with a dose of fresh air and sunlight, so I ventured out to the back porch, where I drank coffee and peeled a ripe banana, in no mood to rush off to work.

In *The Moonstone*, Wilkie Collins had written, "We had our breakfasts—whatever happens in a house, robbery or murder, it doesn't matter, you must have your breakfast." As I leaned against a post, chewing the soft fruit and inhaling the scents of wet grass and honeysuckle, I couldn't agree more.

At that moment, I realized that my mother had been right when she said that I'd needed to stay with her for a spell. She had been a source of constancy over this tumultuous summer, and I'd yet to truly show my appreciation for all the little things she had done to keep me sane.

I felt a rush of shame pinken my cheeks. I had always believed that Althea was the crazy one in the family, and I had held her at arm's length because of her profession, but I now had to admit that she possessed an uncanny ability when it came to predicting my needs. If she was just as accurate with her clients, then perhaps she did have a unique and wonderful gift that I would never understand.

"When my house sells, I'm going to do something special for her," I vowed, sending the promise across the dew-covered fields.

Thirty minutes later I was buying my second cup of coffee, a plump apple, and a cranberry orange scone from Makayla. She was too busy to talk, but I assured her that I'd drop by later and fill her in.

Yesterday, I couldn't imagine mounting the stairs leading to the literary agency feeling so calm and in control, but I was ready to face whatever awaited me there. In fact, I was looking forward to it. For too long I'd been stumbling around in search of clues, and now, to my great relief, the Dunston Police had taken over. Sean and his officers had undoubtedly questioned my colleagues and were merely waiting for a fingerprint match to come through. They'd wrap up the case, and we could all move on.

As I passed through the reception area into the main hallway, I could see that all the office doors were open with the exception of Bentley's. Voices emitted from the staff kitchen, and I was drawn to the murmur of conversation. It was such a normal, regular sound in comparison to the unsettling sirens and radio crackles of the day before, and I realized that just like the first day I'd arrived at Novel Idea, I still wanted to belong to this group, to be one of them. An equal.

"Zach Attack is *totally* scratched off the suspect list!" Zach declared loudly as I entered the room. "Flora and I went to Catcher in the Rye for lunch, and a *million* people saw us."

"More like heard you," Franklin mumbled under his breath, and I had to cover my smile with my hand. "Hello, Lila," he added, catching sight of me in the doorway.

Leaping up from the table, Zach offered me his chair with a flourish. "Please take my seat. You must be sorry you ever accepted this job! But don't leave us. We *need* you!" His dark eyes were filled with concern. "Do you want to talk about it? What happened at Luella's?"

"I'd prefer not to, but thank you," I said, accepting his seat and putting my coffee and takeout bag on the table. "And I don't regret my internship, though I'm really sorry about Luella. You all knew her much longer than I did, and I can't imagine how hard this must be for you. If I can do anything to help, just say the word."

Flora, who was standing by the counter stirring spoonfuls of sugar into a teacup, gave me a sad smile. "That's so sweet of you, dear." Her large bosom rose as her lungs inflated with air and then lowered as she released a sorrowful sigh. "It's too, too terrible. And for the police to think that one of *us* could have . . ." she trailed off with a sniffle.

Franklin left his seat at the table and offered her a tissue.

"Flora, you were at Catcher in the Rye with Zach. No one's pointing a finger at you."

She gave him a grateful little smile. "I was Mata Hari yesterday. I've been waiting all year to be given that name, but when I think of what poor Luella must have been going through while I was all smiles and giggles because Big Ed called out some silly name . . ." She shook her head and stared at her teacup.

"You're in the clear as well, Franklin," Jude stated miserably. With his rumpled clothes and slouched posture, he looked like a different person. "A piano lesson with Maddox Ryan. The perfect alibi. The whole town loves Maddox, and it doesn't hurt that he's a retired judge." Moaning, Jude sunk his head into his hands while Franklin turned his flushed face toward the window. I felt sorry for him. Was Maddox's former profession the reason they kept their affair a secret?

"*I'm* the only one who can't supply a decent alibi," Jude continued. "And I'm the one who chased after Luella yesterday. When I couldn't catch her, I didn't feel like coming back to the office right away, so I wandered through the park. Then Bentley had me drive all the way to Dunston to buy Calliope's favorite truffles. The chocolate shop is only five minutes from Luella's house. Don't you see how guilty I look?"

Zach shook his head. "Why did you take off after her? I didn't think you guys were together anymore." There was a sharp edge of envy in his tone.

"We haven't been an item for nearly a year, but I still care about her," Jude said defensively. I wondered whether his concern was genuine or if he was just a skilled actor. He did have a weak alibi, and he could easily be lying about his relationship with Luella. Perhaps she had been the one to end things and he was still nursing strong feelings for her. Unrequited love could turn people inside out, and there was something very intimate about Luella's death. Whoever had struck her, then smothered her, and finally, arranged her body so carefully was no stranger.

I studied Jude out of the corner of my eye. Was he capable of murder? Of creating a storybook scene using his former lover's corpse?

Flora put down her teacup and placed a hand on Jude's shoulder. "The truth will out, honey. Don't twist yourself up in knots. We know you'd never hurt her."

Her remark was met with silence, but I noticed that the other agents nodded in agreement.

"How's Bentley handling all of this?" I asked.

Franklin gave an embarrassed cough and said, "She seems rather preoccupied with an offer Jude received yesterday from some Hollywood studio."

"Which Jude or *I* should be handling." Zach sulked. "Carson is Jude's client, and *I'm* not called Mr. *Hollywood* for nothing."

I sipped my coffee and wondered if Bentley was really working on a deal or was deliberately seeking seclusion in her office while she grappled with the loss of her agent. Or worse, was she hiding because she was somehow involved in these crimes? "What's the title of Carson's book?" I asked, hoping to introduce a different topic. "I guess I should know it since it's going to be all over the place next year."

"*The Alexandria Society*," Jude answered, perking up at once. "Carson is going to be bigger than Dan Brown or Stieg Larsson."

As he proceeded to give me succinct summary of the plot, I was still reacting to the title. My coffee went down the wrong pipe, and I gagged and coughed, struggling to breathe.

"Are you okay, dear?" Flora inquired.

I nodded and bit into my scone, fearing that if I spoke now I'd blurt out the truth. The idea for Carson Knight's thriller belonged to Marlette! As I chewed mechanically, I realized that Carson was a prime suspect for Marlette's murder. Sending Jude a quick glance, I swallowed the bite of pastry and said, "I'd love to read it. Do you have a copy?"

"I have one on my computer and the original manuscript locked away in my file cabinet," he replied. "You can look at that version, but you can't take it out of the office. That manuscript is worth more than all of our salaries combined."

It took a Herculean effort to muster a grateful smile. "I'll stop by later, thanks. I have so much work to catch up on before then." I looked around at the rest of the agents. "Are the police done with us, do you think?"

"*You* seem to have an in with Officer Griffiths," Zach stated sourly. "Why don't you tell *us*?"

I folded the rest of the scone in a napkin and stood up. "I don't know any more than the rest of you. I only got involved because no one else seemed to care that an innocent man dropped dead in this office!" The anger had come out of nowhere, surprising both my coworkers and me with its vehemence.

"But—" Flora spluttered.

"No, Lila's right," Franklin said solemnly. "If we hadn't turned our backs on that poor man, he might be alive today. Maybe Luella, too. I don't know if there's a connection between the two of them, and I pray the police will sort this mess out, but at least Lila had enough gumption and enough heart to take action on Marlette's behalf." He touched my arm. "I, for one, am ashamed of my callousness."

It wasn't for me to offer forgiveness as, one by one, each of the agents voiced regret. I could only listen and sympathize, and eventually there was nothing else to say, so we dispersed and headed for our individual offices.

At my desk, I eyed the overwhelming stacks of queries, knowing that when I turned on my computer, there'd be an endless stream of emails to tackle as well. I knew I must put aside the emotions and thoughts that were swirling around in my head like a whirlpool and focus on the work I needed to do.

But first I had to call Sean to tell him about Carson's book. Getting that off my mind, and giving the police that valuable information, would clear the way for concentrating on my job.

I reached for the phone. It rang just as I was about to pick it up to dial, and as a result, my hello was somewhat breathless.

"Good morning, Lila," Sean said with a glint of humor in his voice. "You sound as if you've been running."

"Me? Run? Only when the oven timer beeps," I quipped back. "I was about to call you, actually." The idea that Sean and I had both thought of each other at the same time made me smile.

"Oh, what about?"

"I think Marlette's story was stolen, and while I still have to follow up on a few things, I'm fairly certain it's the key to his murder. I believe I might even know who's responsible." The names of my three suspects flashed across my mind. Jude. Bentley. Carson.

"Hold on there, Lila. Don't start making accusations until you have all the facts. Yesterday you thought Iris was a murderer, and your suspicions were completely unfounded. She has an airtight alibi. While Trey was at the grocery store, Iris was visiting an elderly, wheelchair-bound aunt."

"Oh." Feeling properly chastised for suggesting that Iris was a murderer, I toned down my fervor. "Then I'll hold off on sharing my theories for now. What did you want to talk to me about?"

"I wanted to tell you that I've sent Marlette's query to forensics to see if there are fingerprints on it. If so, we'll find out if they match any of the prints we took from Ms. Ardor's house."

I gripped the phone receiver tightly. "A match for the killer's fingerprints?"

"No jumping to conclusions until we have all the facts, remember? I'll talk to you later, Lila."

I reluctantly said good-bye, thankful that at least he thought there would be a "later" for us.

Hanging up the phone, I pulled a stack of queries toward me and opened the first envelope. The letter carried the faintest whiff of a woody scent, reminding me of Marlette. I closed my eyes for a moment and willed him to disappear so I could focus on the task at hand. Mind cleared, I began to read.

By the end of the letter, the author had drawn me into Valetta's world in much the same way that I'd been pulled into Marlette's Alexandria League. Pondering how a writer was able to accomplish this, I thought about Carson's novel. Surely it was more than a coincidence that the title and the plot were nearly identical to the novel in Marlette's query. And Carson, not Marlette, would be raking in the big bucks for an idea that wasn't his own. Had Carson stolen Marlette's novel? Had the two men known each other? Or was Carson in collusion with Jude or Bentley? Had one of my coworkers stolen from a gentle, befuddled recluse for profit?

The answer popped into my mind like a thought bubble in a comic. It *had* to be Jude! Since he was Carson's agent, he would also make a ton of money from *The Alexandria Society*. And he'd had regular opportunities to come in contact with Marlette, to read his query and, later, his entire manuscript.

Then again, Bentley was also profiting from Marlette's novel. Was she a part of it, too, or just an innocent bystander? And how had Luella become involved? *Had* she murdered Marlette? Or had the bee venom evidence been planted in her house and computer? If so, who was her murderer?

As each question raised another, I felt more on edge. I was so close to figuring the puzzle out, but I just didn't have enough information. I needed to see Carson's manuscript.

I worked through the rest of the day, but part of me was merely waiting for time to pass and for the rest of the agents to head home. Finally, at half past five, I stepped out of my office and glanced down the hall. It appeared as though all of my coworkers had left for the day. The agency was ominously silent, and except for the break room, all the doors were closed. Checking each one to be sure, I found everyone's door locked, and nobody called out to me when I knocked. Confident that I was the only one at Novel Idea, I felt an uncanny déjà vu from yesterday, when, alone at the agency, I'd searched Luella's office. I felt chilled, as though the air conditioner had been set ten degrees lower.

In the break room, I took down the coffee can that hid the master keys and pulled out the one to Jude's office.

Looking up and down the hall once more, I crept to his door and let myself in.

Once inside, it struck me how cold and austere Jude's office was. Compared to the other agents' homey spaces, Jude had chosen a desk and accoutrements that appeared to have come straight out of Office Depot. His unadorned, impersonal office could easily reflect the personality of a cold-blooded killer.

Is that what Jude was? I didn't want it to be true. Jude was such a charming man, so filled with laughter and playfulness. I'd been attracted to him the moment we met. I touched my lips as I remembered our impulsive kiss in this very room.

The first drawer of the file cabinet was locked, as were the others. I ran my fingers through my hair in frustration. Perhaps the keys were in his desk.

Perching myself on the ergonomically designed chair, I opened the first and second desk drawer, but neither of them contained the keys. As I opened the bottom drawer, a plethora of sweet scents was released, and my stomach grumbled. Guiltily I took a Twix bar, ripped it open, and bit into it while I considered where Jude might keep the file cabinet key.

The starkness of the furnishings did not offer many options for hiding places. To one side of the desk was a sitting area, the only part of the office that gave any semblance of comfort and relaxation. I sat on the edge of one of the two leather wing chairs as I finished the candy bar and scanned the bookshelves directly across from where I was sitting. The spines of the books were dark and shadowy, their titles containing words like "death," "murder," "killer," "spy." A sense of foreboding filled the room, and I suddenly wanted to get out of there as quickly as possible.

As I stood up, I noticed a small wooden box on the top shelf, sitting between a tennis trophy and an oddly shaped rock. My fingers tingled. Would the key be in there? Could I now unlock the file cabinet, and in so doing, unlock the most significant clue in this investigation?

I reached up on my toes to take it down.

"What are you doing?" Jude's voice pierced the silence like a gunshot. My heart plunged to my shoes, and I jumped, knocking the box to the floor. It sprang open, revealing a black, empty space. I spun around.

Jude stood in the doorway, looking outraged, his dark eyes glinting. A gym bag was slung over one shoulder, a racquet handle sticking out of its opening. He glanced at the box on the floor and then at me. His rugged chin thrust forward, and again he demanded, "What are you doing in my office?"

"I was . . . I just . . ." In a panic I could only stammer. Alone in a room with a potential murderer, an *angry* potential murderer, I was too scared to respond coherently! Gripping the bookshelf for support, I squared my shoulders and steadied my voice. "You said I could read Carson's manuscript."

"I said I would show it to you, but I didn't say you could go through my things! That manuscript is entirely handwritten! It could be extremely valuable one day. Carson had it transcribed, but he agreed to let me keep the original. You can't just barge in here and help yourself to it!" He stepped across the threshold and advanced toward me, the racquet handle swinging ominously at his side.

In that moment, I was like the rabbit Trey and I had cornered in our yard last spring, after it had eaten all the petunia buds. My eyes darted from left to right, just like the rabbit's, looking for a way to escape as Jude came closer.

My alarm heightened. The seconds that had passed since Jude first startled me seemed to stretch into minutes. As if in slow motion, Jude edged forward until he stood in front of me. My mind raced, and I looked around for a potential weapon.

I could *not* let Jude hurt me as he'd hurt Marlette and Luella!

His arm reached out, and I lunged for the coffee table. Grabbing an oversized book, I swung it with a strength I didn't know I possessed. It made contact with the side of Jude's head with a resounding smack, and he crumpled to the floor.

He landed on his back, the gym bag skittering under the desk. His hand cradled the side of his head. "Ahhhh," he moaned. "Why did you do that?" Slowly, he struggled to a sitting position. Shock and dismay radiated from his eyes.

"What were you planning to do to *me*?" I demanded, standing over him. My arms were tensed, preparing to strike him with the book again if need be.

Confusion spread across his face. "*Do* to you?" He touched the reddish bruise forming on the side of his head and winced in pain. "I wasn't going to do *anything* to you. Except kiss you again if I could." He attempted a smile but grimaced instead. "I sure won't try that again without making my intentions clear." He eyed the book, which was getting heavier in my hands by the minute.

I wasn't going to put it down just yet. "Tell me where you got the manuscript for *The Alexandria Society*."

"The what?" His brow furrowed. "From Carson Knight,

of course. He sent me an intriguing query, and after reading the manuscript, I offered him representation. Why are you so focused on Carson's book?" He attempted to stand. I raised the book a fraction higher, and he lowered himself back to the floor. "Geez, Lila. What is *wrong* with you?"

"Carson's novel is the same as the one described in Marlette's query letter. A query letter to which *you* had access. Did you take the one from the flowers the day Marlette was murdered and destroy it? Did you help Carson steal the book from Marlette?"

"What? No! The first I ever knew of *The Alexandria League* was from Carson's query. It had nothing to do with Marlette." Comprehension made his face go slack. "You think *I* murdered Marlette? Oh my god, Lila, I swear—"

"And Luella? Did you frame her for Marlette's death and then bump her off?" I lowered the book, my conviction that Jude was a killer now wavering. At the moment, he seemed more like a hurt and confused little boy than a calculating murderer.

He covered his face with his hands and shook his head. Eventually, he looked up at me with pleading eyes. "I can't believe you think I'm even capable of . . . that kind of violence. I'm a lover, not a fighter." A quick smile revealed his dimples, and then he became serious again. "I *cared* about Luella. I'd never hurt her." He spread his hands wide. "And Marlette was a harmless eccentric. I wouldn't raise a hand against him." He shrugged. "Lila, how can I prove my innocence to you?"

I stepped aside to clear his way to the file cabinet, and though I still wanted to appear in control, I nonetheless softened my voice. "Show me the query. Show me the manuscript. Maybe then I'll believe you."

"Okay." He raised himself to his knees and groped in his pants pocket. He pulled out an Audi key chain and selected a small silver key, holding it between his thumb and forefinger. "Second drawer."

Not wanting to turn my back on him, I said, "You open it."

He started to stand again but hesitated. "You won't whack me with the book again, will you?"

"Not unless you give me reason to." This time I smiled at him. I felt awful about the contusion on his head, now turning an ugly shade of reddish blue, and I was rather ashamed for intimidating him in this way. Yet I didn't want to give up my advantage until I felt confident that Jude was innocent.

He inserted the key into the file cabinet lock. My pulse quickened with excitement as Jude slid open the drawer and began riffling through the files.

"What the hell?" He looked up with a puzzled expression and then pushed himself to his feet and carefully examined every file in the drawer.

Bewildered by his reaction, I peered into the drawer, watching the label of each file flip by. After he'd examined the last one, Jude stared at me in shock.

"It's gone, Lila. The original manuscript is gone!"

Chapter 14

AFTER JUDE LOCKED UP THE OFFICE, I DROVE MY VESPA home through the sticky evening. Wisps of damp hair clung to my cheeks and neck, and my shirt was plastered to my lower back. I decided to take a shower before supper. How I hoped to wash the day off me, to let the fear and confusion I'd felt in Jude's office go down the drain in a spiral of soap and water.

Althea was closeted in the kitchen with a client, so I sat out on the back porch with wet hair and a notebook. I wanted to put my thoughts about the case on paper, hoping to sort out my suspicions and theories. First, I made a list of my coworkers and then drew lines through their names as I ruled them out as killers. When I reached Jude's, I left a question mark beside it. He had seemed genuinely distraught over the missing manuscript, but I couldn't be absolutely sure that he hadn't been involved in a crime.

"Who stole the manuscript?" I murmured softly, but my words were swallowed by the creaks of the rocking chair.

Scenes from *The Great Train Robbery*, *The Maltese Falcon*, and Arthur Conan Doyle's "The Adventure of the Mazarin Stone" played themselves out like a movie montage in my mind. In heist novels, everyone's after money, rare artifacts, or jewels, but in this real-life investigation, the stolen item was an idea.

Marlette had dreamed up an original, saleable idea and had turned it into a book. I could easily picture his angular scrawl filling page after page of watermarked paper as the scenes bloomed in his head like the wildflowers in his hidden meadow.

With his masterpiece complete, he began to query Novel Idea. Desperate to have his novel read, he appeared in person day after day until finally, someone took a few minutes to scan the lines of his letter. If Jude had been telling the truth, then that "someone" was Bentley, Luella, or the previous intern, Addison.

Making a quick note to speak to Addison during tomorrow's lunch break, I returned my focus to the next conundrum, which was puzzling out how someone had gotten their hands on Marlette's copy of the manuscript without his knowledge. After all, he'd hardly continue to appear at the literary agency bearing flowers and a fresh query letter if his novel had gone missing. There was only one explanation: Marlette didn't know that his book had been stolen. Again and again, he blindly climbed the stairs to the reception area clutching a bouquet and a dream.

In one of Agatha Christie's novels, Hercule Poirot claims that "every murderer is probably somebody's old friend." For once, I disagreed with the intrepid Belgian detective. I believed that Marlette's killer had been his enemy from the first. Bentley? Carson? Luella? She had never been his old friend. Even in the past, when she was just a young woman named Sue Ann Grey, Luella had tried to manipulate Marlette. Failing to do so, she immediately set out to tarnish his reputation. She was an enemy.

Years later, she could have read his query letter and hurriedly discovered the location of the manuscript. How she met Carson and the extent of his involvement in the scheme to claim Marlette's book as his own were vague, but I was certain my revealing Luella as Sue Ann Grey to the authorities had put someone's well-laid plans at risk.

I stared at the names on my list. "Did you kill Luella, Carson? What was she to you? Lover? Business partner? Both?"

Then my eyes fell on Bentley's name. "And where do you fit into this terrible plot? I really hope I'm not working for a criminal." I sighed. "Maybe I should have become a freelance reporter. Far less dangerous."

WHEN I GOT to the office the next morning, I was surprised to find Sean seated on the leather sofa in the reception area. His presence unsettled me for a moment because the sofa always reminded me of Marlette's death. However, Sean didn't seem to be bothered by the couch's tainted past. With one ankle crossed over the opposite knee, he was engrossed in a pictorial on the best hiking spots in America. Upon seeing me, he jumped to his feet.

"Good morning," he said with a smile and handed me a takeout cup from Espresso Yourself. "Might I interest you in a caramel latte?"

"You may, thank you." I returned the smile, absurdly delighted to see him. In Sean's presence I had the sensation that everything would be okay, that he and a dozen colleagues were working tirelessly on elements of the case I couldn't even begin to comprehend. I considered all the facts and interviews he had to sort through, the evidence that he and his team had had to gather and process, and how careful he needed to be before accusing someone of murder.

"Any luck with the fingerprints?" I asked him quietly.

Ignoring the question, he pointed down the hall. "Can we go to your office?"

Once inside, he closed the door and we both sat down.

"We found prints from every literary agent in Ms. Ardor's house, which is no surprise considering she hosted a garden party a few weeks ago that all your coworkers attended. However, there was another set of prints we've been unable to match with anyone registered in the national database."

"I have an idea who those prints belong to." I told Sean about the missing manuscript and my theory that Luella and Carson had worked together to steal Marlette's novel and make a fortune from its publication. I realized that I probably should have shared this information with Sean last night, but it had been my hope that I'd be able to present him with some solid facts and all I had was more conjecture. I could tell from his expression that he wasn't exactly dazzled by my investigative work.

"There's only one problem with your hypothesis," Sean said. "Mr. Knight has a solid alibi for the afternoon on which Ms. Ardor was killed."

I put my coffee cup down on my desk, no longer trusting myself to hold it steady. "That leaves only Bentley."

"Ms. Burlington-Duke was here with Ms. Ardor's client.

A Miss, uh, Calliope Sinclair gave us a very precise statement. Apparently, she was rather put out because she had to wait here so long."

The implication of Calliope's corroboration swept over me. I couldn't help but release a heavy breath of relief. "My boss didn't kill Luella."

"No," Sean replied with finality. "She was at the other end of the agency engaged in a conference call when Marlette was given the injection of bee venom."

"So that's been confirmed?" I asked. "Marlette died because of that injection?"

"Yes. After finding the syringe bearing Ms. Ardor's prints as well as a receipt for the venom in Ms. Ardor's house, we escalated the priority on Marlette's autopsy and requested a complete toxicology report from the medical examiner's office." He showed me a color printout of the flowers Marlette had carried into the agency on the day of his death. "This is white milkweed. I'd never heard of this plant, but apparently bees love it. Does it look familiar?"

I reached for the paper. "Marlette was holding onto those clusters of white petals on my first day of work. I remember thinking how beautiful they were, despite the fact that they were being carried by a man who looked like he hadn't had a bath in a very long time." With a shake of my head, I thought of my initial impression of Marlette. "I'm still ashamed of how uncomfortable I was in his presence. He was harmless. Maybe if I'd given him a few minutes of my time, I could have made it impossible for Luella to act. To think that a woman who doused herself in perfume and made men go weak in the knees was walking around with a syringe in her pocket, preparing to commit murder . . . It makes me feel sick."

Sean reached out and touched the back of my hand. His warm fingertips gave me an instant feeling of calm. "Ms. Ardor knew that Marlette always brought wildflowers to Novel Idea. She also knew it was plausible for a bee to be concealed in one of his bouquets," Sean continued. "By injecting her victim and causing him to go into anaphylactic shock and then dropping the dead bee on the floor, Ms. Ardor wanted us to assume that Marlette had a serious allergic reaction to the bee sting. She was smart, but not smart enough to realize that she ran the risk of becoming a victim herself."

"And everyone has an alibi for Luella's murder." I sighed. "What happens now?"

"If these two murders occurred because of plagiarism, then I need to find at least a portion of Marlette's original manuscript. I've got to have something to compare to Mr. Knight's book."

"Carson will just say that he only had the one handwritten copy and he gave it to Jude. And now it's gone. Stolen." My lips formed a tight line of anger. "How convenient for Carson."

Standing up, Sean said, "You said that Carson hired someone to transcribe the manuscript. Perhaps this person remembers what the original handwriting looked like. I could conduct a handwriting comparison."

Excited, I jumped out of my seat. "Yes! There's no way Carson could imitate Marlette's scrawl! Let's see if Jude is in his office."

Sean grabbed me by the elbow before I could open the door. He moved his body close to mine and whispered, "You've been an incredible help, Lila, and I admire your determination, but this is my case. I'll be asking the questions." He softened the stern words with a playful wink, and I smiled. If anyone else had spoken to me like that, I would have bristled like a porcupine, but I trusted Sean. I trusted him to pursue every lead until each secret and every lie had been laid bare.

But I wasn't going to back off, either. Not now, when the agency was in such a fragile state and its agents were confused and scared. I might have begun my employment as an intern, but this place and its people were becoming a part of my life. One I wanted to make permanent. Sean knocked on Jude's door, but it was Bentley who called out, "Enter!"

"Ah, Officer Griffiths." Without rising, she gave him an imperial nod and then looked at me. "Good morning, Lila. Jude and I were just discussing how the agency should handle Luella's client list until we're able to begin a search for a new agent. He made an interesting suggestion—one that I'd like to talk over with you when the good officer is done."

I dipped my head in acknowledgment, momentarily taken aback by Bentley's haggard appearance. Her usual sense of style was evident in her white slacks and zebra-pattered silk blouse, accessorized by black ankle boots and a choker made of jet beads, but her hair was dull and limp, and her claret-colored fingernail polish was chipped as though she'd picked most of it off. She wore little makeup, and the thin skin below her eyes was puffy and tinged with the gray and blue of someone who hadn't slept well in days.

As Sean asked Jude for the contact information of the person who'd transcribed *The Alexandria Society*, I slipped behind him and came to stand near my boss. I wanted to offer her words of comfort and support. "I'm sorry about all that's happened," I told her and then squatted by her side.

"Has Jude told you my theory? That Carson Knight has signed a six-figure deal for a book he didn't write?"

Bentley removed her reading glasses, folded them, and put them on her lap. Rubbing her temples, she released a heavy sigh. "Yes, Jude told me. He also voiced the possibility that Luella was the mastermind behind the entire affair. That would be most disappointing. I've long suspected she wore a different face in private, but she was an excellent agent. I've never known someone with such a penchant for negotiating. She masked her ruthlessness under a façade of charm, but her clients and this agency reaped the benefits."

"Marlette didn't benefit," I reminded her softly.

Raising her brows, Bentley's only reply was, "Touché."

"So you weren't aware of a relationship between Luella and Carson?" I asked.

"Certainly not." Her eyes darkened with annoyance. "I don't give a fig about the personal lives of my employees. As long as my agents work hard, sell books, and represent this agency with dignity and professionalism, I don't care what they do outside the office."

After checking to see that Sean and Jude were still preoccupied, I sank into the vacant leather chair next to Bentley. "Have you read *The Alexandria Society*?"

"Every scintillating word. To think that it could have been written by such a . . . by someone who lived on the fringes of society." She stared at the glasses in her hands. "He was brilliant. The book is brilliant."

It was wonderful to hear Bentley compliment Marlette. I wanted people to respect him, even though he was no longer alive to appreciate it.

"Got it!" Sean said, grabbing a paper from Jude's printer tray. "Thank you for your assistance. I'll be in touch."

He waved at us, his gaze meeting mine and lingering there for a moment, and then he was gone.

Bentley fluffed her lifeless hair and smoothed the wrinkles from her skirt. Before my eyes, she began to transform from a fatigued and perplexed woman to the confident, self-assured boss I was used to seeing.

"Well, *I* do not intend to idly wait around to be told that someone's made a colossal fool of me." She looked at me. "Lila? How would you like to accompany me to Carson's residence? It's time he and I had a little tête-à-tête."

I nodded, happy to have another person from Novel Idea in my corner. "I'd be glad to come with you. I can't wait to see whether Carson can produce notes or an outline or a sample chapter proving that he wrote *The Alexandria Society.*"

Bentley told Jude to hold down the fort and then stopped in her office to grab her purse. She popped open a compact and deftly applied red lipstick. "If Carson is the author, I won't need to view proof of his work. He'll be able to answer trivia questions from his own novel. If he can't, then I'll accuse him of plagiarism, and you'll be there to witness his reaction."

I followed her down the hall, hustling to keep pace with her quick, determined stride. "Shouldn't we wait for the police? Or take Jude along? If Carson feels cornered, he might turn violent."

Bentley stopped short and swung around to face me. Her eyes were icy with rage. "I hope he does. I've got a can of pepper spray and a pair of brass knuckles in my bag, and I'd love the chance to use them."

DURING THE DRIVE to Carson's place in Dunston, Bentley stared straight ahead, her hands firmly clutching the steering wheel. I surreptitiously texted Sean about what we were doing, hoping he would receive the text in time to meet us there. She pulled up alongside a gray apartment block on a lane not far from the railway tracks. Bentley's silver BMW seemed incongruous with the neighborhood, and its horn beeped three separate times as she repeatedly clicked the lock button on her key while walking up the path leading to the middle building.

"He lives *here*?" I couldn't keep the surprise out of my voice.

"Apartment 302," Bentley replied, pushing the front door open. I had to stop it from closing on me as I hastened to keep up with her. Her sharp heels echoed in the stairwell as we climbed to the third floor. "Apparently he's put in an offer on a house on Walden Woods Circle. The charming yellow one. 'More suitable for a successful author,' he said. Hmph, if he's a fraud, his real estate deal will fall through as fast as his book deal."

I gripped the banister tightly, thinking about Carson moving into *my* Walden Woods Circle house. It couldn't happen! He was a thief and a murderer, and should be punished for his crimes. The yellow house deserved someone with a good heart and a clear sense of right and wrong. Someone like me.

At apartment 302, Bentley slid a hand inside her purse, most likely preparing to use her pepper spray. The hallway was dimly lit, barely enhanced by the sun shining through a grimy window at one end. Sounds of a morning television talk show came from the apartment behind us, and the cry of a baby filtered through a door farther down.

"Let's see what Mr. Knight has to say for himself," Bentley remarked as she rapped sharply on the door. We waited.

Nothing.

She knocked again, meeting my gaze.

"Guess he's not home," I ventured. I glanced behind me, hoping to see Sean arriving.

She nodded. "I have to agree." Turning on her heel, she marched back to the stairwell. "Come on, Lila. Back to the office. Our encounter with Mr. Knight will have to wait."

The drive to the office was as quiet as before, but the atmosphere in the car had altered. Bentley's anger had diminished, and her hold on the steering wheel was less white-knuckled.

I stared out the window, disappointed over not having had the opportunity to confront Carson, but also somewhat relieved. Who knows what might have transpired if he'd been home and we'd challenged his integrity? The image of Luella arranged on her bloodstained sheets flitted across my mind, and I shook it away, knowing that Carson was best left to the police.

At the entrance to the agency, I hesitated. It would take five minutes via scooter to get to the Secret Garden where Addison could possibly tell me more about Carson's query.

Turning to Bentley, I said, "Ms. Burlington-Duke? I'd like to run an errand before returning to the office."

She peered at me with raised eyebrows. "An errand?"

"It's related to this case. I want to talk to Addison Eckhart—"

"That incompetent? What on earth could *she* tell you?" Bentley stepped impatiently across the threshold.

"She worked at the agency when Jude received Carson's query and might remember something important." I gestured at my Vespa, which was parked at the curb across the street. "I'd be back in less than half an hour."

Bentley glanced at her watch. "Off you go, then. You're probably too distracted to be very productive in any case." Just before the door to the lobby closed, I heard the words, "I admire your tenacity, Lila. You're going to go far in this business."

ADDISON WAS PUTTING the finishing touches on a floral arrangement when I walked into the garden center. The bell on the door tinkled, and she looked up in the middle of inserting a spiraled bamboo shoot amidst three elegant bird-of-paradise stalks.

"Hey! How are you liking my scooter?" She flipped her long braid off her shoulder.

"I love it," I enthused. "In fact, after work I'm heading up to the Red Fox Co-op to have dinner with my son, and my little Sunshine is going to take me there."

"That's what you call it? That's cool!" She laughed, a ringing sound not unlike the bell on the door.

I fingered a dried fern stem on the counter. "Actually, I came here to ask you a few questions about your time as an intern at Novel Idea."

"Working there was *not* a fun experience." She shook her head and adjusted the green sprigs in the arrangement. "And with what happened to Luella Ardor . . . well, things must be *really* awful there. What do you want to know?"

"Do you remember when Jude received Carson Knight's query?"

She looked up sharply. "Yes. Why?"

"How did it arrive at the office? By mail or email?"

Addison shrugged. "I'm not sure how Jude got it. I didn't give it to him. Sometimes agents receive recommendations from their current clients." She looked away, lost in a memory. "I just remember how excited he was after he read those first three chapters. Ms. Burlington-Duke, too. The whole office believed they had a winner. And Carson, he's awesome." The sprinkling of freckles on her nose gathered together as her mouth curved into a smile.

Did Addison have a crush on Carson? If that were the case, I'd have to tread carefully. "Did you know that Carson and Luella had a relationship?"

"Totally!" She plunked herself down on her stool and clasped her hands. "Carson is *so* in love with Luella." Bringing her fingers to her lips, her mood sobered. "Was, I mean."

"How do you know that?" Maybe Addison didn't have a crush on Carson after all. Perhaps what she felt was more like hero worship. A small-town girl in awe of meeting a future celebrity. "Did he talk to you about Luella?"

She nodded. "After I came to work here, I sold flowers to Carson every day. He always said, 'I need sweet blossoms for my sweet Luella.' Isn't that romantic?" Addison was obviously impressed by the gestures. "He's run up some tab."

"A tab?" Remembering where Carson lived, I didn't think he could afford to be so extravagant.

"We normally wouldn't let someone without a corporate account buy on credit, but . . ." She looked beyond the stores to the greenhouses. Following her gaze, I saw Martin in the distance, watering potted shrubs. Addison's voice became a whisper. "I knew he was going to come into big money once his book sold, so I set it up for him. He's good for it. I mean, he's *such* a great guy."

I looked into her wide blue eyes, brimming with innocence. If Carson was truly the cold-blooded murderer I believed him to be, capable of bludgeoning and smothering the woman he loved, then a naïve young woman like Addison could be at risk should she ever cross him. I needed to warn her.

"He may not be as great as you think," I said quietly.

Her brow furrowed. "What do you mean?"

"I believe that he's a thief and—"

"That's impossible! I don't believe you, and I don't want to hear you talk like that about him." She shot me a look that nearly singed the ends of my hair, and then she jumped off the stool and walked over to the door. Opening it wide, she said firmly, "I need to get back to work."

I made a conciliatory gesture. "I didn't mean to offend you, Addison, but I've found evidence indicating that Carson stole Marlette's book. You remember Marlette? He used to wrap his query letter around a bunch of flower stems? *He* wrote the book all the agents were so excited about, not Carson."

As my words registered, Addison narrowed her eyes. "No way! That old bum couldn't have written his own name! Carson's an amazing writer!" She stood with one hand holding the door, the other at her hip. "Just go!"

I towered over her in height, but in her indignation, she radiated authority. I stepped across the threshold. "Do be careful, Addison. He may have murdered Luella."

The shock that emanated from her as I said those words was like a force pushing me outside. I hadn't learned much more from Addison, aside from reinforcing the theory that Carson had had a relationship with Luella and that his query had mysteriously appeared on Jude's desk.

I hoped my probing wouldn't put Addison in a precarious situation if she were to discuss our conversation with Carson. It infuriated me that a lowlife like Carson could pull the wool over the eyes of an impressionable girl like Addison. But then, he'd done the same with Bentley, a worldly sophisticate.

Worries about Addison and Carson hovered over me when I grabbed a quick lunch to eat at my desk from Espresso Yourself, giving Makayla a very brief synopsis of what had transpired since we last spoke.

Back at my desk, a phone message from Trey allowed me to set those anxieties aside for a while. "Hey Mom," his voice sang in my ear. "Grandma told me how you've been playing detective when she called to reschedule our dinner. When you get here, I'll take you to Marlette's cabin to look for this notebook Iris mentioned." He chuckled. "Apparently Marlette filled it with notes about a big project and sketches of what he called the Library of Alexandria; at least that's what he told Iris. She said it had a red cover, and I know the one you found is brown, so maybe it's still at his cabin. Thought I'd give you a heads-up. See you tonight."

As I hung up the phone, I couldn't help wondering why Iris had suddenly remembered this other notebook. Why hadn't she told me about it before? At the co-op tonight, I'd be sure to ask her.

Visions of finding the notebook interfered with my concentration as I waded through scores of queries, eager for the workday to end so I could head up the mountain.

When five o'clock finally arrived, I was the first to leave the agency. Hopping on my scooter, I raced past Center Park, but my momentum was brought to a halt when the traffic light at Redbud and Lavender Lane turned red just as I approached the intersection. Impatiently, I tapped my fingers on the handlebars.

Mountain Road was potholed and wound its way up the

steep incline. My little scooter had to work hard, and I rode diligently to ensure I didn't skid around the many curves. I was relieved to finally arrive under the willow branch arch with the Red Fox Co-op sign.

As I parked my bike, I inhaled the mountain air. A strong sense of Marlette's presence seized me, and I hoped I'd unearth the red notebook. If it was filled with drawings of the Library of Alexandria, then it might also contain an outline or character sketches from his novel.

Running my fingers through my hair, I headed into the clearing. The woman who was weaving hemp the first time I visited was once again sitting in her chair, working on a hammock. Jasper walked out of the barn and, catching sight of me, raised his hand in greeting.

"Welcome, Ms. Wilkins. We're looking forward to having you join us for dinner. Trey should be back soon."

"Oh. I was hoping to take a walk with him." Disappointment deflated my shoulders. "Is Iris around?"

"She's checking on our beehives, and Trey's gone to the creek to fill up some canteens. You can meet him there if you'd like." He pointed to a path leading away from the campfire pit. It was the same one Iris had used to take me to Marlette's cabin.

"I'll do that, thanks." I started off in the direction of the trail.

Jasper raised an arm as I passed. "Be sure you stay on the path," he said with a smile. "We don't want you turning an ankle on a root."

As I hiked along the trail, the shadows lengthened. In the gloom, the foreboding I'd experienced earlier returned, but I tried to ignore it, knowing I'd be meeting up with Trey soon.

After a few minutes, I spied the laurel bush where Marlette had left poems for Iris. A narrow path veered off to the right, and I recognized it as the way to Marlette's cabin. I decided to explore, figuring that Trey would know to look for me there.

I hastened down the trail, brushing aside overgrown bushes and low-hanging boughs. Twigs cracked under my feet, and branches raked my arms. I was hot and sweaty and had to constantly swat at aggressive mosquitoes as I trudged through the shrubbery. As I stopped to scratch a painful bite, I heard the distinct snap of a twig to my left.

I froze, my disquiet returning full force. I called nervously into the greenery, "Trey? Is that you?"

A crow cawed and a squirrel chattered from the canopy overhead. Other than that, it was quiet.

I peered into the woods to my left. Thin trees and scraggly shrubs cast elongated shadows, but I saw no movement. I hurried the rest of the way to the clearing where Marlette's cabin stood.

In the dusky light, Marlette's abode looked decrepit and far too isolated. A fire pit was overgrown with weeds and lent an extra dose of abandonment to the grassy area outside the cabin. The stream echoed a forlorn sound in this lonely place, and I called out Trey's name again. My voice was swallowed by the woods, and I received no reply. Certain that I'd hear my son when he came nearer, I approached the cabin.

A spiderweb stretched from a tree to the frame of the cabin door, blocking my way. Its creator sat in the center, fat and sinister, busily wrapping the corpse of a dead moth in a sticky, silken coffin. I wiped the strands away and moved forward.

The soiled yellow canvas flap that acted as a door fluttered in the breeze like a phantom. The darkness inside made it difficult to see, and I berated myself for not having brought a flashlight. Perhaps if I fastened the canvas flap open, the light would chase off the largest of the shadows.

I rolled the canvas to the top of the doorway, discovering as I did so that a cord was sewn into it. I tied the knot, imagining Marlette doing the same thing so he could sit on his wooden crate and pen his novel on the makeshift table. A rustling behind me made me spin around, only to see a chipmunk dart across the clearing. I exhaled, mumbling to myself to stop being so jumpy.

On the wall opposite the entrance, a ray of sunshine drew my attention to the cabinet and the books cluttering its shelves. I approached it, moving deeper into the cabin. Suddenly a shadow blocked the doorway. I turned to see who was there, my throat tightening.

Silhouetted in the opening stood a man, his dark figure exuding menace in the backlight of the waning day.

It was not Trey.

"So nice of you to come," uttered Carson ominously, and then he entered the cabin, untying the tent flap.

The material fell across the opening, shutting out any illumination and inviting terror in with the darkness.

Chapter 15

CARSON DIDN'T HAVE TO SAY ANOTHER WORD FOR ME to know that his intentions were wicked. Every cell in my body was buzzing in alarm. The blood rushed through my veins in an attempt to keep my heart pumping at its frenzied pace as my mind tried to comprehend what was happening.

In movies, when an attacker confronts a helpless female, the action always seems to take place at lightning speed. He lunges, she screams and runs, and the scene moves rapidly forward. But in this moment of terrifying discovery, I was rendered immobile. My limbs felt like anchors, and I could not take my eyes from Carson's face, painted in shadow and utterly devoid of any emotion.

I don't know how long we were frozen in our places like two prehistoric creatures encrusted in ice, but when he finally took a calm, unhurried step deeper into the cabin, the spell his arrival had put me under lost its power. My hand, which had been on the rough surface of Marlette's makeshift table, could once again register the feel of its coarse texture. I took in a fortifying breath of pine and damp soil, which seemed to invoke Marlette's presence with such intensity that I felt as though he could be standing right next to me. It was as if he were in the cabin, wordlessly reminding me that he had been murdered, cautioning me to wake up and act.

My fingers reached out and closed around the walking stick leaning against the desk, but I never broke eye contact with Carson.

He took a second step toward me, his mouth curving upward into a chilling smile.

I wondered if Luella had seen the same smile the day she'd died. I didn't need Carson to tell me what had happened—the cold gleam in his eyes and the hulking shape of his shoulders served as his confession. He was a killer.

Carson's hands curled into loose fists at his sides, becoming twin cobras waiting to strike.

He had not come to talk.

He had come to see that I would never speak again.

Marlette's walking stick had a polished knob at its crown, and it fit perfectly against my palm. I took comfort in its solidness and then slid my hands down the shaft, positioning my arms so that I could lash out with the knob the moment Carson reached for me.

"Now, Lila." His predatory gaze turned smug. "Do you really think you can stop me with that thing?"

I gripped my weapon tightly and answered him in a voice made steady by anger. "I'm sure as hell going to try. You can't sneak up on me. I'm not turning my back on you like Luella did."

He laughed a dry, brittle laugh, the expectant glimmer

in his eyes shredding my confidence. "I didn't think I had it in me, you know. To take someone's life. But she forced my hand. All this time she's hidden things from me. Her real name. A copy of the bum's manuscript. Not the original, of course, but she told me the photocopied manuscript was her insurance and that after I paid her a ridiculous amount of money, we'd burn it in her fireplace and make love as it went up in flames."

I frowned in distaste at the warped relationship those two had shared and waited for him to move within striking distance. Luella had been a fool to think she could go on manipulating Carson once he discovered her duplicity. Her arrogance had no bounds.

"You were beautiful, Luella. Oh yes, I enjoyed our time together, but I never loved you." He glanced over my shoulder, no longer seeing me. "You thought I was in your control, but I will never be anyone's puppet again. No one's employee. No one's errand boy. Even though I never found that damned copy, you haven't won. *I've* won!" He reached behind him with his left hand and pulled out something from his back pocket. Even in the dimness, I recognized that it was a notebook with a red cover.

"You have Marlette's notebook?" I asked breathlessly, feeling as though I'd been punched in the stomach.

Flipping the pages irreverently, he let loose a haughty snort. "Of course. Luella took the original manuscript from Jude's file cabinet, and I put that fat stack of pages through a shredder at the copy center. Bye-bye, evidence. And as far as Luella's insurance? I'm not worried about some supposed photocopy. I certainly made sure that she could never breathe a word about it to anyone. Ever." He wiggled his long fingers. In the shadows, they resembled the spindly legs of a tarantula. "After I got rid of both the original manuscript and Luella, I came back here to search for any other incriminating tidbits, and I found this."

"Why did you keep it?" My eyes darted to the book. "Why not destroy it, too?"

He stroked the red cover affectionately. "The bum outlined a sequel. *The Babylonian Society.* I can hire a ghostwriter. Despite what you may think, this isn't over for me. This is just the beginning. Too bad you won't be around to see me living the life of a rich and famous author."

I shook my head incredulously. "You're going to get caught."

"The cops don't have enough on me. So they find my prints at Luella's place. So I admit that I was her lover. That's as far as it will go. If anything, keeping me in jail for a few days will make me more of a media draw." He grinned greedily. "More press means more sales. More money for me. I am *never* going to be poor again. This is the end of shithole apartments and rusted-out cars. The end of cheap clothes and crappy food. It's my turn. I've waited long enough for this break."

Carson's eyes had filmed over with a temporary madness, and I dared to look at the doorway to see if I could get by him and outside before he surfaced from his trancelike state. The moment I tensed my body to spring forward, he blinked and pointed at me with his index finger.

"Tsk, tsk. Naughty Lila. No running, no screaming." His gaze bore into me, and his right hand sank into his pants pocket and drew forth a loaded syringe. Tossing the notebook aside, he held up the needle. The last rays of the sinking sun caught the splinter of steel, and it winked like Christmas tinsel.

This image sent my thoughts careening into the past, and a dozen Christmases flickered in my memory. Trey in footed pajamas, Trey dumping out his filled stocking onto the living room rug, Trey sipping hot chocolate as I read him *'Twas the Night Before Christmas*, Trey singing carols in the school choir, his rosebud mouth forming a perfect O, Trey barreling into my arms to thank me for the remote control dump truck he had wanted so badly.

These memories fueled my courage. "You're not going to take me down with bee venom, Carson. I'm assuming that's what you've loaded into your little syringe, because you're not creative enough to think up an original murder weapon."

Carson's features twisted with fury, and then he abruptly laughed again. "Who needs to be original? I don't want to make a mess, and Luella proved how easy it is to kill someone with this stuff. She was more than willing to bump off that old piece of human trash." His smile turned into a leer. "And then *you* had to stick your nose where it didn't belong. *You!*" He spat the word. "A pathetic, middle-aged intern. A nobody." His speech slowed to a crawl. "You ruined everything."

"But I'm not allergic. It won't kill me." I clung to the hope that this would stop him, or at least give him doubts.

His eyes flashed. "You don't have to be allergic. Ever heard of mass envenomation?" He tapped the syringe. "This contains the equivalent of a thousand bee stings and can easily kill a healthy human. You'll die of renal failure." He shook his head in mock sorrow. "Such a terrible way to go."

His mercurial shifts of emotion revealed a person the likes of which I'd never known. In the shadows multiplying inside the cabin, Carson seemed less and less of a human being. His nonchalance when referring to his plans to plunge a hypodermic into my neck lent him an alien crookedness. He had turned into a nightmare creature with a dark face and angular limbs. And what could I do against him? Stall for time. For what, I didn't know, but it was an instinctual defense. I was the cornered rabbit, trying to distract the cat before it could spring.

And then, without a whisper of warning, he lunged.

I reacted instantly, swinging the walking stick in a powerful arc toward Carson's head. He dodged, nimble as a boxer, and my blow connected with his shoulder instead.

He grunted in pain and hesitated, allowing me the opportunity to hit him again. This time, he stepped away from the stick, but the knob came down hard on his wrist, and in a spasm of agony, Carson dropped the needle.

Seeing it skate across the floor, I knew this might be the only chance I'd have to escape, so I jumped over his crunched-up form and moved to break into a run.

I didn't even make it to the doorway.

Carson's uninjured hand shot out, his fingers locking onto my calf like a vise. He was incredibly strong, and I cried out as he yanked me backward, drawing me into his chest like a spider retrieving the stunned fly.

I screamed as loud as I could. My mind emptied of all thought, and my body took over—kicking, twisting, shouting—and when Carson clamped a hand over my mouth, I wrenched my face to the side and bit down hard on his finger.

It was as if he could no longer feel anything but the desire to silence me, to spend his wrath robbing me of life. He pushed me down onto Marlette's pile of blankets, sending mini hurricanes of dirt and dust into the air. Then, to my horror, he held up the syringe once again.

Seeing the needle sent me into a frenzied panic. I bucked and howled, clawing at him, kicking him, squirming to the left and right, but he straddled my chest with his legs and pinned down my arms. He leaned forward, crushing me under his full weight. My breath was forced out of my lungs, and without fresh oxygen, I had no strength to fight back.

Above me, Carson smiled with satisfaction.

"Say good night, Lila."

I wanted to say so many things. I wanted to beg him to stop, I wanted to speak my son's name once more, I wanted to spit in Carson's face. But his hand clamped down over my mouth.

I had lost.

I was going to die.

"FREEZE!" a voice bellowed from across the room, and then, in a matter of seconds, the weight was lifted from my chest. As I sucked in air, I heard scuffles inside the cabin, but I couldn't move. It was as if I were still being held down. Spots danced before my eyes.

After a few seconds, I heard the voices of several men, and I raised a hand to tentatively touch my throbbing cheek. I could feel the bruised flesh where Carson's fingertips had dug into the tender tissue.

This awareness—that I could feel pain, that breath was rushing in and out of my lungs—allowed my vision to clear. I had survived. I was alive!

Sean appeared at my side, murmuring words of comfort while he helped me sit up. "Are you hurt? Do you need medical care?" he asked urgently, his eyes searching my body, his hands centimeters from my tear-streaked face.

I opened my mouth, but too many emotions were battling inside, and I couldn't talk. With trembling arms, I reached for Sean. He enfolded me gently, but I clung to him fiercely, my tears wetting his shirt.

His lips touched the back of my hands, my neck, my bruised cheeks, my eyelids. They traveled to my forehead and then found my lips.

I kissed him hungrily. He had rescued me. This man, full of strength and intelligence, was my hero. Sean had made certain that I could remain a mother, a daughter, a friend. He had swept in and tackled a coldhearted killer, preserving my life in the process.

My desire for him had existed long before this moment. It was just that now, I didn't stop to consider whether the time was right or who was witnessing our embrace. The rest of the world fell away in the circle of his arms. I lost myself in the warmth of his mouth, drinking in the taste of him—peppermint, safety, strength.

"MOM!" Trey's urgent shout forced me to break off the kiss.

I reached out for Trey with both arms, and my son sank down on the ground in front of me and held me tightly.

"Honey, I'm okay," I whispered.

Trey's handsome face was creased with worry. I could see the fear in his eyes. Even though it was obvious I was only a little bruised and battered, he had never seen me in such a state. To him, I was the person who never got hurt or sick or succumbed to weakness in his presence. I was the constant in his life, and it had clearly terrified him to hear that I had come so close to death.

"Mom," he croaked and put his head on my lap. I stroked my son's hair and murmured soothingly to him, saying a silent prayer of thanks that I had not been separated from my boy.

* * *

LATER, AS WE sat in front of the campfire Trey had built near the co-op's living quarters, I looked from the flames into Sean's blue eyes. "How did you know to come for me?" I asked him.

The rest of the police officers had gone back to Dunston, but Sean had stayed behind to make certain that I was okay. Seated with his arms resting on his thighs, he poked at the small campfire with a stick. "We've been tailing Knight all day. Followed his car right to the base of Red Fox Mountain but lost him in the forest. He didn't take the main path, and there are so many trails up here . . ." It clearly bothered Sean to admit that his suspect had given him the slip. "Luella must have shown Carson how to reach Marlette's cabin without running into anyone from the co-op. By the time we reached this area and Jasper told us where you were headed, I knew you were in danger."

Trey gave Sean a nudge with his elbow. "Jasper said you ran through the woods like a deer. Not bad for a guy your age."

Sean smiled at the playful jest. "I'd be more fleet-footed if I didn't eat Makayla's scones every time I came to town."

Though I was delighted to see the burgeoning camaraderie between Sean and my son, I was unable to share in any expressions of joviality. It was just too soon. "Sean, I need to know . . . Is Carson going to jail for a long time, or is there a chance that some hotshot lawyer will get him off?"

Sean put his hand over mine. "His prints need to match the ones we found on Luella's Eros statue if a murder charge is going to stick. He's facing a string of charges based on what he did tonight, but I want to bury him using as much indisputable evidence as I can, and a print match could help seal the deal."

I nodded. Carson's fate was as of yet undetermined. And what of mine?

As if reading my thoughts, Trey said, "Are you going back to Novel Idea, Mom? I mean—you've met some real losers working there."

"At least one loser, that's for sure. But yes, I plan on returning—tomorrow, in fact, because Bentley has asked us to come in for a Saturday meeting after all that has happened this week. She also mentioned that she wants to talk to me about something, and I have a feeling it's important."

Despite all that had happened, I wanted to be a literary agent. I wanted to discover fresh voices and unique plotlines. I wanted to read the untold stories—those gems brought to the surface so that they glimmered in the light. Stories destined to be shared with the world. "I belong there," I added, giving Trey a smile.

He glanced beyond the campfire, his gaze finding Iris as she and other co-op members set out food for supper. "I get that." His eyes returned to me. "But if anyone ever tries to hurt you again, they'll have to answer to me!"

Sean clapped Trey on the shoulder. "Good man."

At that moment, Iris approached our intimate little circle and offered me a mug of black coffee and a piece of toast. I accepted the food but caught her by her slender arm before she could retreat.

"Why didn't you tell me about the red notebook sooner?" I demanded, refusing to let her pull away.

Her birch pale cheeks filled with color. "I'm sorry! I never meant to put you in danger. It's just that pretty soon after I showed you Marlette's birdhouse in the meadow, someone trashed his cabin." Her arm went limp. "I didn't know whether I could trust you after that happened. After all, no one else but you and the cops came up here asking questions about him." She shot Trey an apologetic look.

"So you told my son about the red notebook today just to see if I would go looking for it?"

Iris nodded miserably. "It was a test. If you didn't search for it, I'd know you already tore apart his cabin and took the notebook, but if you went looking for it with Trey, I'd know that someone else stole it." She sighed. "I should have hidden the red notebook before the place got trashed. I was planning to tell you everything after you guys got back from the cabin, but I didn't think . . . I never thought the person who took the notebook would follow you here. I'm really sorry."

I squeezed her gently and then let her go. "You were just trying to respect Marlette's memory by protecting his possessions. You're the only other person who genuinely cared about him, and I don't blame you for what happened tonight. Not for a second." I managed a weary smile.

Sean, who had been prodding at the fire during this exchange, got to his feet and brushed my shoulder tenderly with his fingertips. "Are you up to confirming your statement tonight? Or would you like Trey to drive you to Dunston first thing in the morning?"

Trey's eyes were wide with pleading, and I knew he wanted to act as my guardian for a while. "We'll have some supper, and then I'll decide. I'm not really hungry, but eating will help me feel normal again, and I have a feeling the food here is better than what you've got in your vending machines."

That earned me a chuckle. Sean patted his belly and said, "Body by Frito-Lay."

The laughter welled up inside me and poured from my throat like a bubbling spring. I couldn't help it. Relief was showing itself through uncontrollable giggles that turned into hearty, deep-bellied laughter. I'd already trembled, cried, kissed a good-looking police officer, and cradled my son's head in my lap. The pure joy of being alive overtook me, and I let it flow forth. Trey and Sean joined in.

Chapter 16

THE NEXT MORNING I WAS AWAKENED FROM A SLEEP SO deep and dreamless that finding my way to consciousness was like dragging myself through molasses. I opened my eyes, trying to discern what had roused me.

"Mom?" Trey peeked his head around the door. "Sorry to wake you, but it's getting late and I need to bring the truck back to the co-op."

I rolled over, squinted at him, and then let my heavy lids fall shut again. "What time is it?" My words came out in a gravelly mumble.

"Eight. Didn't you tell Officer Griffiths you'd be at the station by nine?"

I rolled over, wanting nothing more than to crawl back into the numbness of sleep. Only the fact that I would see Sean again prompted me to reply, "Okay, I'll be down in fifteen minutes."

Under the streaming water in the shower, last night's

events played through my mind. The image of Carson hovering over me with the needle made me shudder. I turned the shower knob, coaxing the water to turn hotter, and tried to focus on the memory of sitting by the campfire instead of being trapped inside Marlette's cabin with a killer.

Not long after Sean left, Jasper and Trey had secured my Vespa onto the bed of the community's Ford F-150 pickup truck. Jasper handed Trey the keys and told me to take care.

Back at my mother's, I had called Sean and told him I'd come to the station in the morning. Trey had insisted on staying the night. He waited until I slipped into bed before tiptoeing down the stairs to fill my mother in on what had transpired on the mountain. I'd drifted to sleep to the murmur of their voices, feeling comforted and protected by their presence.

Now, as I wiped the shower steam from the mirror, the bruises on my neck glared an angry plum color in the reflection of the damp glass. The imprints left by Carson's hands were like a brand, a sign of how close I'd come to losing my life. With Carson in custody, was it really all over?

Gingerly, I did my best to hide the marks beneath a layer of creamy foundation. I then tried to decide what to wear, though this seemed to be an insurmountable task. All I wanted was the familiar comfort of my loose gray sweats, but their color reminded me too much of Carson's cold eyes. Besides, I needed something more appropriate for work. In the end, I chose a pair of navy slacks and a cream-colored tunic that I accessorized with a patterned silk scarf to cover my bruises.

As I stepped out of my room, coffee and pancake aromas filtered up the stairs. I slowly made my way to the kitchen, determined to face this day as though it were any other.

My mother's voice drifted out into the hall.

"You'd best pick the right time to tell your mama," she cautioned. "She's gonna have a hissy fit when she hears your plan."

"Yeah," Trey agreed. "I'm thinking now's *not* the right time."

"For what?" I asked, stepping into the room. They both looked at me with wide eyes. Sitting at the table, my mother sipped from a mug decorated with gold and silver astrological signs. Trey stood at the stove with a spatula in his hands. The frying pan sizzled. I was too stunned to say anything more. My son was cooking breakfast!

"Um." Trey turned back around and flipped pancakes. "I've decided not to go to college," he said to the stove. "I'm staying at the co-op."

"Trey, you can't! The co-op isn't a career choice; it's an experience!" I sputtered. "You can't support yourself with an experience. Think about your future."

"Now, sug." My mother stood and poured me a cup of coffee. "Sit on down and have your coffee. You're strung tighter than a banjo. The boy is simply explorin' his options."

I took the mug and attempted to compose myself.

"Okay, Trey, what are you thinking?"

Rather than answering, Trey placed a plate in front of me. "Here, Mom. I made blueberry flapjacks. Your favorite. And this syrup is from the co-op. Eat up."

I picked up my fork and put a piece of his creation in my mouth. Tart blueberries burst in the cakey sweetness of the pancake, and I nodded appreciatively, cutting another wedge off with my fork. "Delicious, Trey. Thank you. But making me breakfast doesn't get you off the hook. You know that college—"

"Mom, *please*." He sat down across from me. "I like it at Red Fox, and I'm only just discovering what I'm good at. I don't want to quit right now. College would totally disrupt my journey of self-discovery and—"

"Journey of self-discovery?" I exclaimed. "What kind of mumbo jum—" A glare from my mother made me stop midsentence.

Trey snatched his opportunity and stood. "I've gotta go. I have to make a delivery this morning. Talk to you later." He kissed my cheek and was out the door.

I glowered at my mother. "You're encouraging him to take this flight of fancy, but in this day and age, he needs to go to college if he wants any kind of secure future."

"He's still a young colt, Lila. He's got plenty of time to have a little fun before he gets stuck behind some cubicle like a racehorse in a stall." She began to clear dishes from the table. "Let him sow his oats for a while."

"Oats? Hmph!" I stuffed the rest of my pancakes in my mouth to prevent my saying something I'd later regret.

CLIMBING THE STAIRS to the entrance of the Dunston police station, I felt a little uneasy as I considered the fact that Carson was incarcerated somewhere in this building. The last time I had been here I'd come to collect Trey, and now I had to give a statement detailing how a man had tried to kill me.

Thankfully, I spied Sean leaning against the reception counter, and the sight of him lifted my spirits as if they were inflating with helium. I knew his desk was on the other side of the building, and that meant he was only in the lobby to meet me. He looked up and, upon seeing me, cut off his conversation with the receptionist. He strode over and took me by the elbow. This small physical connection did wonders. It was as if Sean knew that my world had come unbalanced last night and would offer whatever help he could to force the ground to level out beneath my feet again.

"Lila," Sean said, his voice a caress. "How are you feeling?"

"Better, now that I'm with you." I smiled feebly. "But mostly I feel like an overcooked piece of spaghetti."

"That's to be expected, considering what you've been through." His fingers curled more possessively around my arm. "Come on back. My chief said we could use her office to record your statement. The interview rooms can be a little unnerving." He nodded at the receptionist as he led the way. "Vanessa will bring us some coffee."

Inside the chief's office, Sean closed the blinds and wrapped his arms around me. In his embrace I felt safe, and I leaned into it, not wanting to be released. We kissed, slowly, tenderly, and then he held me for a minute longer before letting go. Reopening the blinds, he smiled at me. "Now that we have that out of the way, let's get to work." He led me to one of two vinyl chairs positioned in front of a glass-topped table, sat down in the other, and shoved aside a mound of documents. "I'll be recording your statement. After it's been typed, you can read it over for accuracy. Ready?"

I nodded, reluctant to relive last night's terror-filled moments. "Where shall I start?"

Sean pulled the recorder toward him. "Give me a minute to identify myself, but you can begin with your visit to the Secret Garden and your conversation with Addison."

"What does Addison have to do with this mess?" I asked, perplexed.

"Please, just describe everything you can remember. I'll explain why later."

He was about to press the record button when a knock on the door interrupted us. Vanessa entered, carrying two mugs and a plate of fruit Danishes. "I thought you might want something sweet with your coffee," she said, placing them on the table.

The aroma of coffee made me think of the office, and I realized that I hadn't called the agency to inform them I'd be late for our meeting this morning. "Oh no!" I exclaimed. "I need to phone Bentley and tell her why I'm not at work yet." I rummaged in my purse for my cell phone.

"I'll do it," Sean said. "I can explain what happened and officially confirm that Carson plagiarized Marlette's novel. I'm sure this will raise a few issues for your boss, but she needs to know the truth. Mr. Knight provided us with a very detailed confession, but more about that later." He couldn't hide a glint of satisfaction.

"That would be great. Tell Bentley I'll be in as soon as we're done."

I recited the number, and he made the call. While listening to him talk, I had the strange sensation that he was referring to someone else when he succinctly described what had occurred at Marlette's cabin. When he finished, he handed the phone to me. "She wants to speak to you."

Bentley sounded uncharacteristically solicitous. "Lila, there's no need for you to come in today after all that you have been through."

Gratitude flowed through me. "Thank you. I can come in on Monday."

"Take as long as you need—even a few days off. As soon as the police give me the information I need, I'll be flying to New York to deal with the mess that Luella and Carson have created. Between the lawyers and the editors, I may be gone for several days."

An hour later I was ready to sign my official statement. My hand was cold on the pen, and my signature reflected the hint of a tremor. I pushed the paper over to Sean. "It's done."

"I know it wasn't easy for you to relive that." He touched my wrist. "I wanted to tell you about something I learned from Carson's confession. Remember the skull that was painted on the door of your house in Dunston? He was responsible for that. I'm telling you so you don't have to look over your shoulder in the future."

"He was already targeting me *then*?" I ran shaky fingers through my hair, thinking about what might have transpired had I not moved in with my mother.

Sean's face was solemn. "Luella thought you were far too interested in Marlette's death, and she wanted to scare you off, so she got Carson to deface your front door."

"And he claimed to have been no one's puppet," I scoffed angrily. "How did those two find each other?"

"They met in a bar," Sean replied. "After a few drinks, Carson told Luella that he'd do anything to live the good life, to have nice things and stop working menial jobs. Judging from his employment record, he was bright but lazy."

It was easy to picture the scene—Luella seizing the opportunity to manipulate the embittered man she'd met over shots of tequila, taking him as a lover. Together, they formulated their plan to steal Marlette's book and then kill him. All in the name of money.

"Carson told us about the deal they made," Sean continued. "Carson would take on the role as its author. If the book was a success, he was going to be rich, although she was taking a bigger cut. She somehow arranged for the advance and future royalties to be deposited into an account that only she had access to. But Carson wasn't the pliable lump of clay Luella supposed him to be. Her hubris had been her undoing."

"She convinced him to play the part of the modest but brilliant thriller writer," I mused. "But why did he turn on her?"

Sean smirked. "Ms. Ardor felt the net tightening. We were digging around; *you* were nosing about. Actually, her plan starting falling apart as soon as Jude mentioned that the spot on Marlette's neck looked like a needle mark. The dead bee she'd planted wasn't going to do the trick. Once you'd shown her the photo from Woodside Creative Camp, she knew she was going to have to run. Sadly, Carson was waiting for her at home. He had his own key and would often spend time at her place, preferring it to his own apartment."

"He told you all of this?" I shook my head in disbelief. "Why? And how did he know I was going to Marlette's cabin last night?"

"Addison told him where you'd be. She's his half sister. After you left the garden center she called Carson and told him that you viewed him as a murder suspect. She also shared your plans to have supper at the co-op. Carson was already in the woods when you arrived at Red Fox, and then he followed you to the cabin."

"Addison is Carson's *sister*?" It was hard to believe that she'd almost gotten me killed. Then I remembered her immediate reaction to my accusation about Carson. "Did she know he'd murdered Luella? And stolen Marlette's manuscript?"

"She didn't know what Carson had done, but she was his alibi for Luella's murder. Addison did lie for him, although he'd given her some other reason to do so. Now, he wants to protect her. I told Carson we'd drop all charges against her in exchange for a confession. He took the bait. He really cares about Addison. We still need to bring her in for questioning, but no one's seen her since yesterday."

I considered all I'd learned, probing the gaps in my knowledge. "But how did Luella know about Marlette's book in the first place?"

"Apparently, when Marlette first came to the agency, he was hustled out of the office by Zach, and Luella passed by them on the stairs. She'd told Carson that as soon as she saw Marlette, she recognized him as the monster who'd assaulted her, even though he looked like a bum. She realized that Marlette also knew who she was when he ranted at her, but she didn't even acknowledge him. She managed to follow him later and discovered where he lived." Sean ran his fingers through his hair. "She kept an eye on him for months, learning about all his hidey spots, and coercing Carson into spying on him, too. She knew Marlette's novel had the potential for success, because all those years ago at the camp she'd read some first-draft excerpts. According to Carson, she'd never forgotten about that book."

"So she seized the opportunity to steal the manuscript from Marlette when it presented itself," I concluded.

Sean nodded. "Setting in motion all that happened these past weeks."

"Did she do it just for the money? Or was she still out to get Marlette?"

Sean shrugged. "We can only guess. According to Carson, she did it to get back at Marlette for having stolen her girlhood. However, since Marlette never did what she accused him of, and we know this for certain because we found her diary from that summer, I believe it was all about the money."

"Maybe that was also her motivation when she was a teenager," I surmised. "She wanted to steal his idea, and when that didn't work, she destroyed his reputation." I leaned back and closed my eyes, letting all the pieces fall into place. "Well, I'm glad it's all over."

He nodded. "Yes, for you it's over." He reached for my hand and squeezed it. "You faced down a monster last night, Lila. That experience is going to change you. Take some time to work through what's happened. Enjoy the little things. Your family. They'll see you through."

IN ADDITION TO the weekend, I took three days off from work. Three days of sleeping late, sitting around in my pajamas, losing myself in a comforting Alexander McCall Smith novel, and drinking tea with slice after slice of Althea's chocolate banana bread. When I found myself concocting a dinner for my mother and me of angel-hair pasta with goat cheese and sun-dried tomatoes, accompanied by wine, I knew I was ready to face the world again.

Before heading in to Novel Idea the next day, I stopped in at Espresso Yourself. The coffee shop was quiet. Only two tables were occupied, and Makayla was in the corner by the bookshelves, removing books from a paper bag.

"Hey, girl! Long time no see," she said upon noticing me. "Take a look at these." She held up two books. The first was *The Book Thief* by Markus Zusak and the other, *The Help* by Kathryn Stockett. "One of my regulars dropped off this bag for my little lending library. There are some fine books in here." She put them on the shelf and pulled out another. "Oh, I am going to get lost in this one during my break. Ever read any of hers?"

I took *The God of the Hive* by Laurie King from her and perused the back cover. "No, but it sounds like an interesting series." I handed it back.

"Did you read the paper this morning?" Makayla asked. When I shook my head, she said, "There's an article about Marlette and his book." She handed me a copy of the *Dunston Herald*. "Page three."

Eagerly, I opened the paper. In the bottom left-hand corner, Marlette stared out at me from a black-and-white photo, younger than when I met him but older than in the camp photo. His eyes gazed out knowingly beneath his wild hair. For a moment I felt him in the coffee shop, as if he were standing behind me, looking over my shoulder.

ARTS CENTER BEQUEATHED TO INSPIRATION VALLEY read the headline. I pored over the article, which briefly described Marlette as a former university professor turned author. There was no mention of his recent lifestyle or how he died. I wonder whose influence directed this account.

The article continued:

A lucrative publishing contract has been signed for Robbins's novel, The Alexandria Society. *Due to his untimely death, Robbins will fail to reap the rewards of his success. However, the town of Inspiration Valley will benefit, as the heir to Robbins's estate, a distant cousin, has donated the entire advance, as well as all rights to the book, to the town of Inspiration Valley. The proceeds will be used to construct the Marlette Robbins Center for the Arts.*

"We are thrilled by this act of generosity," said Ms. Bentley Burlington-Duke, president of Novel Idea, the literary agency representing Robbins's novel. "Marlette Robbins was a gifted member of our community. His creative achievement will put Inspiration Valley on the map as an epicenter of culture." Burlington-Duke will make an official announcement to the town upon her return from New York.

Beaming, I looked up at Makayla. "This is wonderful! Marlette gets credit for his book, and an arts center in his name will ensure that the town will always remember him."

"Too bad we didn't appreciate him more when he was alive," she remarked, tamping down coffee grinds.

My smile faded. "I know. But given everything that's happened, this is a pretty good result."

"Here you go, sugar. That'll fuel you for your first day back."

"Thanks." I picked up the takeout cup and turned to go, glancing through the window. As if summoned by the memory of Marlette, a sparrow flew past the coffee shop and landed in the tree on the corner. A group of people ambling down the sidewalk broke out into spontaneous laughter. A young woman trailing closely behind them had a long braid. Addison!

"Hey!" I shouted, running out the door and across the street. "Wait!"

Addison stopped but didn't turn to greet me. I couldn't blame her. After all, I was the reason her brother had been apprehended—that her world had been turned upside down.

"What do you want?" she demanded, her voice a low growl.

"To tell you that I'm sorry."

She frowned. "For what? Ruining my life? Showing me a side of my brother I never knew existed?"

I was relieved to hear that this young girl hadn't had foreknowledge of Carson's crimes. "I'm sorry that you have to go through this. I wouldn't wish this pain on anyone."

She kicked at the curb with the heel of her boot, and I could see her eyes welling up with tears. "That's what the cop who interviewed me said. But here I am."

"You're going to be okay," I told her. "You're strong. Just don't stop believing in people. They can surprise you in good ways, too."

I wanted to hug her but sensed she wouldn't welcome the familiarity, so I gave her my card, telling her to call me if she ever needed a friend. She took it and stuck it in the pocket of her jeans and then crossed the street without another word.

I watched her until she disappeared around a corner, and I silently prayed that she could recover from this ordeal.

Walking into Novel Idea felt like coming home. The other agents were genuinely glad to see me, and they hugged and fussed over me for a good fifteen minutes before I finally ventured into my office and got to work.

My concentration was interrupted by a call from the reception area. "Hello?" The woman's voice sounded vaguely familiar, although I couldn't place it. I hurried out to see who it was. Standing near the entrance was Calliope, Luella's client, wearing a purple velour pantsuit and a canary yellow headband.

I held out my hand. "Hello, Calliope. I'm Lila Wilkins. We met last week."

She narrowed her eyes. "I don't . . ." Recognition registered on her face. "You're the one who found Luella. I read about it in the paper. It must have been awful." She offered me her hand as though I might bend over and kiss her garish diamond and amethyst ring. "Poor Luella. She didn't deserve to die like that."

"No one does," I said, though part of me believed that Luella had merited some kind of retribution for what she'd done to Marlette. "How can I help you?"

"I'm looking for Bentley." She pointed down the hall. "Is she in?"

"She's in New York, but perhaps I could be of assistance?"

She shifted her bag from one shoulder to the other. "What will happen to Luella's clients?"

I shook my head. "I don't know, but I'm sure you'll be taken care of." I suddenly realized I'd seen a photograph of Calliope's face before. It had been on the inside back cover of the book Luella had lent me on my first day of work. "Isn't *Can't Take the Heat* one of your books? I read that recently and loved it."

She nodded, her face aglow with pride. "It's nice to be represented by an agency whose staff loves my work. However, a New York firm is offering me some *very* attractive perks. I'm tempted, but they want me to stick with contemporary romance." She put her hands over her heart. "*I* want to leave my comfort zone. I've written a historical romantic suspense set in Elizabethan England, and personally, I think it's my best writing. Ask Bentley if this agency would like to represent my new project. If so, she knows how to reach me. I do want to stay with the agency out of loyalty, but I'm wondering if anyone's got enough free time for little old me."

"Of course we do," I hurried to assure her.

She turned to go but then abruptly spun around. "Oh, I almost forgot! I didn't come here just because I was in the neighborhood. I have an important delivery. Please give this to Bentley." She pulled a thick brown envelope from her cavernous Prada handbag. "Luella gave it to me for safe-keeping a while ago. Told me that if anything happened to her, I was to get it to Bentley."

"Do you know what it is?" I asked, noticing the envelope was sealed. It was heavy in my hands.

Calliope shook her head, her dark curls bouncing wildly. "Feels like a manuscript to me. I thought it was a *very* strange thing for her to do, but no matter how much I probed, she wouldn't tell me what it was or why she wanted me to hold on to it. When she was murdered, I was dying to open it, but I'd made a promise to a friend." Her magenta-hued lips crumpled a little, and I saw that she and Luella had shared a bond that went beyond agent and client.

After Calliope left, I took the envelope back to my office. I knew I should have put it directly on Bentley's desk, but I couldn't. Everything that had happened revolved around the contents of this package, for I was certain that it held a pho-tocopy of Marlette's manuscript. This had been Luella's insurance policy, and though it had failed to keep Carson under her control, it would add to the stack of evidence that was mounting against him.

But beyond all of this, the envelope contained Marlette's book. This was the project of years of labor, and it had been good enough to ignite a major bidding war among several publishing houses. It had been good enough to be called brilliant by my boss. I felt I deserved to read just one page of the novel that had caused so much strife and yet would soon be devoured by thousands and thousands of readers.

I slit one end open with the edge of my scissors and shook the envelope over my desk. A thick stack of papers secured with two rubber bands fell out with a thud, and I immediately recognized Marlette's handwriting.

"Ahhh," I breathed as though I had just been reunited with a long-lost friend. After pivoting the bundle using a pair of ballpoint pens to prevent getting my fingerprints on the manuscript, I read the first page.

It was wonderful. I wanted more, but the book did not belong to me. It was evidence, and so, reluctantly, I did the right thing. I called Sean. When he didn't answer his cell phone, I rang the main switchboard and spoke to Vanessa. She informed me that Sean was in a meeting but she'd send an officer to the agency to collect the envelope.

When the policeman left my office an hour later, I experienced a strange sense of loss. It would be months before I'd be able to read *The Alexandria Society* in its final polished form. But that was all right. I knew it would be worth the wait.

THE FOLLOWING DAY Bentley returned and immediately summoned me to her office. It was hard to imagine that not so long ago I had sat here, waiting to find out if I'd landed the intern's job. That Friday, I was nervous, yet determined. Today, I felt like I'd been at this agency for years.

Bentley, who was wearing a white suit with black piping and a red silk pocket scarf, pulled a sheet of paper out of a file folder and placed it in front of her. She peered at me over her reading glasses.

"The other agents think very highly of you, Lila, and I've been impressed with both your instincts and dedication."

"I enjoy working here," I said, "despite all that has happened. I love the excitement of discovering a story that sparks the imagination, of encountering a fresh voice that I want to introduce to the world."

"Yes, I sense that. Now, your three months internship has not run its course, but with Luella's . . . demise, we need someone to take over her position. Based on your good work here, and on your newspaper experience, I'm offering that to you. Are you interested?"

It was all I could do to not jump out of my seat and scream my acceptance. Instead, I folded my hands tightly on my lap. "I'm most definitely interested."

"The first six months will be a probationary period, but I expect things to go well. You'll handle our romantic suspense and traditional mystery clients. The latter is an area in which you seem to have some expertise, considering your activities of late. Flora will take over the rest of Luella's romance and erotica clients."

"Flora? Erotica?" Relief mixed with surprise as I pictured the plump children's lit agent blushing over manuscripts.

"Yes, she specifically requested this assignment." Bentley slid over the piece of paper she'd earlier placed on the desk. "Here are the details outlining your new position—job description, salary and benefits, vacation schedule, travel reimbursements, et cetera. I trust it meets with your satisfaction?"

I read through the information, my eyes widening at the salary increase. Things were definitely looking up. Once my house in Dunston closed, I'd have enough money to pay for the damage Trey had wreaked on his high school and make an offer on the yellow house on Walden Woods Circle. If I was frugal enough, I could also handle Trey's college tuition after I convinced him to change his mind. And I would be a full-fledged literary agent! I could feel the joy shining through my eyes. "Thank you, Ms. Burlington-Duke."

"Since you are now a bona fide agent of Novel Idea, please call me Bentley." She stood and reached out her hand. "Congratulations, Lila."

I shook it, understanding that this was a dismissal. "I'd better get to work."

Just as I reached her door, she called me back. "One more thing. I'm giving you the responsibility of hiring a new intern as your replacement."

The other agents were gathered in the break room, and as I walked past, the expression on my face must have told them what had transpired in Bentley's office, because they applauded. Jude held out a plate of cinnamon buns. The pastry in the center bore a lit candle.

"Congratulations, Lila!" called Franklin, raising his mug in a toast.

I stood in the doorway and drank in the moment. "Thanks."

"I had a feeling about you from the first, dear," Flora said as she dipped a tea bag in and out of her cup.

Zach brushed past me. "I gotta run, babe, but Zach Attack is totally stoked that you're going to need a brand-new shiny name plaque!"

"Thanks. Me, too."

Jude gazed at me with his chocolate brown eyes and smiled. "You deserve this promotion, Lila. And we're glad you're staying, even though your first weeks here have been somewhat eventful."

"That," I said, "is an understatement."

In my office, I could no longer contain my excitement. In the midst of all that had happened, my ambition had been realized. I did a little victory dance, feeling the gladness bubble up from deep inside. I picked up the phone and dialed my mother's number.

"Why, hello, Ms. Hotshot Literary Agent," she said by way of greeting.

I opened and closed my mouth like a fish tossed into a bucket. "How did you—?"

"This was meant to be, Lila. Now, if you wanna hear what I've got to say about your love life . . ." she trailed off with a laugh, and I felt a wave of affection flow through me for this amazing woman.

"Not right now, Mama," I said with a smile, pushing aside thoughts of Sean, of my impending conversation with Trey, of Marlette's legacy, and of anything else that did not involve Novel Idea.

I was a literary agent now.

The words were waiting for me. Words strung together like luminous pearls. Words as sharp as blades and as soft as rose petals. The stories, the authors, and the future readers were waiting, too.

I closed my door and sat down to read.

Turn the page for a preview
of Lucy Arlington's
next Novel Idea Mystery . . .

EVERY TRICK
IN THE BOOK

Coming soon from
Berkley Prime Crime!

BY THE MIDDLE OF OCTOBER, THE HEAT AND LASSITUDE of a Southern summer had finally loosed its hold over Inspiration Valley. Cool air traveled down from the foothills and encouraged the people of North Carolina to search their closets for lightweight sweaters and to spend their weekends at football games or strolling through pumpkin patches in search of the perfect gourd.

Signs of fall were everywhere. Advertisements were stapled to nearly every telephone pole enticing the public into taking hayrides, attending apple festivals, and purchasing potted mums from the local plant store, the Secret Garden. An electric charge was present in the crisp mornings and a bowl of warm grits or a cup of hot cider never tasted better. Folks went about their business with a spring in their step.

Although I loved autumn and welcomed the brisk breezes, and the harvest moons hung from a canvas of deep indigo, I was too busy to enjoy the season. Novel Idea, working in conjunction with the town of Inspiration Valley, was on the verge of hosting the area's first Book and Author Festival and I was in charge of registration for both the participants and the guest speakers. In addition to this time-consuming assignment, I had to find our agency a new intern because the woman I'd hired in August to take my place had been forced to accompany her husband in an abrupt job transfer to Minnesota.

This meant that come Monday, my desk and email inbox would be crammed with unfulfilled tasks. Thank goodness today was Saturday and the work I had before me was of the kind I'd been looking forward to for months. Today was moving day.

Most people view this activity as a miserable one. True, it involved plenty of hard labor and emotional stress, but I was giddy with excitement when my son, Trey, pulled up in front of my mother's house in a borrowed pickup truck.

"Ready to put these guns to good use?" he asked, and then flexed his biceps. As usual, he was wearing a T-shirt. Freezing rain could cover the surface of Inspiration Valley and my son would insist that he wasn't cold.

"Manual labor suits you," I told him. "If you still have energy after a day of shoveling out the goat pens or chopping wood, you could always hike down the mountain and mow my lawn."

Trey puffed out his chest, pleased that I'd noticed how strong he'd become since joining the co-op up on Red Fox Mountain. "You won't have a man around now, Mom. So if there's anything you need, just say the word and I'll totally be here."

Touched by his offer, I smiled at my only child. Trey was tall with the wide shoulders of a football player and had sky-blue eyes that were prone to twinkle with mischief. His fair hair was too long for my taste, but I reached up and ruffled it fondly. He squirmed away from my touch, re-adjusting his shaggy locks while introducing me to two young men from the Red Fox Mountain Co-op who'd be helping us transfer the furniture and boxes stacked in a Dunston storage unit into a charming cottage located minutes away from Novel Idea.

I'd had my eye on this creamy yellow house with the periwinkle shutters since it came up for sale, but because Trey had totaled my car and trashed the Dunston High School's football field and bleachers in the process, I hadn't been able to make an offer on this picket-fence paradise until I sold my house in Dunston. The moment I was freed from my financial burdens I rushed into the Sherlock Homes Realty office and put down a deposit to ensure that after a mid-October closing, I could lay claim to the two-bedroom house in the lovely subdivision of Walden Woods Circle.

Throughout the months of August and September I'd fallen asleep to visions of the cottage's sunny rooms and secluded rear garden. I couldn't wait to hang family pictures on the walls and dig up the previous owner's spent annuals to plant row after row of perennials that would burst through the ground the following spring. My head was filled with images of Van Gogh's irises and sunflowers, O'Keefe's poppies and lilies, and a riot of Manet's roses, and I planned to transform my back yard into an impressionist painting.

As for the interior, I wanted to decorate using a combination of furniture from my old place as well as some new pieces in bright, cheerful hues. Unfortunately, I'd have to sell a few more of my clients' books to major publishing houses before I could afford to head over to High Point to pick out comfy living room chairs or a farm table for the kitchen. Up until now, I'd only sold two book series. One was a cozy mystery featuring a sushi chef and the second was a romantic suspense set in a Scottish castle. And I couldn't really take credit for the sale of the romantic suspense. That deal was already in the works when I was promoted to literary agent.

At the storage unit in Dunston, I pulled out boxes of clothes and milk crates stuffed with books for the boys to load into their truck. As I worked, my thoughts focused on another client I'd inherited from the previous agent. I still couldn't believe that I now represented the international bestselling romance author Calliope Sinclair. If I could just convince her to make some changes to her latest manuscript, I felt certain that several publishing houses would enter into a bidding war to acquire the latest masterpiece from one of America's best-known authors.

"Stop gatherin' wool, girl!" My mother's voice startled me out of my reminiscing. "You're standin' in the middle of the path and this box isn't gettin' any lighter. What've you got in here? Cannonballs from the Civil War?"

Putting my own box on the ground, I rushed forward to take my mother's burden and set it on the bed of her turquoise pickup truck. I added the last box and then shut the tailgate, causing the magnetic sign plastered to the side of the truck to fall askew. I realigned the purple and black sign advertising the services of Amazing Althea, Psychic Advisor. "Sorry," I told Amazing Althea. "I was thinking about work again."

"*This* is work. Good work. The kind that gets you out in the open air and invites the sun's rays to paint your face. Before long, it'll be winter and we'll all be starvin' for this feelin'." My mother held out her free arms as though she could embrace the whole world. "I always feel like a kid durin' the fall. This is gonna be the best Halloween ever! I am gonna decorate the front door and scare the masks right off the kids who toilet papered my holly bushes last year. They won't come near my place totin' rolls of Charmin ever again."

I waited until we were both inside the truck before saying, "Is that an official prediction?"

My mother swatted me with the paperwork from the storage facility. "I don't read the cards for somethin' like that. I've gotta save my spiritual energy for when someone needs me, and my appointment calendar is as stuffed as a Christmas goose."

We chatted about her clients as I maneuvered the winding roads leading to Inspiration Valley, Trey following right behind me in his pickup truck. The town sat in a circle of low mountains like a teacup in a saucer and I never grew tired of the view. After that last sweeping curve, the town suddenly became visible through my driver's side window— an oasis of tree-lined streets and beautifully designed houses and storefronts. There were no concrete boxes in Inspiration Valley. Nearly every home boasted a garden, and the business district was lush with public green spaces.

Making my careful descent, I was struck anew by its charm. An army of multicolored trees surrounded the town, standing guard over the bookstore, garden center, organic grocery, restaurants, art studios, and tidy subdivisions like timeless sentinels. Today, the foliage show was magnificent. Corn yellow, pumpkin orange, and spiced cranberry leaves encouraged rich and aromatic fantasies about the first meal I'd cook in my new house.

By the time we'd unloaded all the boxes and I'd arranged my pots, pans, dishes, and utensils in the green and ivory kitchen, however, I was too tired to do anything but order takeout.

"What would you boys like to eat?" I asked Trey and his friends.

"Everything!" Trey answered wearily, putting his feet up on my coffee table.

I knocked them off with the sweep of one hand and held out the menu for Godfather's Pizza with the other. "Your wish is my command, gentlemen."

The three young men suddenly shucked off their fatigue and began to argue over the merits of pies made of sausage and mushroom, ham and pineapple, quattro formaggio, pepperoni, or spinach and feta. Before they could get too fired up, I promised to have all five delivered to my new house.

After the pizza arrived, my mother and I set the table and put a pitcher of iced tea and a pile of extra napkins in the center and then called the boys into the kitchen.

"Thank you so much!" I told them, feeling my heart swell at the sight of my family gathered around my table.

Trey raised his glass of iced tea. "To making new memories!"

His two friends shouted a hearty "here, here" and then dug into their food.

Trey devoured the pizza with such gusto that I couldn't help but wonder if my son was getting enough to eat living in the self-sustained community he'd joined in June. Although I'd had my reservations at the time, I had to admit that the Red Fox Co-op had done Trey a great deal of good. He was stronger, more independent, and treated his elders with respect. He'd gained a quiet confidence and was willing to throw himself into hours of demanding physical labor. Yet at the same time, he was missing out on a college education.

In early August, he'd received a letter from UNC-Wilmington containing a welcome packet and the name and contact information of Trey's future roommate. Several weeks later, when my son should have been attending his first class as a college freshman, he was grooming the co-op's herd of goats and preparing for a trip to Dunston to sell goat products to a selection of natural food stores and chic boutiques.

I had called the school and managed to defer Trey's admission until January, but I feared he'd refuse to attend then as well. From the beginning, I'd assumed his interest in the rustic, rather primeval way of life on Red Fox Mountain was a passing phase, but it seemed that his enthusiasm had been compounded upon meeting the lovely and ethereal Iris Gyles, the co-op leader's younger sister.

Autumn in North Carolina is a gentle season, but I was worried about Trey spending a cold winter up on the mountain. The members of the co-op stayed warm with the help of woolen clothing and pot-bellied stoves, but if our area received more than a dusting of snow or a freezing rain, the dirt road leading to the mountaintop community would be impassable. I hated the idea of my son being cut off from electricity, medical care, and me. I was ready for him to resume the life of an average American teenager but was terrified that he would never do so.

Pushing these irksome concerns aside, I focused on one last task before a dessert of raspberry sorbet. I had picked up a fabulous mirror at Dunston's largest consignment shop and was given an enormous discount by the owner. When I was still an intern, I'd passed along her query letter on decorating with vintage objects to Franklin Stafford, the agent representing nonfiction books. He had found her idea compelling and later signed her as a client. As a result, the oval mirror, set in a wood frame embellished with carved flowers and small birds, didn't cost me much more than tonight's pizza order.

Trey had drilled a hole and secured a wall anchor just inside the cottage's front door and I was just about to lift the mirror onto the hook when my mother entered the hallway.

"Everything's comin' together," she said with a smile.

I balanced the heavy mirror on the top of my foot and nodded. "Yes, it is. And not just the house. Everything. I love my job, I'm dating a great guy, and Trey and I haven't gotten along this well since he was a little boy."

My mother raised her brows. "So you and the good-lookin' man in blue are finally knockin' boots?"

Blushing, I turned away from her bemused gaze. "If you must know, we haven't progressed beyond the kiss goodnight stage."

"Why the hell not? You're a grown woman. More than grown." She grunted. "Shoot, Lila. Don't you know that havin' gray hair means that you get to sleep with a man without anybody's permission?"

I frowned at her. I spent a pretty penny keeping my shoulder-length hair a gray-free, roasted chestnut hue. "I'm not looking for permission. Work just keeps getting in the way. Sean's been assigned a string of night shifts, and with the festival coming up at the end of the month I—"

"How about a little afternoon delight?" my mother suggested with perfect aplomb. "When your daddy was alive—"

Thankfully, Trey called out for Althea before she could elucidate the ecstasies of her marital bed. I'd heard them before, usually after she'd consumed a few fingers too many of her lifelong beau, Mr. Jim Beam, but I really didn't want to hear her conjugal anecdotes before dessert.

Returning my attention to the mirror, I hefted it against the wall and slowly eased it onto the brass hook. The moment I drew back, the wire attached to the frame snapped. My fingers shot out to catch hold of the mirror, but I couldn't move quickly enough. The vintage work of art tilted sideways and hit the hardwood floor. The sound of glass shattering echoed down the narrow corridor.

I screamed in dismay and both Trey and Althea came running.

"Did you cut yourself?" Trey asked, worry clouding his handsome face.

"I'm fine, honey, but I doubt I can say the same about this." I bent over the mirror. It had fallen facedown, concealing the extent of the damage. Gently, I flipped it onto its side, listening to the sickening crunch of broken glass coming loose from the frame and crashing onto the ground.

I sighed in relief. The delicate birds and flowers were unscathed. There was a small scratch on the right-hand side that could be easily repaired with a dab of stain and the glass could be replaced by the local art supply store. I'd seen their custom frame jobs and knew they'd have my mirror fixed in no time.

Trey disappeared to fetch a broom and a dustpan, but my mother stayed rooted in place, her features pinched in concern.

"Mom," I said softly, touched that she was so upset over the thought of my being injured. "I'm okay. See?" I presented both of my pink, healthy palms as proof.

She shook her head and did not meet my eyes. She

couldn't seem to tear her gaze from the jagged shards of glass. "Oh, darlin'. It's not fine. Not at all."

To my surprise, she knelt down on the floor and picked up a piece of glass shaped like a lightning bolt and began muttering under her breath.

"Mom?" I began to feel a stirring of alarm.

She waved Trey away when he appeared with the broom, insisting that she needed to collect the pieces and take them far away from the house.

"Whatever for?" I asked her, utterly perplexed. "All that nonsense about broken mirrors and seven years of bad luck is just that. Nonsense."

She took a deep breath and answered in a tremulous voice. "You should believe. I'm takin' these to protect you, Lila. Trouble's comin'. It's comin' hard and fast as a runaway train."

My uneasiness grew. "That was this summer. It's all over now."

She pointed at the debris on the floor, and I was disturbed to note that her finger shook as she said, "You're wrong, Lila. This is only the beginning."